THE LAST GUNFIGHTER: DEAD BEFORE SUNDOWN

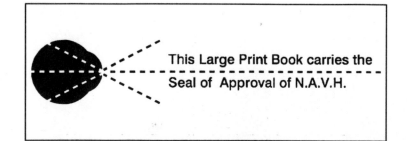

This Large Print Book carries the
Seal of Approval of N.A.V.H.

THE LAST GUNFIGHTER: DEAD BEFORE SUNDOWN

WILLIAM W. JOHNSTONE
WITH J. A. JOHNSTONE

WHEELER PUBLISHING
A part of Gale, Cengage Learning

GALE
CENGAGE Learning™

Detroit • New York • San Francisco • New Haven, Conn • Waterville, Maine • London

GALE
CENGAGE Learning™

Following the death of William W. Johnstone, the Johnstone family is
working with a carefully selected writer to organize and complete Mr.
Johnstone's outlines and many unfinished manuscripts to create
additional novels in all of his series like The Last Gunfighter, Mountain
Man, and Eagles, among others. This novel was inspired by Mr.
Johnstone's superb storytelling.

Wheeler Publishing Large Print Western.
The text of this Large Print edition is unabridged.
Other aspects of the book may vary from the original edition.
Set in 16 pt. Plantin.

LIBRARY OF CONGRESS CATALOGING-IN-PUBLICATION DATA

Johnstone, William W.
   The last gunfighter : dead before sundown / by William W. Johnstone ;
with J.A. Johnstone. — Large print ed.
   p. cm. — (Wheeler Publishing large print western)
   ISBN-13: 978-1-4104-4020-4 (pbk.)
   ISBN-10: 1-4104-4020-6 (pbk.)
   I. Johnstone, J. A. II. Title.
PS3560.O415L354 2011
813'.54—dc22   2011017522

Published in 2011 by arrangement with Pinnacle Books, an imprint of
Kensington Publishing Corp.

Printed in the United States of America
   1 2 3 4 5   15 14 13 12 11
FD206

THE LAST GUNFIGHTER: DEAD BEFORE SUNDOWN

CHAPTER 1

The storm blew up unexpectedly. At least, Frank Morgan didn't see it coming, but he was no sailor. He was at home on the back of a horse, not the pitching deck of a boat.

As the *Jupiter* made a run for shore, Frank stood at the railing, his hands clutching the smooth wood, and watched the dark clouds looming behind the ship. A hard wind blew, and the waves that jutted up from the water reminded Frank of gray fangs waiting to chew the life out of him.

Frank was a broad-shouldered man of medium height whose high-crowned, cream-colored Stetson was pulled down tight on his graying dark hair to keep the gusts from blowing it off his head. His faded blue shirt, jeans, and well-worn boots were the outfit of a cowboy, but except on rare occasions, he hadn't punched cows since he was a young man in Texas.

That was a lot of years in the past, and a

long way from here, as well.

The holstered Colt strapped around Frank's hips told a different story. The revolver's walnut grips were worn smooth with use. The holster was oiled and supple.

Habitually, Frank's right hand never strayed far from the gun butt. Even when he was at ease, he was ready to hook and draw at a split-second's notice.

Frank Morgan was a gunfighter. People called him the Drifter, and that summed up his life pretty well. Considering his age and the deadly speed and skill he still possessed, some said he was the last true gunfighter, the last survivor of the era that had included such notorious pistoleers as John Wesley Hardin, Smoke Jensen, Ben Thompson, Falcon MacCallister, and Matt Bodine.

Hardin and Thompson were dead now, treacherously gunned down by their enemies. Smoke Jensen was living the peaceful life of a rancher in Colorado, the last Frank had heard. That made him a rarity among men who had lived by the gun. Nearly all of them had died by it, too. Frank didn't know what had happened to MacCallister and Bodine. He had lost track of them over the years.

As for Frank, he was still drifting, still winding up in one fracas after another despite his intention to avoid trouble, and lately his wanderings had carried him to the far north, to the gold-rich Yukon country along the border between Alaska and Canada. He had survived a harrowing adventure there and had returned briefly to the Alaskan port of Skagway to settle a score, only to find that fate had already taken care of that for him.

Now he was on the *Jupiter,* sailing south toward Seattle, Washington, but this squall had come up and forced the ship to turn toward the Canadian coast to avoid it.

A woman's voice came from behind him on the whipping wind. "Frank? What are you doing out here?"

He glanced over his shoulder and saw Meg Goodwin standing there on the deck. Her hands were thrust into the pockets of her jeans to protect them from the cold. It was summer, but in this part of the world when the storm winds blew, they were chilly, no matter what the season.

Meg was a mighty attractive sight, what with the blond hair that escaped from under her flat-crowned brown hat whipping around her face. She was dressed like a man in jeans, a buckskin shirt, and a denim jacket, but there was no mistaking the fact that her trim, shapely figure belonged to a woman.

Frank was old enough to be Meg's father, and because of that there was nothing romantic between them — although she had made it clear on more than one occasion that she wouldn't mind that in the least — but he was objective enough to know she was a very pretty gal.

She could shoot as well as most men, too, a fact she had proven during Frank's perilous sojourn to Alaska.

He didn't answer the question she had asked him. Instead he said, "Where's Salty?"

Their friend Salty Stevens, the third member of the unofficial trio that was traveling together, was an old-timer, even older than Frank. Salty had been knocking around the frontier for decades, working as a stagecoach driver, Army scout, and range detective, among other odd jobs he had held. He had run into some bad luck when he went north to the Yukon to prospect for gold, but then good luck had found him in the person of Frank Morgan.

"He's down in his cabin, like you should be," Meg said. "If that storm catches us and the ship starts pitching around, you're liable to fall off!"

Frank smiled. "Don't worry. If she starts

bucking like a wild bronc, I'll go below. I reckon there's a good chance the captain's going to get us ashore before that happens, though."

He pointed to the dark line that was visible through the gloom on the horizon.

"Is that Canada?" Meg asked.

"I think so. I overheard one of the ship's officers telling another that we'd duck behind some island and run into a little port called Powderkeg Bay until the storm passes."

"I hope he was right. I'm not sure I have my sea legs well enough to ride out a storm."

Despite the potential danger, Frank was sort of enjoying the elemental drama playing out on this gray afternoon. He had never spent much time on ships during his life, and it was a new challenge for him.

But Meg was obviously worried, and Frank was curious about how well Salty was riding out the weather, too, so he said, "Why don't we both go below? We'll stop at Salty's cabin and see how he's doing."

"I think that's a good idea," Meg said with a nod. She held her hat on, pushing it down on her blond hair, as they turned toward the stairs that led below decks.

When they reached Salty's cabin, a feeble

moan was the only answer to Frank's rap on the door. Frank opened it and stuck his head into the dim cabin.

"Salty? Are you all right?"

"I've rid stagecoaches that bounced over some of the worst roads west of the Mississippi, but I ain't never felt no bouncin' around like this dang ship does!" The querulous voice came from the cabin's bunk. "Ding-blasted thing needs better thoroughbraces!"

"And the storm hasn't even caught us yet," Frank said as he stepped into the cabin.

He scratched a match to life and held the flame to the wick of a lamp that hung on gimbals from a wall sconce. The lamp swayed with the motion of the ship, casting a shifting pattern of shadows over the small room.

Salty sat up on the bunk and raked fingers through his white beard. He swung his legs off and let his booted feet thump to the floor. His rumpled thatch of hair was as snowy as his beard. Keen, dark eyes were set in pits of gristle in his leathery face.

"We're gonna sink, ain't we?" he asked glumly.

"I don't think so," Frank said. "We're in sight of land. It shouldn't be much longer until we're in a bay, and the water ought to

12

be calmer there."

"I hope this don't put us too far behind schedule. I'd like to make it to Mexico afore winter sets in. After freezin' my —" Salty glanced at Meg as he caught himself. He went on, "After freezin' in Skagway and Whitehorse last winter, from now on I plan to spend the rest of my days somewheres warm. I don't know what in blazes ever possessed me to go north to Alaska, anyway."

"Gold," Frank said. "The same thing that possesses just about everybody else who heads up there these days."

"Yeah, well, that didn't work out too good, did it?"

Salty had been robbed by a gang of criminals operating in the Alaskan settlement of Skagway. Frank had hoped to recover some of the old-timer's money when they returned to the settlement, but the leader of the outlaws was dead and the rest of the men had scattered. The chances of getting back any of the money they had stolen from Salty had dwindled to just about nothing.

That was a shame, but there wasn't anything they could do about it. As long as Salty and Meg were traveling with Frank, they wouldn't have to worry about money.

Despite his cowhand garb, Frank Morgan was actually one of the richest men in the

West, owning half of the vast business empire founded by the woman he had once been married to, Vivian Browning. When Vivian had been murdered, Frank and the son he hadn't even known existed until recently, Conrad Browning, had inherited those lucrative holdings.

Conrad had run the business for a while and done a fine job of it, until another tragedy had changed the direction of his life. Now, firms of lawyers and financial officers in Boston, Denver, and San Francisco administered things and banked Frank's share of the profits. His needs were simple, but he didn't skimp on helping out his friends and other people who deserved help.

Now, Frank smiled at Salty and said, "Once you get down there south of the border, sipping on a glass of tequila some pretty señorita brings to you, you won't even think about Alaska anymore."

"Don't that sound good," Salty said with a sigh. He looked better now, but he still needed something to keep his mind off the ship's motion. "Why don't I set up the checkerboard? I reckon we got time for a game or two afore this boat hits land."

"Why don't you and Meg play?" Frank suggested. "I'll take on the winner."

"That'll be me," Meg declared confidently.

Salty slapped his thigh. "We'll just see about that, missy!"

Frank and Meg exchanged a quick, satisfied glance. They had succeeded in distracting Salty from his worries.

Salty got out his checkerboard and set it up on the room's small table. The ship's motion made the pieces want to slide a little, but he and Meg succeeded in playing a game. Salty won, much to Meg's apparent chagrin, and he was getting ready to play Frank when they all noticed how much calmer the water had gotten.

"We must have reached that bay," Frank said. "Want to go take a look?"

"Yeah, I reckon I wouldn't mind gettin' a little fresh air," Salty said as he reached for his battered old hat. "Don't think you're foolin' me, though, Frank Morgan. You was just huntin' for any excuse not to get whipped at checkers."

"You're too smart for me, Salty," Frank said with a chuckle.

The three of them went up on deck, being careful not to get in the way of any of the sailors bustling around. Some of the other passengers were emerging from their cabins as well. They clustered on the starboard side of the ship to look at the rocky-sided, pine-covered island that now protected the vessel

15

from some of the wind's force.

Up ahead and to port loomed the mainland, which was also covered with pines for the most part. Lights on shore gleamed through the overcast, and as the ship sailed closer Frank began to make out the shapes of buildings clustered along the coastline. As a sailor paused nearby, Frank gestured toward the settlement and asked the man, "Is that Powderkeg Bay?"

"We're sailin' in it," the man said, "and that's the name of the town, too. Rough place."

"Really?"

"Yeah, we don't normally stop there." The sailor jerked a thumb at the gray, angry sky. "Like the old sayin' goes, though, any port in a storm."

He hurried on about his duties, leaving Frank, Meg, and Salty to watch along with the other passengers as the *Jupiter* sailed closer to the settlement.

Powderkeg Bay was in the lee of a small peninsula that jutted out from the mainland and formed a cove of sorts. It was a fishing community, judging by the number of small boats anchored at three docks. The thickly forested landscape rose sharply behind the settlement, looming over the town and giving it a rather gloomy aspect, as if it were trapped between those dark woods and the unforgiving sea.

Rain began to fall as the *Jupiter* approached the port. Most of the passengers hurried below again, including Meg and Salty. Frank lingered for a moment to study the settlement before following them.

Powderkeg Bay was a deep-water port, so the ship was able to drop anchor at one of the docks, rather than standing offshore a short distance. The captain came around to the cabins, telling the passengers that they would be staying here tonight, as a safety precaution. The storm would be gone by morning, he explained, and they would set sail again then.

He also advised them to remain in their cabins for the night, adding, "Powderkeg Bay has a rather unsavory reputation. It's full of saloons, gambling dens, and houses of ill repute. The fishermen, loggers, and trappers who live here are a tough bunch, and there are often drunken brawls in the streets."

Frank wasn't too worried about getting mixed up in trouble. He had visited some of the most hell-roaring places west of the Mississippi, places like Deadwood, Dodge City, and Tombstone.

But he didn't have any reason to leave the

ship tonight, either. When Meg asked him if he was going ashore, he shook his head and said, "I never lost anything in Powderkeg Bay." The decision was that simple to him.

But that evening as he was in his own cabin, stretched out on the bunk reading a book of stories by Stephen Crane in the light from the lamp on the wall, someone knocked on the door. Frank looked up from the book and called, "Who is it?"

"Meg."

He frowned slightly. She didn't make a habit of coming to his cabin, so he wondered if there was trouble.

"Come in," he told her, and the look on her face when she opened the door and stepped into the room worried him even more. He swung his legs off the bunk and set the book aside as he asked, "What is it?"

"I can't find Salty anywhere," she said. "I've looked all over the ship for him. He's gone, Frank."

CHAPTER 2

As he stood up and moved to Meg's side, Frank said, "I don't hardly see how he can be gone. He's bound to be somewhere onboard."

Meg shook her head stubbornly. "He's not, I tell you. I've looked everywhere except the crew's quarters, and he'd have no business being there."

"Unless he found a poker game or something like that going on," Frank pointed out. He sat down on the bunk again and reached for his boots. "Stay here. I'll go find him."

"Nothing doing," Meg said. Her firm tone left no room for argument. "I'm coming with you."

Frank shrugged and finished pulling on his boots. He knew that arguing with a woman was usually a waste of time, breath, and energy. It wasn't the wisdom of his years that told him that, either. He was smart enough that he had figured it out early on.

When he stood up, he hesitated, then picked up the coiled shell belt and holstered Colt from the stool where it lay next to the bunk. He didn't figure he would need the gun, but it was better to have it with him just in case.

He had learned *that* lesson early on, too.

He put his hat on and followed Meg out of the cabin. She started toward the stairs. They would have to go up on deck and follow it forward to reach the crew's quarters.

One of the sailors intercepted them as they crossed the deck. The rain had slowed to a drizzle, and the wind wasn't blowing anymore.

"Something I can do for you folks?" the sailor asked.

"Our friend is missing," Meg said. "Mr. Stevens? Do you know him?"

"The old-timer with the beard?"

"That's right."

The sailor scratched his jaw and frowned in thought under his short-billed cap. "I haven't seen him. The cap'n told everybody they ought to stay onboard the ship tonight, though."

The mist in the air gave the lights of the settlement a blurred look. Frank heard the faint strains of music drifting through the night air from somewhere as he asked, "You don't have a guard posted to keep folks from leaving, do you?"

The sailor shook his head. "No, sir. What the cap'n told the passengers was just a suggestion, not an order."

"That's what I figured." An idea had come to Frank when he heard the music, and he didn't like it very much. Still, they ought to make sure Salty wasn't onboard before checking out his new hunch. "Can you take us to the crew quarters? If there's a poker game going on anywhere, Salty can usually sniff it out."

"I can promise you, the old fella isn't there, Mr. Morgan. I just came from there to go on duty."

Frank didn't have any reason to doubt the man's word. "What about the officers' quarters?" he asked.

The sailor shook his head. "No, sir, he wouldn't be there. None of the crew is allowed to fraternize with the passengers. Cap'n Beswick wouldn't stand for it."

Meg sighed in frustration. "Then where could he have gone?"

"There," Frank said, tipping his head toward the settlement. That made some mist that had collected on his hat drip off the brim in front of his face.

Meg's eyes widened as she looked at him. "You think he went to . . . ?"

Her voice trailed off as she didn't finish the question.

"I reckon they have some saloons in that town, son?" Frank asked the sailor.

"Yes, sir, several. Does Mr. Stevens, uh, like to take a drink now and then?"

"He used to," Frank said.

"He wouldn't have any trouble finding a place to do that in Powderkeg Bay. Or to indulge in any other sort of vice you can think of." The young salt cast an embarrassed glance toward Meg. "Begging your pardon, ma'am."

"Don't worry about it," Meg told him with a wave of her hand. "Frank, we've got to find Salty. I thought he gave up drinking."

"He did," Frank said, "but that doesn't mean he wouldn't get tempted from time to time. All it would take would be a moment of weakness."

He turned toward the gangplank that led from the ship's deck to the dock.

"Wait a minute, sir," the sailor said. "Have you ever been to Powderkeg Bay before?"

"Never even heard of the place until today."

"It has a bad reputation. It would be

dangerous for a stranger to go wandering around alone. Cap'n Beswick even put the town off-limits to the crew."

Frank smiled. "I can take care of myself, son."

"But sir —"

"Do you know who this is?" Meg interrupted. "This is Frank Morgan. People call him the Drifter."

The sailor's face showed his surprise. "The famous gunfighter? Really?"

"I'm Frank Morgan," Frank said. "The famous part doesn't concern me."

"Why don't you let me take you to see the cap'n?" the sailor suggested. "Maybe he could send some men with you to help you search for Mr. Stevens."

That wasn't a bad idea, Frank decided. He nodded and said, "All right, son, let's go."

The sailor led the way forward and down another set of steps. Companionways, Frank thought they were called. Or maybe those were the corridors below decks. He wasn't sure. He was a landlubber at heart, no doubt about that, he thought as he smiled wryly to himself despite his worry over Salty's possible whereabouts.

A brisk voice answered, "Come in!" when the sailor knocked on a door.

The young man opened it and said, "Cap'n, a couple of the passengers need to speak to you."

The captain didn't invite them into his cabin. Instead, he stepped out into the corridor. He wasn't wearing his coat or his cap, but he still stood ramrod-stiff as he frowned at the sailor.

"What's this about, Monroe?"

Frank spoke up. "We asked the young fella if we could talk to you, Captain."

The lantern-jawed man with bushy side whiskers regarded Frank with a cool stare. "Mr. Morgan, isn't it?"

"That's right," Frank said with a nod. "This is Miss Goodwin."

Captain Beswick inclined his head politely toward Meg. "What can I do for you folks?"

"Our friend Mr. Stevens doesn't seem to be onboard the ship tonight."

"You're certain of that?"

"He's not in his cabin or on deck," Meg said.

"We haven't looked in the officers' quarters or the crew's quarters," Frank added.

"Or in the other passengers' cabins, I'll wager," Beswick said.

Frank and Meg glanced at each other. She shook her head.

Beswick smiled an annoyingly indulgent

24

smile as he said, "So you see, there are still plenty of places he could be." His voice sharpened as he looked at the sailor and went on, "Monroe, get some of the crew and conduct a search. Locate Mr. Stevens and then report back here."

"Aye, Cap'n," Monroe said. He hurried off.

"Won't you come in?" Beswick invited Frank and Meg. "You might as well be comfortable while we wait."

They followed the captain into his cabin. Like all the other cabins on the *Jupiter,* the room was small, but it was comfortably furnished with a bunk, a desk, a map table, and a couple of chairs. A bookcase was built into one wall.

"Would you like a drink?" Beswick asked Frank. "I have some decent brandy."

"I'm obliged, but no thanks," Frank said. He wasn't that much of a drinker under normal circumstances. With Salty missing, Frank knew he might need a clear head even more than he usually did.

"I'm sure Monroe will be back shortly with the news that he's found Mr. Stevens."

Frank thought the captain was pretty irritated by the situation, but Beswick was trying to keep that from showing. The shipping line would want him to be polite to the passengers.

"The thing is, Salty doesn't really know anybody else on the ship, either the passengers or the crew," Meg said. "He wouldn't have any reason to be in somebody else's cabin."

Frank said, "We think he's gone ashore."

Beswick frowned. "Into the settlement, you mean? Why would he do that? I explained to everyone about what sort of place Powderkeg Bay is."

"That wouldn't mean much to a man like Salty. He's likely traipsed through every hell-on-wheels between the Rio Grande and the Milk River," Frank said.

Of course, the same comment could be made about *him*.

"Salty used to drink quite a bit, too," Meg added worriedly.

"Ah," Beswick said. "I see."

Anger flashed in Meg's blue eyes. "I don't think you do," she said. "Salty's not just some old drunk. He's been all over the West and done just about everything there is to do."

"I meant no offense, Miss Goodwin. Still, you have to admit, you *are* worried about him because you think he may have slipped off to some saloon in the settlement."

Meg couldn't deny that, so she settled for

26

just glaring in silence as they waited for the young sailor, Monroe, to return.

That took about ten minutes. Beswick said, "Come in," when someone rapped on the door. Monroe stepped inside, holding his cap respectfully in front of him.

"Mr. Stevens isn't onboard, sir," he reported.

Beswick frowned in surprise. "You're sure of that?"

"Aye, sir. I found Mr. Handlesman, told him what you said, and he organized a search party. We checked everywhere, even in the cargo hold."

"And you didn't find Mr. Stevens?"

"No, sir."

Beswick turned to Frank and Meg. "It looks like you may have been right. My apologies for doubting you."

Frank didn't care about apologies. He said, "Now that we know Salty's not onboard, I'll go take a look for him in the settlement."

"Not alone," Beswick said. "That wouldn't be wise."

Meg said, "He won't be alone. I'm going with him."

"That would be even *more* unwise." Beswick looked at the sailor. "Monroe, you and Mr. Handlesman and the rest of that

27

search party will accompany Mr. Morgan ashore."

"I don't want to have to keep up with a bunch of sailors," Frank said.

"With all due respect, Mr. Morgan, that decision isn't yours to make. I'm charged with the safety of my passengers, and I intend to see to it that I deliver each and every one of them safely to Seattle. Besides, you can use the help. Mr. Handlesman is my second mate and a good man."

Frank supposed it wouldn't hurt to have some of the crew with him, especially if Powderkeg Bay really was as wild and woolly a place as everybody said it was.

"All right, but I'm going ashore now. Salty could already be up to his neck in trouble."

"There's no doubt about that," Beswick agreed.

"What about me?" Meg demanded.

"Go back to your cabin and wait," Frank told her. "Sorry, but that's the way it's got to be."

"I don't like it," she muttered darkly, "but I reckon we shouldn't waste time standing around arguing. We've wasted too blasted much of it already."

"I'll see that the young lady gets back to her cabin safely," Beswick said, which earned him another glare from Meg.

Frank and Monroe left them there and hurried back up to the deck. The continuing drizzle made it a little slippery under Frank's boots.

Monroe found the second mate, Handlesman, who turned out to be a stocky gent with a bulldog face and red hair under his cap. Even though he clearly didn't care for the orders that Monroe delivered, he quickly gathered up several sailors to serve as the search party.

"You don't have to go ashore with us, sir," he told Frank.

"I think it would be a good idea if I did. When you find Salty, he's liable not to listen to you. He can be a crotchety old pelican when he wants to."

Handlesman shrugged burly shoulders. "All right, then. Let's go."

They went down the gangplank to the dock. Frank was careful not to slip. His boots were made for riding, not for negotiating the damp gangplank of a ship.

Water lapped softly against the dock's pilings. The thick mist in the air seemed to muffle sounds, including the music Frank could still hear.

"Where's that coming from?" Frank asked Handlesman. "It might have lured Salty off the ship."

The second mate grunted. "Like the Sirens, eh? You won't find any such creatures at Red Mike's place. Only whores, tinhorns, and cutthroats."

"I've heard about Red Mike's," Monroe put in. "Never been there, though."

"That's because the skipper put the whole settlement off-limits before you shipped out with us," Handlesman explained. He spat on the hard-packed dirt of the street as they reached the end of the pier. "We had a couple of crewmen get killed in there."

It sounded like the sort of place where Salty could get in trouble, all right. Frank said, "Let's go have a look."

Not many people were out and about on this damp, dank night, and the ones who were got out of the way of the grim-faced party from the ship. Within moments, Frank and his companions were approaching a squat building made of rough-planed boards.

Frank had figured that the place was called Red Mike's because the proprietor had red hair, but in the flickering light of a lantern that hung beside the door, he saw that the boards were painted red. It was a sloppy job with ragged bare patches and streaks, but Frank doubted if the men who came here to drink really cared about such things.

The door stood open. The music coming through it was louder now, but the notes came to an abrupt, discordant end when Frank and the men from the ship were still a block away. Loud, angry voices replaced the tinny strains from a piano.

"Sounds like trouble in there," Frank said.

"I'm not surprised. Brawls happen all the time at Red Mike's." Handlesman motioned the other sailors forward. "Just in case the fella we're looking for is in there, we'd better have a look before —"

He didn't get to finish his sentence. Guns began to roar inside the saloon, their deadly blasts ripping through the misty night.

CHAPTER 3

Frank started to break into a run toward Red Mike's, but Handlesman lunged and grabbed his arm, stopping him.

"What do you think you're doing?" the *Jupiter*'s second mate demanded.

"My friend might be in there," Frank responded as he jerked his arm free of Handlesman's grip. He hurried toward the saloon.

"Come back here, you damned fool!" Handlesman shouted. Frank ignored him.

It would be just like Salty to get himself caught in the middle of a corpse-and-cartridge session like the one going on inside Red Mike's. The old-timer was a trouble magnet.

Of course, the same thing could be said of Frank Morgan. But it took one to know one, as the old saying went.

He veered to the side as he approached the place. He didn't want to run right into a stray bullet that came out that open door. When he reached the building, he put his back against the sloppily painted wall and slid along it toward the entrance.

Guns continued to bang inside the building. Frank passed a window, but inside the glass, heavy curtains were drawn, preventing him from looking in.

As he neared the door, he caught a whiff of the powder smoke that rolled out into the night. He had smelled that sharp tang too many times in his life. He was downright weary of it.

But weary or not, there was a chance Salty was in the middle of that ruckus, so Frank was going to have to go in there and make sure.

He used his left hand to take off his hat and edged his head just far enough into the doorway that he could take a look at part of the saloon.

He saw a bar to the right. It was made out of rough-hewn planks, not the polished hardwood of most bars, but the planks must have been thick enough to stop a bullet because several men appeared to be hiding behind it.

Smoke and flame gushed from the barrels of the guns they thrust over the top of the bar and fired at somebody who was back to

Frank's left.

Seeing that the volleys were going back and forth inside the bar instead of being aimed at the door, Frank took a deep breath and leaped across the opening, pressing his back to the wall on the other side.

From there he could see what seemed to be one man crouching behind an overturned table, sporadically returning the fire of the men behind the bar. Frank didn't get a glimpse of anything except the man's hand and the revolver in it, but he thought he recognized the old long-barreled Remington.

That was Salty's gun.

Frank mulled over what he should do next. Charging straight through the door probably wouldn't accomplish anything except to get him killed.

But he had spotted a door at the far end of the bar, and that door probably led to an office or a storeroom, something like that. There might be a back door to Red Mike's, and if there was, it would allow him to get the drop on the men behind the bar.

Before Frank could move, he saw Handlesman, Monroe, and the other sailors from the ship making their way cautiously toward the saloon, staying low and behind whatever cover they could find. After a moment, Handlesman and Monroe dashed to his side.

"What's going on in there?" the second mate asked.

Frank thought that was pretty obvious, but he suppressed the irritation he felt.

"Some men behind the bar are shooting it out with one hombre behind a table," he explained. "I think the man behind the table is Salty."

"Then he's in a bad spot."

Frank nodded. "That's right. Eventually those varmints will shoot that table to pieces. I'm going around back to see if I can get in that way."

Handlesman reached under his blue jacket and brought out a short-barreled revolver. "I'll come with you," he said.

Frank started to refuse but changed his mind before he said anything. If Handlesman wanted to get mixed up in this ruckus, it was his decision to make.

"What about me and the rest of the men?" Monroe asked.

"You're not armed," Handlesman snapped. "Stay out here unless you hear me yelling for you. Then you can charge in and do the best you can."

Monroe nodded. "Aye."

Frank put his hat on and jerked his head

toward the black, narrow alley at the side of the building. "Come on."

He and Handlesman made their way through the stygian gloom in the alley. Frank banged his knee against something, but not hard enough to hurt him. Trash rustled under his feet. More rustling, accompanied by squeaking, told him that rats were fleeing in front of him and Handlesman.

They reached the rear corner of the building. It was black as sin back there. Frank had to feel his way along with his left hand on the wall until he came to a window.

When he tried to raise it, it wouldn't budge. The window had been either nailed or painted shut, and he didn't have time to figure out which.

"Give me your jacket," he said to Handlesman.

"What?"

"Your jacket," Frank snapped.

Handlesman shrugged out of the garment and handed it to Frank, who wrapped it around his gun. The shooting was still going on in the saloon's front room. That would help cover up any racket he made back here.

Anyway, he didn't have any time to waste.

Using the jacket-wrapped gun butt, Frank smashed the windowpane. The broken glass clattered to the floor inside the room, but no one reacted to it, telling him the room probably was empty. He raked the Colt's barrel around the edges of the window to clear away any shards.

"You might want to wait until you can check for broken glass before you put that back on," he told Handlesman as he handed the jacket back to the second mate.

Handlesman grunted. "I'll do that."

Frank holstered his gun long enough to haul himself through the window. He drew it again as he turned back to give the burly ship's officer a hand.

If anything, this back room of the saloon was even darker than the alley outside. The blackness was relieved only by a faint line of light that seeped under the bottom of a door leading into the main room.

As Frank looked at that line of light, he saw it pulse, brightening in time with the muzzle flashes from the guns going off on the other side of it. He gripped the Colt tightly and moved to the door. A second later he grasped the knob.

Frank turned the knob and eased the door open. It opened inward, which meant he had a chance to look out into the saloon's main room before anybody noticed him.

From where he was, he could see along

the area behind the bar. Three men crouched there, just as he'd thought. One wore the dirty apron of a bartender and had a head as bald as a cue ball. The other two sported somewhat shabby suits and derby hats. They looked like gamblers or whore-mongers, maybe both.

The important thing was that none of them was Salty Stevens. Frank couldn't be absolutely sure the man they were trying to kill was Salty, but Frank's gut told him it was pretty likely.

He was about to step out and tell the men behind the bar to throw down their guns, when he suddenly realized that one of them looked familiar. It took Frank a moment to figure out where he had seen the man before and remember his name.

One of the derby-hatted men was the brutish criminal known as Yeah Mow Hop-kins. Hopkins had been one of Soapy Smith's top henchmen back in Skagway the year before, and after Smith had been killed in a shootout with a vigilante, Hopkins had lit a shuck from the Alaskan settlement, along with some of Smith's other men. If they had stayed, they would have risked be-ing on the wrong end of a lynch rope.

Seeing Hopkins made Frank more con-vinced than ever that Salty was behind that overturned table, which was starting to be pocked with bullet holes. If the old-timer had walked into Red Mike's looking for a drink and recognized Hopkins as Frank had, his anger over being cleaned out by Smith's gang might have prompted him to slap leather before he really thought about what he was doing.

All the saloon's other customers must have fled when the shooting started. The place was empty except for the four combatants — and Frank and Handlesman in the back room.

Frank couldn't afford to wait any longer. He pulled the door open wider and stepped out into the saloon's main room, leveling the Colt as he bellowed, "Hold your fire! Drop those guns!"

All three men jerked toward him. The bartender and the other man brought their guns up. Hopkins turned and fled toward the end of the bar.

The would-be killers had called the tune, although they almost certainly didn't realize that they were about to dance with the Drifter, one of the deadliest gunfighters around. Flame spouted from the Colt's gun muzzle as Frank put a slug in the bartender's chest.

The bald man went over backward, crashing into the bottles on a shelf attached to the wall and upsetting them. The bottles fell and shattered, and the reek of spilled rotgut suddenly mingled with the stench of gunsmoke.

The other man got a shot off, but it went wild, whipping harmlessly past Frank, who fired again. His bullet shattered the man's right shoulder and knocked him to the floor, where he dropped his gun, clutched at the wound, and howled in pain.

Meanwhile, Yeah Mow Hopkins tried to escape out the saloon's front door, but he stumbled as the old Remington roared again. Hopkins threw a shot toward the table. The man hidden there fired yet again. Blood sprayed from Hopkins's hip as the slug clipped him and sent him spinning off his feet.

Frank lunged behind the bar and kicked away the gun that the second man had dropped. The bartender stared up out of lifeless eyes. He wasn't a threat anymore.

Handlesman had emerged from the back room, gun in hand. Frank told the second mate, "Keep an eye on this one," as he nodded toward the man with the busted shoulder. He stepped out from behind the bar.

"Frank? Is that you?"

The slightly mush-mouthed voice came

from behind the overturned table. Frank recognized it, just as he had expected to.

"Yeah, it's me, Salty," he replied. He trained his gun on the fallen Yeah Mow Hopkins as he added, "You can come out from behind there now. Are you all right?"

The old-timer stood up with the Remington in his hand. His battered hat had fallen off during the fracas, and his white hair was tangled.

"I got a few nicks and scratches from all the splinters flyin' around, but I ain't hurt bad," Salty said. "Them varmints threw a whole heap o' lead, but none of it found me."

"That's good." Frank approached Hopkins cautiously. The man seemed to be in shock as he lay there on the sawdust-littered floor and bled from wounds in his hip and thigh, but Frank knew better than to take unnecessary chances. The barrel of his gun didn't waver.

Salty bent and picked up his hat. As he crammed it back on his head, he said, "You know who that fella is?"

"Yeah, I recognize him," Frank said.

"That's Yeah Mow Hopkins," Salty said excitedly, as if he hadn't heard Frank's answer. "He worked for that bastard Soapy Smith!"

"I remember. It looks like he recognized you, too."

"Naw, neither him nor Palmer knew me when I first come in," Salty said as he joined Frank. He sounded a little sheepish as he went on. "I should'a turned right around and gone back to the ship to get you. But I got so mad when I thought about how that bunch stole all my money, so mad I reckon I wasn't thinkin' straight when I grabbed my hogleg and went to cussin' 'em."

"I reckon not," Frank said drily.

"They knowed who I was after that and started shootin'. I didn't figure I was gonna get out of here alive."

"You probably wouldn't have if Meg hadn't missed you and got me started looking for you," Frank told him. "We heard the shooting going on in here, and I had a hunch I'd find you right in the middle of the festivities."

"I'm sure obliged for the help." Salty toed Hopkins's shoulder. "I just wish Palmer hadn't gotten away when the shootin' started."

"Joe Palmer was here, too, eh?"

"Yeah, that's right. Didn't see any more of them bastards who worked for Smith, though."

Hopkins opened his eyes and looked up at

42

Frank and Salty. Pain twisted his face. "You . . . you crazy old son of a bitch!" he gasped.

Salty hunkered next to the wounded man and put the Remington's muzzle against Hopkins's jaw.

"I wouldn't be mouthin' off if I was you," the old-timer warned as he pressed hard enough with the gun barrel to bring a groan of pain from Hopkins's mouth.

"I need . . . a doc," he said. "You gotta patch me up . . . before I bleed to death."

"After all the hell you and the rest o' your bunch raised, I reckon I could stay right here and watch you bleed to death without it botherin' me all that much."

Frank didn't blame Salty for feeling that way, but he couldn't stand by and watch an injured man die. He was about to say as much when Hopkins stammered, "If . . . if you'll help me . . . I'll tell you where Joe went."

"I wouldn't mind settlin' the score with Palmer," Salty said, "but I ain't sure it's worth —"

Hopkins broke in, saying desperately, "He's got your money, you loco old coot!"

CHAPTER 4

Salty's eyes just about bulged from their sockets as what Hopkins had just said sunk in on him.

"My money!" he repeated. "You mean —"

"Not the same exact coins and greenbacks we took off'a you," Hopkins grated through clenched teeth. "But when we got outta Skagway two jumps ahead of those damned vigilantes, Joe and me managed to get our hands on a lot of the loot Soapy had cached. There's more than what you lost, old man, a lot more."

Salty's hand shot out and grabbed the front of Hopkins's vest. He dragged the man up off the floor a little, which brought a pained cry from him.

"Where'd he go?" Salty demanded. "Tell me how to find him, durn your sorry hide!"

Hopkins's lips stretched in an ugly grin. "I'll tell you where to look for him . . . after you get me a sawbones."

Frank said, "The other fella behind the bar could use a doctor, too, Salty. Let's get these men patched up, and then Hopkins can talk."

"How about he talks now, or I just blow his damn fool head off?"

"If you do, you'll never find your money," Hopkins warned.

Frank put a hand on Salty's shoulder. "I understand how you feel, but you're not a cold-blooded murderer."

"Wouldn't be cold-blooded," Salty muttered. "My blood's plenty hot right now." He sighed, took the gun away from Hopkins's neck, and eased the hammer down. "But I reckon you're right, Frank."

Frank looked over behind the bar. "How's that man doing, Handlesman?"

"He passed out, but he's still alive," the second mate answered. "Monroe!"

The young sailor, who along with the other men from the *Jupiter,* had come closer to the saloon's door when the shooting stopped, hurried in and asked, "Sir?"

"Come here and put some pressure on this man's shoulder so he doesn't bleed to death," Handlesman ordered.

While Monroe did that, Frank asked Hopkins, "Where's the doctor's office?"

"I ain't sure. Joe and me haven't been here

that long." Hopkins's face had lost most of its color. "For God's sake, go and find him. I'm dyin' here!"

"You may hurt like hell, but you're not losing enough blood to die," Frank told him. "Not right away, anyway. But if we were to let you lie there for an hour or so . . ."

"I'll tell you what I know, I swear it," Hopkins said. "Just as soon as the doc's tended to those bullet holes."

"I'll go find the doctor," Handlesman volunteered. "If I have to, I'll fetch our ship's doctor from the *Jupiter.* Come to think of it, that might be even quicker."

Frank nodded. "That's a good idea. Go ahead."

Handlesman hurried out of Red Mike's, leaving Frank and Salty to keep an eye on the wounded men, along with the other sailors.

Salty told Hopkins, "Why don't you go ahead and tell me now, just in case you're hurt worse'n you think you are?"

"Go to hell," Hopkins muttered.

Handlesman was back in ten minutes with the ship's doctor, a lean, craggy-faced man named Johnston. He was about to check on Hopkins when Frank said, "The man behind the bar is hurt worse."

"Hey, wait a minute!" Hopkins protested.

"The more you argue, the longer it'll be before somebody tends to those wounds," Frank told him.

Hopkins subsided, muttering curses. Johnston went behind the bar and worked for quite a while on the injured man back there. When he came over to Frank and Salty again, he reported, "I think he'll live, but he'll never get much use out of that arm again."

"He shouldn't have tried to use it to shoot me," Frank said. He gestured toward Hopkins. "See what you can do for this varmint, Doc."

Johnston knelt beside Hopkins, cut away the man's trousers to get at the wounds, and started cleaning them. Hopkins gritted his teeth and made groaning sounds through them as carbolic acid bit at the raw flesh on his hip and thigh.

The wound on his hip was just a deep graze, messy and painful but not serious since it didn't seem to have nicked the bone. The hole in his thigh went all the way through, again resulting in a lot of blood and misery but not posing a threat to his life. Johnston cleaned and bandaged both wounds.

The only fatality was the bartender.

Frank's first shot had taken him cleanly in the heart.

When the doctor was finished, Frank and Handlesman took hold of Hopkins's arms and lifted him into a chair.

"Time for you to keep your end of the bargain," Salty said.

Hopkins glared at him. "You took so damn long gettin' me fixed up, I ought to not tell you."

"You'd better think twice about that," Frank cautioned him. "We can always take you back to Skagway and let the folks there deal with you."

Hopkins frowned. He knew good and well how the citizens of Skagway would deal with him. It would involve a rope and a gallows.

"Y'understand, I don't know exactly where Joe is. But I know where we were going, and I'd bet that derby of mine he's headed there right now, the dirty bastard. Runnin' out and leavin' me like that."

"Keep talking," Frank said.

Salty still had his Remington in his hand. His thumb rested on the hammer, ready to pull it back.

"Calgary," Hopkins said. "We were gonna cut across the mountains to Calgary. Joe said he knew some fellas there we could throw in with."

Frank had heard of the Canadian city but had never been there. Calgary was on the other side of the Rockies, at the edge of the Great Plains that extended from Canada down through the United States. Located not far north of Montana, it was a cowtown, Frank had heard, as wild in its early days as Abilene or Dodge City had been.

The formation of the North West Mounted Police had tamed Calgary and the rest of western Canada, at least to a certain extent. But Frank was sure there were still plenty of lawless men in the region, so Hopkins was probably right. He and Joe Palmer would have been able to find some new partners, or set up some illegal operation of their own.

Especially with the money they had stolen from Salty and the other citizens of Skagway to finance them.

The old-timer said, "We got to go after him, Frank. I worked hard for that dinero. I thought I'd never see it again."

"We'll talk about that," Frank promised. "Right now we need to figure out what to do with Hopkins and that other fella." He turned to Handlesman. "Do you know if there's any law hereabouts?"

"There might be some Mounties on patrol around here," the second mate said. "On the other hand, there might not be. The closest garrison is down at Vancouver."

"Do you think Captain Beswick could be persuaded to take Hopkins to Seattle and turn him over to the authorities there?"

Handlesman rubbed his heavy jaw as he frowned in thought. "I don't know. This is Canada. The *Jupiter*'s an American ship."

"It was an American that Hopkins was trying to kill," Frank said with a nod toward Salty. "Anyway, Hopkins is wanted in Alaska, and that's an American territory. He's probably got warrants out for him in Colorado and other places, too. That's where Soapy Smith and his bunch were before they went north to Alaska."

"I suppose it can't hurt to ask him," Handlesman said. "What about the other fella?"

Frank shook his head. "I don't even know his name. We'll leave him here. He probably has friends who'll take care of him."

"What about us?" Salty asked. "We're goin' after Palmer, ain't we?"

"We'll talk about that back on the ship," Frank said.

"What were you thinking, sneaking off like that?" Meg asked Salty with a scolding tone in her voice as if she was his mother, rather than young enough to be his granddaughter.

"Aw, shoot, I don't know," Salty replied. His leathery old face wore a hangdog expression. "I heard music, and it sounded like folks was havin' fun. And I hadn't had a drink in so long. . . . I wasn't gonna go off on a bender, I can promise you that. Them days is over."

Frank wasn't completely sure they were, but he and Meg couldn't watch Salty all the time. Sooner or later the old-timer had to be responsible for his own actions.

The three of them were in Meg's cabin on the *Jupiter.* She had been waiting for them on deck when they got back to the ship. Handlesman had already told her that Frank and Salty were all right, when he came to get the doctor for the two wounded men.

Yeah Mow Hopkins was locked up in the *Jupiter*'s tiny brig. Captain Beswick had agreed, reluctantly, to deliver him to the law when the ship reached Seattle.

The question now was, what were Frank and Salty going to do?

"I'm sure sorry for all the trouble I caused," Salty went on, "but if I hadn't snuck ashore and gone to that saloon, I wouldn't have spotted those two varmints. It was just pure-dee luck. Either that, or an omen tellin' us to go after Palmer and get my dang money back."

"We'd have to track him across the Rocky Mountains," Frank pointed out. "That's mighty rugged country. We might not be able to catch up to him until we got to Calgary."

"I don't care how long it takes." Salty glared determinedly. "I'll go after the dang skalleyhooter by myself if I have to, by grab!"

Frank chuckled. "Take it easy. I never said I wouldn't go with you. I'm just saying it's liable to be a hard chase."

"I'm up to it," Salty insisted. "I've traipsed hell-west and crosswise all over the frontier in my time. I can ride all night and fight all day if'n I have to."

Frank didn't doubt it. Salty might be old, but he was tough as whang leather. Sort of like Frank himself.

"We'll have to get some horses and pack animals," Meg put in.

Frank and Salty both turned to look at her. "What makes you think you're goin'?" Salty asked.

"I figured you'd stay on the ship and go on to Seattle," Frank added. "You can wait for us there."

"You figured wrong," Meg shot back at

him without hesitation.

"Didn't you hear what I was telling Salty about how hard the trip might be?"

"We were all going to Mexico together. That's still the plan as far as I'm concerned. This is just a little . . . side trip, I guess you could say."

Crossing the Canadian Rockies, even in summer, was likely to be more than a little side trip, Frank thought. But he had to admit it probably wouldn't be as bad as traveling from Skagway over Chilkoot Pass to Whitehorse with winter coming on, and Meg had survived that. She was a good rider, could handle a gun, and certainly wasn't lacking for courage.

Maybe it wouldn't be a bad idea to have her along.

"All right," he said as he nodded.

Salty stared at him. "Have you gone touched in the head? You want to bring a gal along while we're chasin' a owlhoot like Palmer acrost Canada?"

"Meg can take care of herself," Frank said. "And she probably won't go sneaking off and get mixed up in a gunfight."

"Yeah, yeah," Salty muttered. "I done said I was sorry."

"It's settled, then," Meg said. "Tomorrow morning we head east toward Calgary and try to pick up Palmer's trail."

"Providing we can find some decent horses," Frank said. "That might not be as easy as it sounds."

CHAPTER 5

Captain Beswick intended to sail early the next morning, so Frank was up at first light to head into the settlement. He thought he had seen a livery stable the night before, while he and the party from the ship were headed toward Red Mike's, and he wanted to find out if he was right.

As it turned out, he was. Parkhurst's Livery dealt in saddle horses and pack animals for the fur trappers who made Powderkeg Bay their headquarters. The proprietor, a white-haired man with the bulbous red nose of a heavy drinker, was glad to sell Frank three mounts and a couple of pack mules.

The horses weren't much for looks or speed, but they were sturdy animals that ought to stand up well to traveling over the mountains, Frank thought.

"You can ride the mules if you need to," Parkhurst assured Frank. "They'll take a saddle. Their gait'll loosen your teeth, though, if you have to ride 'em for very long."

"We don't intend to," Frank said. "We'll need saddles and the rest of the rigs, along with packs for the mules."

Parkhurst nodded. "I can fix you up, Mr. Morgan."

"What about a general store for supplies?"

"Right along the street here." Parkhurst pointed. "Haney's Emporium. Tell Todd Haney I sent you."

The sun had just begun to peek over the mountains to the east by the time Frank had bought the supplies and loaded them on the mules. He left all five animals tied up in front of the store while he went back to the ship to let Salty and Meg know they were ready to ride out.

Both of them had their gear gathered. It didn't amount to much, since they had been traveling light. Meg was wearing a holstered .32-caliber revolver and had a short-barreled Winchester carbine tucked under her arm. She looked as if she was ready for trouble.

And they were liable to find it, Frank mused. That was just the way things seemed to go where he was concerned.

Captain Beswick was waiting at the gangplank to bid them farewell. He shook hands with Frank and Salty and tipped his cap to Meg.

"Good luck to you," the captain said. "To be honest, I think this is a bit of a fool's errand you're going on, but perhaps it will work out. I hope so."

Salty said, "No offense, Cap'n, but it ain't your money that's involved. To my way of thinkin', I'd be a fool not to go after Palmer and try to get it back."

"If you get a chance, write to me in care of the shipping line. I'd like to hear how this all comes out."

"We'll do that," Frank said with a nod.

When they reached the dock, Frank looked back at the ship and saw Handlesman and Monroe at the railing. He lifted a hand in farewell to the second mate and the sailor. Both of them had been helpful during the ruckus the night before.

No one had bothered the horses, the mules, or the supplies. Frank, Salty, and Meg swung up into their saddles. Captain Beswick had a map of Canada among the numerous maps in his cabin, and Frank had studied it. Calgary was approximately four hundred miles east and a little bit south of Powderkeg Bay. In mountainous country, it would take three weeks, possibly more, to get there.

Frank was confident that he could find the settlement. They might not follow exactly the same trails between here and there as Joe Palmer did, but on the other hand, there were a number of mountain ranges in their path and probably only a limited amount of routes through them. If Palmer wasn't in too much of a hurry, they might be able to catch up to him before he reached Calgary.

Only one trail led out of Powderkeg Bay, winding up the side of the mountain that loomed above the town. When they had climbed quite some distance, Frank reined in and motioned for the others to do likewise.

"In terrain like this, we'll have to stop pretty often to let the horses rest," he told Salty and Meg as he dismounted. "We don't want to wear them out. According to Captain Beswick's map, there are a few small settlements between here and Calgary, but we may not be able to get fresh mounts until we get there."

They stood on the trail, holding the reins, and looked down the mountainside at the bay, the island a short distance off shore, and the vast Pacific beyond it. From up here they had a good view of the town, and Frank could also see the *Jupiter*'s sails as the ship turned south toward Seattle.

Frank pointed out the vessel to his companions. "I hope Hopkins gets what's comin' to him," Salty muttered.

"He will," Frank said. "Sooner or later, all owlhoots do."

"I ain't interested in later. The sooner that varmint's dancin' a jig at the end of a hang rope, the better."

Frank didn't know if Hopkins would wind up being hanged or not. It would depend on what charges the authorities could prove against him. But at the very least he would spend a long time in jail.

When the horses had rested for a few minutes, the three of them mounted up again and resumed their trek. Frank had already spotted a flat shoulder jutting out from the mountain higher up and had a hunch the trail followed it around the peak.

That turned out to be the case, but it took them until the middle of the afternoon to reach the shoulder. They hadn't even gotten out of sight of the sea before dusk began to settle down and Frank started looking for a place to make camp.

He found a clearing in the evergreens that thickly coated the mountainside and bordered both sides of the trail. Plenty of dry branches littered the ground under the trees, so they would have an abundance of firewood. It would come in handy to ward off the chill the night would bring.

As they sat by the fire eating a supper of salt pork and biscuits, Frank said, "You know Palmer's not going to give up that money without a fight, Salty."

The old-timer snorted. "Wouldn't expect him to. Hope he don't. That way I'll have a good excuse to plug the varmint."

"If you do get the money back, what then?" Meg asked. "Are you still coming to Mexico with us?"

"If I recollect right, headin' south of the border was my idea to start with," Salty pointed out. "I ain't changed my mind about it, neither."

Frank smiled. "South of the border in these parts means back in the United States."

"Yeah, I know." A wistful tone crept into Salty's voice. "I appreciate the two o' you comin' with me like this. I know you're prob'ly anxious to get back home."

"I don't have anything waiting for me," Meg said.

"Yeah, but Frank does."

Frank knew the old-timer was talking about Stormy and Goldy, his two horses, and Dog, the big, wolflike cur that had been

Frank's friend and trail companion for a long time. All three of the animals had been left with a friendly stable owner in Seattle, and Frank trusted the man to take good care of them. Paying for that care wasn't a problem, either.

But Frank had to admit to himself that it would be good to see his old pards again. He had no idea how long it was going to be before that happened. In the meantime, he would concentrate on the job at hand.

Another advantage to having a fire was that it would keep wild animals away from the camp. Frank didn't know for sure what sort of varmints might be roaming these mountains, but he figured it was certainly possible there might be wolves and bears around here.

The drawback was that Joe Palmer might spot their fire and take it as a sign that someone was coming after him . . . which was true, of course. It was possible that Palmer might double back and try to ambush them.

For that reason, Frank thought it would be a good idea if they took turns standing guard at night. He suggested that Meg take the first shift, since it was the easiest, then he would take the second and Salty the third.

They nodded their agreement. "What are you worried about, Frank?" Meg asked. "Wild animals?"

Salty said, "More like varmints of the two-legged variety, I'm bettin'."

"That's right," Frank said. "We don't know how far ahead of us Palmer is. If he knows he's being chased, he might try to bushwhack us."

"That'd be fine," Salty said. "That way we won't have to chase him clear to Calgary."

"Assuming he doesn't kill us," Frank said drily.

Salty snorted again. " 'Tain't likely. Not with a couple o' old hands like you and me on his trail."

The night passed quietly, with no sign of Joe Palmer or any other dangerous varmint, and the next morning the three of them resumed their journey.

That was the beginning of a week's travel through rugged but spectacularly beautiful country. The trails they followed led through lush green valleys between towering, snow-capped peaks. Fast-flowing streams danced merrily along those valleys. Eagles wheeled through the clear blue sky, and every day Frank spotted elk, moose, and antelope herds, as well as the occasional majestic, lumbering bear.

Not once, though, did they see another human being in this vast Canadian wilderness.

That changed abruptly on the seventh day of their trip.

"Look yonder," Salty said, reining in and pointing. "Smoke from somebody's chimney."

Frank had already spotted the thin column of gray curling into the sky. It was rising from a spot a mile or so down the valley they were following.

"Are we going to stop?" Meg asked as she and Frank brought their mounts to a halt as well.

Frank nodded. "It would probably be a good idea. That smoke's likely coming from some trapper's cabin. He might have seen Palmer go by. It would be nice to have some proof that we're on the right trail."

"We're on the right trail," Salty insisted. "I can feel it in my bones."

Frank didn't want to dispute what Salty's bones said, at least not to the old-timer's face, but some actual evidence would be welcome. If whoever was responsible for that smoke had seen Palmer, he could tell them how far ahead of them the fugitive was.

They heeled their horses into motion

again. The pack mules plodded along behind at the end of ropes tied to Frank's and Salty's saddles.

The smoke led them to a long meadow with a shallow stream running along one side of it. At the far end of the meadow and on the other side of the stream, between the water and the trees, sat a log cabin. The smoke rose from a stone chimney built onto one side of the cabin.

Frank lifted a hand to stop the others. He leaned forward a little in the saddle, easing his muscles as he studied the cabin. He saw a pole corral and a lean-to shed behind it, but no horses were in there. In fact, he didn't see any movement anywhere around the cabin.

The smoke rising from the chimney was the only sign of life.

"What are we waiting for?" Meg asked.

"It's not a good idea to just go riding up to somebody's place without taking a look around first," Frank explained. "You don't want to pay a visit unannounced, either. People can get spooked easy, especially out in the middle of nowhere like this."

"I understand," she said. "Do you think a trapper lives here?"

"That's what it looks like to me."

"Maybe the fella ain't home," Salty suggested. "I see his horses are gone."

Frank rubbed his jaw and frowned. "Yeah, maybe. But would he go off and leave a fire burning in the fireplace?"

"There ain't no tellin' what some folks'll do. Not ever'body's been to see the elephant like you and me have, Frank."

"That's true, I suppose," Frank said with a shrug. "Let's go."

He hitched his horse into motion again, riding slowly forward along the creek. When he came to a likely looking spot where the stream flowed shallowly over its rocky bed, he sent his mount into the water. This was as good a place to ford the creek as any. Salty and Meg followed.

The closer they got to the cabin, the more Frank felt the skin on the back of his neck prickling. Over the long, dangerous years, he had learned to put complete faith in his instincts, and now those instincts were warning him that something wasn't quite right here.

An instant later, that hunch was confirmed as the barrel of a rifle suddenly thrust out from a window and gushed flame and smoke.

Chapter 6

Frank was in the lead, so he saw the rifle first. He reacted instantly, yanking his horse's head to the side and calling, "Follow me!" to Salty and Meg, at the same time as the shot blasted out from the window.

The bullet came close enough that Frank heard its high-pitched whine. He galloped toward the trees. It wouldn't do any good to cross back over the creek. There was no cover over there in the open meadow.

A glance over his shoulder told him that Salty and Meg were close behind him. He was relieved to see that neither of them appeared to be wounded.

The whip crack of another rifle shot came to his ears, over the pounding of hooves. Then he reached the trees and sent the horse plunging into the thick growth. He pulled his Winchester from the saddle boot as he hauled the animal to a stop and dropped from the saddle.

Salty and Meg were close by, shielded by the tree trunks as well. As they dismounted, Frank called over to them, "Either of you hit?"

"Nope," Salty said. "Not me."

"I'm fine, too," Meg said. "How about you, Frank?"

"That first shot was a mite close, but it didn't get me," he told them without taking his eyes off the cabin. "Meg, hold the horses. Salty, get your rifle."

The old-timer worked the lever of the Winchester in his hands. "Already got it," he said. "Let's pour some lead into that shack."

"Hold your fire," Frank ordered. "We can't just start blazing away without knowing who we're shooting at or why."

"We may not know who, but I dang sure know why!" Salty responded. "Because the son of a buck shot at us!"

"Maybe he thought he had good cause."

"Maybe," Salty allowed as he crouched behind the thick trunk of a pine. "That don't mean I aim to let him get away with tryin' to kill us. Dagnab it, Frank, that could be Palmer his own self in there!"

"It could be," Frank said. "Why don't we try to find out?"

No more shots had come from the cabin

after the second one. Frank eased forward to the edge of the trees. He couldn't see the rifle anymore. Whoever was using it had pulled it back inside the window.

"Hello, the cabin!" Frank shouted. "Hello in there! We're not looking for trouble!"

There was no response.

Frank tried again. "Can you hear me in there? We're friends!"

"That's stretchin' it a mite," Salty muttered. "I ain't friends with nobody who tries to part my hair with a bullet!"

"Hush," Frank said. He raised his voice again. "Hello, the cabin!"

Nothing met the call but silence. There weren't even any sounds in the underbrush. The shots had caused all the birds and small animals to flee.

"Something's wrong," Frank said quietly.

"Yeah, some polecat shot at us!"

"It's more than that," Frank said. "Salty, you and Meg keep an eye on the place."

"What are you going to do?" Meg asked.

"Work my way through the trees and see if I can get behind the cabin. There might be a door or a window back there by that corral and shed."

"Be careful," Meg cautioned him. "There might be more than one man in there. If there is a back way in, somebody may be watching it."

"That's a chance I'll have to take," Frank said. Before she could argue with him, he slid off through the trees, moving quickly but quietly.

He pulled back deeper into the woods so that anybody watching the trees wouldn't be as likely to see him. The cabin was only about fifty yards away. Frank covered twice that distance in circling around it. When he thought he had gone far enough, he ventured a look.

He was past the cabin now, so he was able to look at the back side of it. The shed was built right against the wall. There was no window or door.

But that didn't mean this side was a blind approach. There could be chinks between the logs big enough for a man to look out through them but too small for Frank to see from this distance. There could even be loopholes through which a rifle barrel could be slid.

But he had to take the chance. The only other option was for him and his companions to mount up, work their way through the woods until they were out of sight of the cabin, and then ride on.

They could do that, but Frank didn't like unanswered questions. Nor did he care for the possibility that the man they were look-ing for could be in that cabin.

The cabin and its adjacent shed and cor-ral lay about twenty yards from the edge of the trees. Frank took a deep breath and then charged out from cover, running toward the structures as fast as he could.

Riding boots weren't made for running. All too aware that he was out in the open, Frank felt like he was barely making any progress at all. He knew with every step that somebody could be drawing a bead on him.

In reality, only a few seconds passed before he reached the corral. He paused for a second, crouching beside the pole fence. When no shots roared out from the cabin, he moved closer. He reached the corner of the cabin.

There were no windows on this side, either. It was beginning to look as if the door and the front window were the only ways in or out of the place.

With his rifle held ready, Frank cat-footed along the side of the cabin. He waved toward the trees where Salty and Meg were hidden to let them know he was all right, as well as to signal that they should hold their fire.

He stopped at the front corner and lis-tened. Dead silence hung over the valley.

No sounds came from inside the cabin.

Like it or not, he had to move over to the window and see if he could find out what was going on here. He eased in that direction. Despite his long years of experience in dangerous situations, his pulse was beating a little faster than usual.

He was close enough now to see that while the door was pushed up, it wasn't closed quite all the way. The window had shutters on the inside. One of them was closed, but the other hung open. Frank stopped only a foot from the window and listened again.

This time he heard a very faint rasping sound, like somebody using a piece of sandpaper on some wood. After a moment, he realized what he was hearing.

Someone inside the cabin was struggling mightily to draw one breath after another.

Carefully, he lowered the Winchester and leaned it against the cabin wall. He pulled the Colt instead, steel whispering against leather as he drew it. The revolver was better suited for close work.

The labored breathing could be a trick, the bait in a trap designed to lure him in.

Frank's instincts told him that wasn't the case. The man inside the cabin hadn't cried out or claimed he was wounded or anything like that. It was unlikely that he even knew

Frank was out here, close enough to hear those rasping breaths.

Frank took off his hat and leaned closer to the window. He risked a look around the edge of the closed shutter.

The inside of the cabin was dim and shadowy, but enough light came through the window for him to make out the shape of a man lying in a twisted position on the hard-packed dirt floor. The man wasn't moving. Frank saw a dark stain on the ground around him and knew it had to be blood.

If the man Frank could see was the only one in the cabin, he didn't represent much of a threat. Unfortunately, Frank couldn't be sure the man lying on the floor was the only one in there. To confirm that, he would have to go inside.

He crouched low and went under the window, then straightened and put his hat on again as he came to the door. He paused long enough to flash a confident smile toward the trees where Salty and Meg were watching, then lunged forward, hitting the door with his shoulder and knocking it open as he dived through.

Frank landed on his belly with the Colt tilted up, ready to fire. His head jerked from side to side as his keen eyes scanned the room. The cabin wasn't very big, and it took him only a second to see everything in it.

The man lying on his side in a pool of blood was the cabin's only occupant except for Frank himself.

Frank heaved himself up on his knees. With the door wide open now, enough light spilled through it for him to see the man's pale, twisted face. It was narrow, with an angular, beard-stubbled jaw. The man wore a buckskin shirt, the front of which was sodden with dark blood, and corduroy trousers.

He definitely *wasn't* Joe Palmer.

A rifle lay on the floor not far from the man's outstretched hand. Frank stood up and nudged it well out of reach with a booted toe. He kept his Colt trained on the wounded man. The man seemed to be out cold and probably on the verge of death, judging by the amount of blood he had lost, but Frank didn't believe in taking unnecessary chances.

He stepped to the doorway and called to Salty and Meg, "It's all right! Come on in!"

The man on the floor let out a groan.

Frank wanted to go to him and see if he could do anything for him, but he waited until his companions got there. When they did, he told Meg, "Wait out here."

"Why?" she asked.

"Because you don't want to go in there," Frank said bluntly. "Come on, Salty."

Meg obviously didn't like it, but she remained outside. When Frank and Salty stepped into the cabin, Frank said, "Keep him covered while I check on him."

"What happened to him?"

"That's what I'm going to find out. Looks like he was shot or stabbed in the belly."

Being gut-shot was a long, hard, miserable way to die. Frank hadn't wished such a fate on many men, not even most of his enemies. Certainly not on a stranger.

He holstered his Colt and knelt next to the man. Gently, he rolled the man onto his back and pulled up the buckskin shirt to take a look at the wound. The long, narrow opening through which the crimson blood had welled told Frank that the man had been knifed.

The man's eyelids fluttered. His thinning dark hair was askew, and beads of sweat covered his forehead. He managed to force his eyes open and gasped, "Who — ?"

"Take it easy," Frank said. "I'm a friend. I won't hurt you."

"You . . . I shot . . . at you . . ."

"Yeah, but I won't hold that against you. I reckon you thought you had a good reason."

"I thought . . . you were him . . . comin'

back to . . . finish me off."

Frank had thought it might be something like that. He said, "Are you talking about the man who stabbed you?"

"Y-yeah. He rode up . . . this morning . . . wanted some grub. I fed him. . . . Then he wanted to . . . swap horses with me. . . ."

Every word was a struggle for the wounded man to get out. Frank felt a pang of sympathy, but he knew there was nothing he could do to save this luckless fella's life. He wanted to find out as much as he could in the time the man had left, though.

"It hurts like . . . hell," the man said. "I need some . . . whiskey."

Frank glanced at Salty. Both of them knew that whiskey wouldn't do the man any good.

On the other hand, he couldn't hurt much worse than he already was, and the liquor might brace him up a little, at least for a few moments. Salty went over to a rough-hewn table and picked up a jug that sat on it. He pulled the cork, took a sniff of the contents, and nodded to Frank, who held out his hand.

Frank took the jug with one hand, lifted the wounded man's head with the other, and tipped a little of the fiery rotgut past the man's lips. That brought a gasp from the man. His eyes opened a little wider.

75

"The man who did this to you," Frank asked, "what did he look like?"

"St-stocky fella . . . had a mustache . . . wore one of those . . . funny hats."

"A derby?" Salty asked.

"Y-yeah. A d-derby."

Salty nodded to Frank. "That's Palmer, all right."

"Had a hunch it was," Frank said. He asked the wounded man, "What happened after he wanted to swap horses with you?"

"I said I . . . didn't much want to . . . and he said . . . that was all right. He seemed like . . . a friendly cuss . . . but then he . . . when I wasn't lookin' . . . he . . . he stuck a knife . . . in my belly."

"The low-down son of a bitch," Salty said. "That's just what he'd do, all right."

"I tried to fight him . . . but I was . . . hurt too bad. . . . Reckon I must'a . . . passed out. . . . I came to . . . heard horses . . . thought he was comin' back. . . . I got my rifle . . . made it to the window. . . . Couldn't see too good, but I got off . . . a couple of shots. . . ."

"That's all right, friend," Frank told him. "No need to wear yourself out. We understand now what happened."

"Didn't mean to . . . shoot at strangers. . . ."

"Don't worry about it. Just rest easy."

The man grimaced and seemed to bow in on himself as a fresh surge of pain hit him. When it eased a little, he whispered, "I could use . . . some more whiskey. . . ."

Frank lifted the jug again, but before he could bring it to the man's mouth, a shudder went through the man and a long, rattling sigh eased from him. His muscles went slack and his eyes turned dull with death.

"He's gone," Frank said.

"Yeah," Salty agreed. "Poor varmint. He died for nothin'."

"Not completely for nothing." Frank looked up at Salty and went on grimly, "At least now we know for sure that we're on Palmer's trail."

CHAPTER 7

Frank wished he had taken a moment to find out the man's name before that unfortunate passed away. As it was, all he could carve on the crude cross he and Salty made were the date and the letters RIP. They set up the cross at the head of the grave they dug to one side of the cabin, after they'd filled it back in.

Salty glanced at the sky and said, "It's a mite late in the day to be pushin' on, but I ain't sure I feel too good about spendin' the night here where that poor varmint crossed the divide."

A shiver ran through Meg. "I feel the same way," she said. "I'd rather make camp somewhere else."

Frank nodded. "Let's ride. We've done all we can here."

They headed east, following the creek as it meandered along the valley. Soon the cabin and the lonely grave were out of sight behind them.

That night they made a cold camp. "Palmer is less than a day ahead of us," Frank pointed out. "If he hasn't spotted us before, we don't want him to now."

"We're gonna catch the no-good varmint," Salty said. "I can feel it in my bones."

"No disrespect to your bones, Salty, but there's still a lot that could happen." Frank gazed off into the darkness. "But we know now that he's up there somewhere ahead of us, and that's something, anyway."

For the first time in several days, Joe Palmer wasn't hungry. He had looted the trapper's cabin of all the supplies he could pack onto his horse, after moving his saddle over to the horse in the corral behind the cabin.

Now, with a week's worth of provisions and a spare mount, he felt better about his chances than he had at any time since he'd fled from Powderkeg Bay. As he leaned back against the fallen tree that lay in the clearing where he'd made camp, he wondered idly about his former partner.

Palmer had been trying to get away from Yeah Mow Hopkins ever since they had left Skagway together with that loot Soapy had cached. It wasn't that Palmer had anything against Yeah Mow. He wasn't that bright,

79

but he was strong and loyal.

Palmer wanted all the money for himself, though. He had never planned on partnering up permanently with Hopkins. That was just a way for both of them to get out of Skagway with their hides intact when the vigilantes started their rampage.

But in the months since then, Hopkins had watched him like a hawk. Hopkins didn't mind Palmer carrying the loot, but he didn't let him out of his sight, either. Yeah Mow was cunning, even if he wasn't exactly what anybody would call smart.

So as far as Palmer was concerned, running into that old pelican Salty Stevens was a stroke of luck. It was amazing that Stevens was even still alive. He had disappeared from Skagway with winter coming on, and Palmer had just assumed that the old bastard had frozen to death somewhere.

The worrisome thing was that if Stevens was still alive, Frank Morgan might be, too. Morgan had befriended the old-timer in Skagway. The gunfighter was definitely dangerous. Palmer and the rest of Soapy's men had found that out when they tried to get rid of him.

When the shooting had started in Red Mike's, Palmer had seized the opportunity to get out of town while Hopkins was pinned down behind the bar. Palmer had mixed emotions about the outcome of that gunfight. If Stevens had killed Hopkins, then he didn't have to worry about Yeah Mow coming after him. If it was the other way around, chances were that Hopkins would follow him. Hopkins knew that the plan called for them to cross the mountains and head for Calgary.

Hopkins wouldn't be in a forgiving mood. He would want the money, and he would want revenge for Palmer running out on him like that. Maybe it hadn't been a good idea, Palmer mused now. He hadn't spent a lot of time thinking about it, though. He had just acted when the chance presented itself to him.

As usual, he was damned either way, he brooded. And damned even more if Frank Morgan was still alive and coming after him.

But he couldn't do anything about that now except try to stay ahead of any possible pursuers, no matter who they were. He'd have a lot better chance of doing that with the supplies and the extra horse. Since leaving Powderkeg Bay he had been living on the game he could shoot. Now with any luck, he could make those stolen supplies stretch all the way to Calgary.

Once he reached the settlement, the biggest in western Canada, he was confident that he could link up with some fellas he knew there and be safe, even if Frank Morgan was still alive and on his trail.

Both of the horses suddenly lifted their heads and pricked their ears. Palmer tensed as he noticed the reaction from the animals. They had heard or smelled something.

A moment later, he smelled it, too. Wood smoke. Somebody had a campfire burning not too far away. Palmer muttered a curse under his breath.

He hadn't built a fire because he didn't want anybody seeing it. Somebody was out here in this wilderness who didn't care about that. Stevens? Morgan? Both of them?

No, Palmer decided. The light breeze that carried the scent of smoke to him came out of the east. It was possible that someone trailing him could have gotten past him without any of them knowing about it, but he thought it was unlikely. He had been moving pretty fast.

That meant somebody else was ahead of him. No telling who it might be. Another trapper, maybe. Some travelers on their way through the mountains. It could be anybody, Palmer told himself. He had no reason to think they were a threat to him.

But he didn't *know,* and that bothered

him. He got to his feet and picked up his rifle. The idea of traipsing around on the side of a mountain in the darkness wasn't very appealing to him, but he liked the idea of being surprised by enemies even less.

He was a city boy and didn't like this wilderness, but he had been around it enough that he was confident he could find his way back to the camp. He left the horses tied up where they were and started making his way through the shadows, following the scent of wood smoke that still drifted through the night.

"The fire is already too big, Joseph," Charlotte Marat said as she stood with her arms crossed, glaring impatiently at her brother. "Someone will see it."

Joseph tossed another branch onto the flames and shrugged. "Who is out here to see it, other than our friends?"

"We don't *know* who is out here," Charlotte insisted. "That is the whole point of being careful."

Joseph sighed. It was easier to humor Charlotte than to argue with her, much easier. He knew that. Sometimes he had to remind himself of that fact, however.

"We'll let the fire burn down," he said. "I wanted some hot food tonight. All this running and hiding and living like animals . . . it gets wearisome, Charlotte."

Her expression softened, and when it did, some of the beauty that hardship had drained out of her returned, if only momentarily.

"Of course it does," she said. "I'm sorry, Joseph. But we must stay alive and free if our cause is to have any chance of succeeding."

She sat down on a slab of rock on the other side of the fire. The light from the flames painted her face with red shadows.

Joseph Marat was aware that his sister was a beautiful woman. She should have been in an elegantly appointed drawing room somewhere, wearing a fine gown, instead of hunkered in a forest clearing in boots, denim trousers, and a flannel shirt. Her thick, dark brown hair should have been piled on her head in an elaborate arrangement of curls instead of drawn back and tied behind her head so that she could tuck it more easily under her hat when she was riding.

But neither of them had asked for their fate. The Indian blood that mingled in their veins with the French meant that they would always be half-breeds, pitiful creatures to be scorned and looked down upon, despite the fact that both of them were more intelligent and better educated than the English and the Scots who had driven their people out of their homeland.

Joseph took the skillet from the fire, divided the beans and bacon in it among the two of them. His rifle was close at hand, and even while he was heating the food, he had paid close attention to the woods around them.

What he had told Charlotte was true, as far as it went. They had no enemies out here that he knew of.

But it was what a man didn't know that often wound up killing him, Joseph reflected. Charlotte was absolutely right. He shouldn't have built such a big fire.

The objection she had raised didn't keep her from eating eagerly. They washed the food down with sips of hot coffee. After a while, Charlotte said, "How much longer do you think we'll have to wait?"

Joseph shook his head. "I don't know. Duryea wasn't sure when the guns would arrive. Sometime this month."

"We've been waiting for a week already."

"I know. We'll wait another week if we have to. However long it takes."

Joseph's tone was a little sharper than he'd intended. He saw the flash of hurt in his sister's eyes and wanted to apologize to her. He suppressed the impulse.

A man who was tough enough to lead a revolution didn't start saying he was sorry every time his bossy little sister got her feelings hurt.

A little noise in the brush caught Joseph's attention. A small animal might have caused it . . . but it might be something else, too.

Moving casually so as not to alarm anyone who was watching, he reached over and put his hand on his rifle. Charlotte noticed the movement, and her eyes narrowed. Joseph knew she was about to ask him if something was wrong. To forestall that, he stood up and said, "I think I'll take a little walk."

"Why?" she asked.

"I don't demand explanations from you when you have personal business to conduct, do I?"

Her face turned even redder in the firelight. He felt bad about embarrassing her, but better a little embarrassment than tipping off a possible enemy that he was aware of them lurking near the camp.

He tucked the rifle under his arm as if he didn't have a care in the world, then stepped out of the circle of light cast by the campfire. Instead of heading toward the sound he had heard, he moved off in another direction.

As soon as the thick shadows underneath the trees had enfolded him, he turned and shifted the rifle so that it was in his hands, ready to fire. He began working his way around the camp.

When Joseph was a boy, his father had been friends with Gabriel Dumont, the famous hunter and plainsman who was Louis Riel's second-in-command. Dumont had taught Joseph how to track game, and that involved being able to move silently through the woods, even in darkness.

Joseph used those lessons now, taking care each time he put a foot down not to make any noise. It was slow, painstaking work, but such caution could save a man's life.

He paused frequently to listen, but he couldn't hear anything except the faint crackling of the fire as it burned down. Had he been too suspicious? Was there really nothing dangerous out here?

"Joseph?" That was Charlotte calling out to him. "Joseph, are you all right?"

Blast it, Joseph thought bitterly. He couldn't answer her without giving away his position, but if he failed to respond and there really was someone out here watching the camp, that silence might warn the lurker that he had been discovered.

Joseph was trying to decide what to do

when the brush crackled again, right in front of him this time. His eyes, adjusted to the darkness since he had been away from the fire for several minutes, saw a patch of deeper darkness shift and reveal itself to be the rough shape of a man.

Certain now that something was wrong, Joseph lunged forward and thrust the barrel of his rifle into the stranger's back. "Don't move!" he shouted. "Charlotte, stay where you are!"

Instead of obeying the order, as would any sane man who had a rifle barrel prodding him in the back, the stranger suddenly twisted around and threw himself out of the line of fire. Joseph started to pull the trigger anyway, but his finger froze on the trigger as he realized the rifle was pointing toward the camp. If he fired, he might hit Charlotte by accident.

That second of indecision was enough. The man grabbed the rifle barrel and wrenched upward. That move made Joseph jerk the trigger involuntarily. The shot was deafeningly loud under the thick canopy of tree branches.

The stranger drove the rifle toward Joseph, ripping the weapon from his hands and slamming it into his chest. The impact made Joseph stagger backwards. He felt stunned, as if the blow had caused his heart to stop beating. He couldn't seem to get his breath. While he was off-balance and struggling, the man barreled into him and knocked him off his feet.

Joseph landed hard on the ground, stunning him even more. A knee dug painfully into his belly and pinned him there. The next second, he felt the cold, hard bite of steel as the stranger pressed a gun muzzle into the soft flesh of his neck.

"Don't move, mister," the man warned, "or I'll blow your head off."

He was about to die, Joseph thought, and things couldn't get any worse.

But then they did, as Charlotte's voice, tight with fear, said, "No, m'sieu, it is you who should not move, or *I* will blow *your* head off!"

CHAPTER 8

Joe Palmer had been threatened plenty of times in his life. He had a pretty good feeling for when somebody actually meant to kill him, and for when they didn't.

The gal who had just called out might *think* she meant the threat, but she really didn't. When it came down to the nub, she wouldn't pull the trigger.

He was betting his life on that.

Palmer didn't take his gun away from the man who'd tried to jump him. Instead he said, "Lady, you better be careful. Even if you shoot me, you can't do it fast enough to stop me from killin' your husband."

"He is not my husband," she said. "He is my brother. And all I have to do is pull the trigger —"

"All that's holding back the hammer of this revolver in my hand is my thumb," Palmer interrupted her. "You shoot me, and the hammer falls. Your brother dies. Simple as that."

For a moment, a tense silence filled the darkness. Then the woman said, "What do you want me to do?"

Something inside Palmer eased. He wasn't going to die tonight. Not from being ventilated by this woman, anyway. His bet had paid off.

"Look," he said, trying to strike a reasonable tone, "I don't mean any harm to you folks. Your brother's the one who jumped me. He stuck a rifle in my back. I'm just defending myself here. Why don't you come around where I can see you?"

She didn't respond right away, but after a second he heard her moving. She circled through the brush and stepped into his line of sight. In the shadows under the trees, he couldn't make her out very well, but he saw that she had lowered the rifle.

"Put the gun on the ground," Palmer ordered.

"Charlotte, don't do it!" the man choked out. The gun barrel pushing into his neck half strangled him. "Shoot him!"

"Better not," Palmer warned. "Damn it, I'm tryin' to be friendly here."

He wasn't actually interested in being friends with these two, although from what he had seen of the woman as she sat by the

91

fire while he eavesdropped on their conversation, he wouldn't mind getting better acquainted with her.

However, they had mentioned that they were waiting for somebody, and the word "guns" had been dropped casually. Palmer found that intriguing. He wanted to know more about what they were doing out here, hundreds of miles from anywhere.

"Don't trust him," the man warned his sister again. "Shoot him, Charlotte!"

"I . . . I cannot," Charlotte said.

"You got no reason to," Palmer said. He took another gamble. "In fact, to prove that, I take back what I said. You hang on to that rifle, miss. That way, if I do anything to show that I've been lyin' to you, you can shoot me then."

"I would be more inclined to believe you if you got off my brother."

Palmer looked down at the man he had pinned to the ground. "How about it, mister?" he asked. "If I let you up, are you gonna behave?"

"I don't have much choice, do I?" the man said between clenched teeth.

"There's always a choice, friend. Sometimes we make good ones, and sometimes we don't." Palmer eased the revolver's hammer back down. "I'm gonna take a chance here and hope I made a good one."

He pulled the gun away from the man's neck and stood up, stepping back so that he'd have plenty of room to move if he needed to.

The man sat up and rubbed his neck where the gun barrel had dug in painfully. Palmer kept the revolver in his hand. If the bastard tried anything, Palmer knew he'd have time to shoot him, then plug the girl, too, if he had to.

He hoped it wouldn't come to that. He'd much rather get friendly with Charlotte than shoot her.

When he needed to, he could be pretty damned charming. He tried that now, saying, "Look, folks, I just smelled your fire and thought maybe I could get a little coffee and maybe some hot food. Not to mention some company. This is mighty lonely country out here."

"You were spying on us," the man accused. "I heard you moving in the brush. You were listening to what we said."

Charlotte said to her brother, "Then you lied to me when you told me nothing was wrong."

"Be quiet," the man snapped.

"Sure, I was eavesdropping," Palmer admitted. "I wanted to find out who you were and whether you'd be likely to shoot me if I walked into your camp. A man who's not careful about what he does out here deserves whatever happens to him."

"You don't sound like a frontiersman."

Palmer laughed. "Maybe I ain't one, not by choice, anyway. I spent most of my life in cities. But I've knocked around out here in this big lonely enough to have learned a few things." He paused. "My name's Joe Palmer. What's yours?"

Telling somebody your name usually caused people to let their guard down a little, Palmer knew. He didn't mind telling these people who he really was. He wasn't wanted in Canada, and anyway, if he decided that they were a threat to him, he'd just kill them. Simple as that.

After a moment, and with obvious reluctance, the man said, "My name is Joseph Marat."

Palmer grinned. "See? You're Joe, and I'm Joe. Just a couple of Joes. That ought to tell you right there we should be pards."

Marat nodded his head toward the woman. "This is my sister Charlotte."

Palmer lifted his free hand to the brim of his derby. "Mademoiselle Marat. It's an honor to meet you."

"You speak French?" she asked, sounding

surprised.

"Not really," he replied with a chuckle. "I've picked up a little, here and there."

Marat started to get up. Palmer stepped forward and extended his left hand.

"Let me help you there."

Marat hesitated, then clasped Palmer's hand. Palmer hauled him to his feet. Marat still seemed suspicious, but the tension in the air definitely had eased.

"Let's go back to the fire," Charlotte suggested. "We have a little coffee left, but no hot food. I am sorry."

"Don't be," Palmer told her. "I'm just obliged for the offer of coffee."

He turned his back on them and started toward their fire, which was visible through the trees. It was a risky move, he knew, but so far tonight his bets had paid off and he was going to continue to ride his luck.

The Marats, brother and sister, followed him. They didn't shoot him in the back, so he figured that for now, he was ahead of the game.

"Where is your horse?" Marat asked as they reached the clearing where the camp-fire was burning down to tiny, flickering flames.

"I've got a couple of them, a saddle horse and a pack animal," Palmer replied. "I left them tied up a ways off. When I smelled your smoke, I wanted to check it out, but I knew the horses would make too much racket." He grinned. "If I had seen that you folks were dangerous, I would have snuck back to my horses and gone around. You never would have known I was there."

"I knew," Marat snapped.

Palmer shrugged. "So I'm not much of a woodsman. No offense, but you two don't exactly look like Daniel Boone, either."

It was true. All three of them were a little out of place here in this vast wilderness.

Marat took offense at the comment, though. "This is our home," he said. "We are Métis."

"Half-breeds, you mean?"

Marat's upper lip curled in a sneer. "Mixed-bloods. Our ancestry is mostly French, with only a little Indian."

"Oh," Palmer said. He didn't care. A redskin was a redskin, as far as he was concerned. These two might not look it, but they were tainted with savage blood.

He had heard about the Métis. You couldn't spend much time in this part of the world without hearing about them. Descendants of the French fur trappers who had been the first white men to venture into western Canada and had taken Indian women as wives, they had spread all over the plains and mountains.

When the British had come to spread the dominion of the Crown all the way from one side of the continent to the other, the Métis had tried to get along peacefully with them at first. It hadn't taken long for the mixed-bloods to realize, though, that as far as the British were concerned, they had no real voice in their fate.

Led by the highly intelligent and charismatic Louis Riel, twice the Métis had tried to rise up against the British. Both times the rebellions had been short-lived. The Métis had scored a minor victory or two, but then the British had crushed their resistance. The first rebellion had led to the formation of the North West Mounted Police.

After the second rebellion, Louis Riel had been found guilty of treason against the Crown and hanged.

That had happened less than fifteen years earlier, but to Palmer, it was ancient history and had nothing to do with him. Or at least, it hadn't had anything to do with him until now. The earlier talk about guns had sure made him curious.

"Didn't mean any offense," he went on. "I've heard about you folks. The way those damned Britishers treated you never seemed right to me."

He might as well make them think he was on their side, he told himself. That was the quickest, easiest way to worm himself into their confidence and find out what was going on.

Charlotte got a tin cup out of their gear and lifted a coffeepot from the edge of the fire. She poured the last of the coffee in the pot into the cup and handed it to Palmer.

"Thank you," he said with a smile. He knew he wasn't a particularly handsome man, but he was big and rugged-looking and women seemed to respond to him when he smiled.

Charlotte Marat was no different. She lowered her eyes and blushed.

"What are you doing out here?" Joseph Marat demanded, still scowling suspiciously at Palmer.

"I could ask the same thing of you, you know," Palmer responded. He sipped the coffee, which was bitter and had grounds in it. He didn't let his face show how bad it tasted.

"Our business is our own," Marat said.

"Likewise." Palmer shrugged. "I don't mind telling you that I'm on my way to Calgary, though. I've heard that some friends of mine have gone into business around there. I thought maybe I'd join up with them."

That was actually true. The criminal grapevine that stretched across even vast areas of frontier wilderness had carried the rumors that Owen Lundy and Jericho Blake were operating in Calgary now. Palmer had worked with Lundy and Blake in Chicago, before they had all moved farther west and north, and he figured they could probably use another good man.

But they would be even more likely to let him throw in with them if he already had a lucrative scheme lined up.

These two innocents might be the key to that.

"If you're headed to Calgary," Palmer went on, "maybe we could travel together. On the frontier, it's always safer for a group."

With a stubborn look on his face, Marat began, "Our destination is —"

"Your own business, I know," Palmer cut in. "Look, if you want, I'll go back to my horses and won't bother you folks anymore. I don't like sticking my nose in where it's not wanted."

"It's not that, M'sieu Palmer," Charlotte said. "It's just that we are engaged on a matter of great importance. We must be careful about everything we do."

Her brother glared at her, as if she had already said more than he wanted her to.

Palmer took another sip of the bad coffee and nodded. "Hey, at least I got to see some more humans. This is lonely country, and a man gets tired of looking at nothing but elk and moose." He drank the last of the coffee and managed not to grimace. "I'll be pushing on, I guess."

"Good luck to you in Calgary," Marat said, but his surly tone made it clear that he didn't mean it.

"And good luck to you in whatever you're doing." Palmer handed the empty cup to Charlotte and smiled again. He nodded, adding, "So long."

He left the camp, making quite a bit of racket as he tramped through the woods. That was just for show, because he stopped when he was a couple of hundred yards away and listened intently. He heard them moving around and talking to each other, and a few moments later, the sound of horses' hooves drifted through the night air. The orange glow of the fire was gone now.

They were moving their camp. Palmer wasn't the least bit surprised. He had expected Marat to insist on it.

It didn't matter. They might be native to this land, but he had cunning to spare and never lost a trail when there was the promise of a payoff at the end of it. He would find them again and track them until he discovered what was going on here. The delay would give any pursuers coming after him more of a chance to catch up, but it couldn't be helped.

Whatever Marat and his sister were up to, Palmer intended to cut himself in on it.

And when he had done that . . . well, maybe he would just take himself a share of pretty little Charlotte as well.

CHAPTER 9

Frank, Salty, and Meg took up the trail again the next morning, riding east through the mountains. The terrain was rough enough to make their progress frustratingly slow.

That frustration increased when Salty's horse pulled up lame in the middle of the day. When the horse began to limp, Salty let loose with a flood of angry exclamations that sounded like curses even though they actually weren't.

"Take it easy," Frank told him.

"Take it easy?" the old-timer repeated incredulously after he had dismounted and checked his horse's bad leg. "We're gonna have to let this jughead rest a day or two. Wouldn't do no good to switch out the packs on one o' the mules and slap a saddle on it. Those supplies weigh just about as much as I do, so it wouldn't help the hoss to have to carry 'em." He jerked his battered old hat off and slammed it down on the ground in exasperation. "That varmint Palmer's gonna get that much farther ahead of us!"

"We'll make up the time," Frank said, "and even if we don't, we know where he's headed. We'll just have to catch up to him in Calgary, that's all."

"It's gonna be that much harder to find him once he gets to a settlement," Salty pointed out. "Calgary's big enough he'll be able to find a place to hide."

Frank couldn't argue with that. He just said, "We'll find him, Salty. You've got my word on that."

They dismounted, unsaddled the horses, and took the packs off the mules.

"If we had to make camp sooner than we expected, this isn't a bad place to do it," Meg said as she looked around.

She was right about that. The ground was fairly level and there was an open stretch along the bank of the creek, with evergreens towering above it. The valley was narrow here, running between rocky, steep-sided slopes.

Frank took a can of liniment from one of their packs and massaged the thick, foul-smelling stuff into the tight muscle on the bad leg of Salty's horse.

"That'll help," he said. "In the meantime, we might as well take it easy."

Salty looked as if that was going to be a difficult task for him. He was still muttering to himself as he sat down, leaned against a large rock, and pulled his hat down over his eyes.

Frank grinned and shook his head at the old-timer's chagrin. He understood why Salty felt the way he did, but there was nothing that could be done about it.

"I think I'll take a walk up the creek," he said as he pulled his Winchester from its sheath. "Might find some game. We could have elk steaks tonight."

Meg said, "We won't need a fire tonight, but I suppose I'll go ahead and start gathering some wood."

"Keep your eyes open," Frank advised. "You wouldn't want to run into a bear."

"I'll keep that in mind," she said with a smile.

With the repeater tucked under his arm, Frank walked along the stream. Between the twists and turns it took and the way the trees closed in, he was soon out of sight of the camp.

In fact, as far as he could tell by looking, he might as well have been the only human being in five hundred miles.

Frank didn't mind the solitude. In fact, he liked it.

He'd had no choice but to get used to being alone, since so many of his long years had been spent that way. Too many days and nights had been spent far from anywhere and anyone, trying to avoid trouble.

Many times he had been on the run from a posse led by some overzealous lawman who blamed him for crimes he hadn't committed, simply because he had a reputation as a fast gun. When that happened, he sometimes asked himself . . . if he was going to be damned anyway, why not go ahead and become the sort of man they thought he was?

But he couldn't, of course. It wasn't in him to be an owlhoot. He hadn't been raised that way.

Folks could think what they wanted. In his heart, he knew who Frank Morgan was, knew *what* Frank Morgan was . . . and was not.

And in recent years, things had begun to change a little, slowly but surely. Though in the habit of keeping people from getting too close to him, he had allowed the woman named Dixie to steal his heart.

That had ended tragically, sending him into a spiral that had almost claimed him and left him beyond redemption.

His friendship with the young Texas Ranger Tyler Beaumont had rescued him from that fate. Then, because of Beaumont, he had been reunited with old friends from his past. His estranged son Conrad had reached out to him, in need of help, and that was the beginning of the growing respect and friendship between the two of them.

For a while, Frank had even pinned on a lawman's badge and served as the marshal of a Nevada mining town, something that ten years earlier, he would have sworn up and down had no chance in hell of happening.

It had taken him a lot of years to learn it, but he had come to the realization that no man can predict the course of his life . . . and it was a fool's errand to try.

There was nothing wrong with planning for the future — that was only good sense — but a man had to live with the knowledge that those plans might never come about.

He smiled to himself as he realized how deeply he had sunk into this reverie. Being surrounded by nature had something to do with that, he supposed.

It was beautiful here. These Canadian Rockies were some of the most spectacularly beautiful country he had ever seen.

But they held plenty of danger as well. Beautiful or not, carelessness could get a man killed in a hurry here.

As he walked along the creek between the trees, he saw birds and small animals, but no elk or moose. He decided he had come just about far enough and was about to turn around and go back to camp when he heard something.

The crackle in the brush behind him made him spin around and bring the rifle to his shoulder, ready to fire.

"Frank, wait! It's me!"

He found himself staring over the Winchester's sights into Meg's blue eyes, which were wide with surprise and even a little fear right now.

Biting back the curse that sprang to his lips, he lowered the rifle and said, "Blast it, Meg, you know better than to sneak up on me like that."

"I didn't sneak up on you," she protested. "I was just walking along behind you. I'm surprised you didn't hear me before now."

So was he. Surprised and angry, mostly at himself. He had let himself get caught up in contemplating his lonely past, and if Meg had been an enemy, he would probably be dead now.

"I thought you were going to gather some firewood," he said in a gruff voice as he dropped the rifle to his side.

"I did. Then I decided to come after you."

"Something wrong back at camp?"

Meg shook her head. "No, not unless you count Salty's snoring." She came a step closer to him. "I just thought you might want some company."

It would have been rude to tell her that he didn't, so he just said, "I was about to start back. Didn't see any game worth shooting."

Meg looked around and took a deep breath. "It sure is lovely here," she said. "And the air smells wonderful."

"That's because of all these evergreens," Frank said. "And because there's no town close by to foul the air."

He was trying not to think about the way her breasts had lifted underneath the soft buckskin of her shirt when she inhaled deeply like that.

"You don't care much for civilization, do you, Frank?"

He shrugged. "I like civilization just fine."

"Then it's the people you don't like."

"I like people, too. Just not some of the things they do. Most folks are too greedy, and they're too quick to judge other folks."

"Isn't that what you're doing right now?"

Meg asked with a twinkle in her eyes.

Frank had to chuckle. "I reckon you're right."

"Anyway, you shouldn't hold people to your standard. Not everybody can be as perfect as Frank Morgan."

He grunted and shook his head ruefully. "I'm a long way from perfect. That just goes to show that you don't know me as well as you think you do."

"I know that most men would have had me in their bed a hundred times in the months that I've known you, Frank. I've pretty much thrown myself at you."

He looked away, fastening his gaze on the stream that danced and bubbled merrily a few yards away.

"We don't need to talk about that."

"I think we do," she insisted. "Damn it, if you don't know by now that I love you, you're a lot dumber than I think you are."

"I'm smart enough to know that I'm twice your age."

"But not smart enough to know that I don't care about that?"

Frank sighed. He was going to have to put it to her plain.

"Listen. I've been married twice. I don't intend to ever get married again."

"Who said anything about getting married?" Meg shot back. "You see a preacher anywhere around here? I don't. But I see a nice, thick bed of grass on that creek bank, and I see mountains and blue sky and all the beauties of nature. I'm just saying we ought to add to those beauties, Frank, and if that shocks you, I'm sorry. I just don't believe there haven't been other women in your life besides the ones you married."

"There have been," he admitted. More than he could remember, really. In those days, he had taken comfort where he could find it and then ridden on without regret, taking with him only memories . . . and those always faded.

"Then why is it a problem?"

"Because, blast it, I'm too damned old for this!"

"I don't think so."

How had she gotten so close to him without him noticing? He couldn't answer that, but suddenly she was close enough that he could feel the warmth of her breath against his face. She lifted her arms and put them around his neck before he could pull away.

Did he even *want* to pull away? He sure wasn't trying very hard to do so.

He didn't put up a bit of a fight when she lifted her face to his and pressed her lips against his mouth, either.

He had the Winchester in his right hand. His left arm came up and went around her waist. He wasn't thinking now. It was an instinctive reaction when he pulled her closer to him. She came eagerly, her body molding to his.

In the cool mountain air that surrounded them, the heat of her kiss seemed searing to Frank.

Why not? The part of his brain that was still working asked that question. Demanded an answer.

He didn't have one. Other than the ones he had already stated, he didn't have a single good reason not to give Meg what she so obviously wanted.

Then he heard something besides the thudding of his own heart.

The clink of bit chains, followed by a man's voice.

With the arm that was already around her waist, Frank picked up Meg, drawing a started gasp from her, and hustled her away from the creek, deeper into the shadows underneath the thickening trees.

"Quiet," he told her in an urgent whisper. "There's somebody out here."

CHAPTER 10

Frank listened intently, but the sounds didn't grow louder. In fact, he heard voices only a couple more times, and then they faded away. Wherever and whoever those pilgrims were, they weren't coming closer to Frank and Meg.

"Who was it?" Meg whispered to him.

Frank shook his head. "No idea. Sounded like several horses and men, though."

"Do you think it was Palmer?"

That was an interesting possibility. As far as they knew, Palmer had been alone when he fled from Powderkeg Bay. He could have run into some other outlaws and joined up with them, though.

"I don't know, but I intend to find out," Frank told Meg. "Come on. Let's get you to camp. We need to tell Salty about this so he'll be on his guard, too."

With Frank setting the pace, they moved quickly but quietly through the trees, heading back to the spot where they had left Salty. Frank hoped that nothing had happened to the old-timer while they were gone.

As they neared the camp, he heard snoring and knew that Salty was all right. A feeling of relief went through Frank. They emerged into the clearing and saw him slumped against the rock where he had been sitting earlier.

Frank nudged Salty's foot with a booted toe. That caused the old man to come awake sputtering and thrashing. Salty's hand moved toward the butt of his gun before Frank said, "Take it easy. It's just us."

Salty took his hat off and ran his fingers through the tangled thatch of white hair.

"Dadblast it," he complained. "You come mighty near givin' me a heart attack, Frank. You hadn't ought to Injun up on a fella like that."

"We heard men and horses moving around somewhere near here."

That made Salty glance up, his complaints forgotten.

"You get a look at 'em?" he asked.

"No, we just heard them."

"Frank heard them," Meg put in. "I didn't really hear anything myself, so they must not have been too close."

Salty climbed to his feet and put his hat

back on. "Noises are funny things in these mountains. They can bounce around so they seem like they're right close, but there ain't really no tellin' where they're comin' from."

"I know," Frank said with a nod. "That's why we have to be careful. Hold off on building a fire, keep the horses and the mules quiet, and be on your guard."

"From the way you're talkin', it sounds like you ain't gonna be here."

"I'm not," Frank said.

With a worried frown, Meg asked, "Where are you going?"

"To find those hombres and see who they are. Chances are, they're just some trappers or prospectors and don't have anything to do with us."

"But you have to find out for sure, don't you?"

He nodded. "It's the best way to stay alive."

"I could come with you," Meg offered.

Frank shook his head. "I'd rather have both of you here keeping an eye on the animals and our supplies. If anything happened to them, we'd be in mighty bad trouble."

She looked as if she wanted to argue some more, but then she nodded and said in resignation, "I'll do whatever you think is best, Frank."

"Are you goin' on foot?" Salty asked.

"Quieter that way," Frank replied with a nod.

There was nothing else to say. He gave Meg a quick smile, then set off on foot along the creek. Again, it wasn't long before the camp was out of sight behind him.

When he passed the spot where he and Meg had heard the men and horses earlier, he couldn't help but think about what had almost happened there.

It was a good thing they had been interrupted. He knew good and well he would have regretted giving in to the impulse, and he figured there was a good chance Meg would have been sorry about it, too.

Such moments of human weakness were something else he had to guard against, along with all the other dangers that seemed to dog his trail constantly.

Frank was able to move quietly enough that he didn't spook the birds and small animals. When the songs of the birds and the rustling of creatures in the brush suddenly ceased, he noticed it and knew that he hadn't caused it.

That made him stop short and listen, but it wasn't his ears that told him someone was nearby. It was his nose. He caught a whiff of tobacco smoke on the breeze.

Whoever they were, they were probably following the creek. That was the easiest way to get through these rugged mountains. Knowing that, Frank moved away from the stream, angling to his left through the underbrush. The trees closed in around him. It was harder to be quiet, but he wasn't likely to be seen.

A few minutes later he heard voices. A horse nickered. The sounds came from his right, toward the creek. Carefully, he worked his way in that direction again but found a giant slab of rock blocking his path. It must have sheered off from the face of the mountain looming above him and toppled down here sometime in ages past.

The rock sloped away from him and was rough enough that he thought he could climb it without much trouble. Being careful not to let the Winchester strike the rock — the clink of metal on stone could be heard for quite a distance — he began the ascent.

Frank didn't get in any hurry. In a situation such as this, haste was dangerous. He still heard the men talking and smelled the quirlies they were smoking. They must have stopped to rest their mounts and let the horses drink from the creek.

He reached the flat top of the big rock. It was high enough that the trees didn't shade it much, so the stone was hot from the sun as he crawled out onto it. He ignored the discomfort and crept stealthily toward the front of the slab.

Before he got there, he stopped and took his hat off, left it lying on the rock with his rifle. Then he inched forward again until he could peer over the edge of the rock without being too noticeable.

From where he was, he could see through the trees to the stream. The trunks and branches blocked his view to a certain extent, so he couldn't be sure how many men had stopped there on the creek bank. At least half a dozen, he decided as he watched them moving around.

There were that many horses, of course, and some pack animals, too. Frank's forehead creased in a frown as he spotted several mules with wooden crates lashed to them. He wondered what they were carrying in there. Two more mules were carrying wagon wheels, of all things, but the men didn't have a wagon with them.

One of the men laughed. It was a coarse sound. From what Frank could see of them, they were roughly dressed, and he spotted several rifles and holstered pistols.

Well-armed hardcases and a caravan of pack mules usually meant one thing: smugglers. Frank had no idea what sort of contraband these men were transporting, but it was none of his business. He knew they probably wouldn't take kindly to being discovered. It would be better to just let them go on their way. He and Meg and Salty would try to avoid them.

Satisfied that he had found out what he needed to know, Frank edged back until he could no longer see the men. He picked up his hat and rifle and returned to the ground.

Even though he was moving away from the apparent smugglers, he was still careful not to make too much noise as he walked through the woods.

Because of that, he heard the shot plainly when it sounded suddenly from up ahead of him somewhere.

Frank stopped short, every muscle in his body tensing as his hands tightened around the Winchester. He figured he was about halfway back to the spot where he had left Salty and Meg . . . and that was about where the gun blast had come from.

He broke into a run.

He didn't worry about being quiet now. That shot had sounded as if it came from Salty's old Remington. There had only been one shot, so it was possible Salty had blasted a snake or some other varmint.

But it was also possible that Salty wasn't able to shoot anymore, and that was what worried Frank.

There was also a chance those hardcases had heard the shot and would come to investigate. Frank wanted to get his two companions moving — assuming they were all right — so the smugglers wouldn't discover them.

A horseman's high-heeled boots weren't made for running, of course. That slowed Frank down a little. But he made pretty good time anyway and within minutes began to spot some landmarks that told him he was getting close to the camp.

He stopped to listen again. Rushing blindly into a situation was just plain foolish.

Nothing. No horses, no men, no birds or animals. The single shot had been enough to spook the critters, Frank thought. He began working his way closer to the campsite, using all the cover he could find.

Several minutes later, he crouched in the brush and carefully parted the branches so he could look between them. From where he was, he could see part of the grassy clearing on the creek bank. He didn't spot Salty or Meg and didn't hear them talking.

A horse blew loudly through its nostrils, though, so he knew the camp wasn't completely deserted.

Frank sniffed the air. The tang of burned powder still hung there faintly. This was where the shot had gone off, all right. He was sure of it.

He shifted his position, circling the camp in as close to absolute silence as he could manage. When he stopped and peered through another gap in the thick foliage, he could see all the camp that he hadn't been able to see before.

The lame horse stood there, but the other saddle mounts and the pack mules were gone.

More importantly, so were Salty and Meg.

CHAPTER 11

A short time earlier, Anton Mirabeau had had nothing more on his mind than the lovely Charlotte Marat. She filled his thoughts as she often did. He should have been paying more attention to where he and the other men were going.

If he had, they wouldn't have ridden right into trouble.

As it was, Mirabeau and the half-dozen other Métis with him had emerged from the trees into a clearing on the creek bank only to find themselves looking down the barrels of a rifle and a revolver, held by a couple of people who had taken cover behind some pines.

"Hold it right there, mister!" a man's voice ordered.

From the sound of it, Mirabeau thought the voice belonged to an old man. But an elderly finger could pull the trigger of a gun the same as a young one, provided, of course, that age had not stiffened it.

Mirabeau reined his horse to a stop and motioned for the other men to do likewise. His gaze darted around the campsite. He saw three horses and three saddles, along with a couple of pack mules and the packs of supplies lying on the ground.

Three saddle horses meant three people, but he saw only two pointing guns at him and his companions. The third man was probably somewhere nearby, out of sight, likely with a rifle pointing at him right now.

"Easy, my friend," Mirabeau said, taking care to keep both of his hands in sight. "We are not hunting trouble."

"Then what do you want?" the old-timer demanded.

"We are looking for some friends of ours. A man and a woman. Brother and sister, actually. Perhaps you have seen them. They both have dark hair. The young woman is very attractive."

"I don't know who in blazes you're talkin' about," the old man said. Mirabeau caught a glimpse of white hair and beard as the man peered around the trunk of the tree where he had taken cover. The man added in a disgusted mutter, "Who'd'a figured these woods would turn out to be so blamed crowded?"

Mirabeau knew what he meant. This area of the mountains had been chosen for the rendezvous precisely because it was so remote, so isolated, so empty of humanity.

He looked at the other tree, the one where the man with the rifle crouched.

Or perhaps the rifleman was not a man at all, Mirabeau thought suddenly, as he took note of how the denim-clad hip he could see behind the tree curved. Though he had lived his entire life in Canada, he credited the blood of his French ancestors for giving him an appreciative eye for the female form.

The blue eyes and the blond curls stuffed under a flat-crowned hat just confirmed his suspicion. He and his companions were faced with an old man and a girl.

But even such as them could be dangerous.

"We will be on our way," Mirabeau said. "Please forgive the intrusion."

"Hold on just a dang minute," the old-timer said. "Who are you fellas, and what are you doin' out here in the middle o' nowhere?"

"We could ask you the same," Mirabeau pointed out, "but we did not."

The old man ignored him and demanded, "Are you lookin' for that varmint Palmer? Is he a friend o' yours?"

Mirabeau shook his head. "I do not know anyone named Palmer."

"Yeah, well, you'd probably lie about it if you did. That'd make you the same sort of thievin' polecat he is."

Suspicion suddenly reared up in Mirabeau's mind. "This man Palmer is a thief?"

"Dang right he is!"

"And he is an American?"

"What else would he be?"

The response brought a faint smile to Mirabeau's lips. So typical of the Americans to think without hesitation that they were the only ones occupying the continent. But despite their arrogance, they had their uses.

Such as providing the weapons that Mirabeau, the Marats, and the rest of the Métis so desperately needed if their plans were to succeed. It was possible this man Palmer was part of the group that was supposed to rendezvous with Joseph and Charlotte. If that was true, then these two were after him. Could the old-timer be an American lawman? Mirabeau couldn't rule out that possibility.

That meant he and his friends couldn't just ride away. They had to find out the truth. Nothing could be allowed to disrupt the plan. Not now. Not when they were so close to achieving their objective.

Even though Mirabeau's thoughts were whirling madly in his brain, he didn't allow that to show on his face. Instead he kept smiling and said, "I give you my word, we know nothing about the man you seek. We are innocent trappers, nothing more."

The old man hesitated, but finally he nodded and stepped out from behind the tree. He didn't lower the big revolver in his hand, which, despite his age, was rock steady. He motioned with his free hand for his companion to stay where she was, then said, "All right, I reckon you can go on about your business. Don't get no ideas, though. There's a dozen of us in this here posse, and they'll be back any time now."

The old man had overplayed his hand, Mirabeau thought. There might be one more man in the group, but the story about there being a dozen was an obvious lie.

Mirabeau hitched his horse into motion and lifted a hand as if in farewell as he started past the old man. The other Métis fell in behind him.

Without warning, Mirabeau kicked his feet out of the stirrups and launched himself from the saddle in a dive that sent him crashing into the old man. His arm flashed out and struck the old-timer's arm, knocking it to the side as the revolver roared. Both of them went down, with Mirabeau's considerable bulk pinning the old man to the ground.

The young blond woman darted out from behind her tree with the rifle in her hands. She hesitated, obviously not willing to take a shot at Mirabeau for fear that she would hit the old man instead.

"Take her!" Mirabeau roared to his friends.

She swung the Winchester toward the others, but she was too late. A couple of them were already on her, diving from their horses to grab her and wrench the rifle out of her hands. She screamed, but the sound lasted only a second before one of the men clapped a hand over her mouth.

Mirabeau hit the old man, pulling his punch so that he stunned him, but did no real damage.

"Get their horses and supplies!" he ordered. "We'll take them with us."

He hadn't forgotten about that third horse. He halfway expected rifle fire to start raking them, but silence hung over the rugged landscape.

In a matter of moments, his companions had gathered up the supplies and thrown saddles and packs on the animals. They left the mount that had gone lame. They put the girl on one of their own horses, in front of a Métis plainsman. Mirabeau lifted the half-conscious old man and draped him across his horse in front of the saddle.

"Across the creek," he ordered. He led the way, and with the others following, the group of Métis and their prisoners splashed across the stream and disappeared into the thick woods on the far side.

Frank emerged cautiously from the brush. He knew that Meg and Salty couldn't have been gone long. He was convinced the shot he'd heard had come from Salty's revolver.

His eyes scanned the ground, searching for any clues as to what had happened here. He looked for splashes of blood on the ground but thankfully didn't see any.

Something on the other side of the creek caught his attention. The grass was thick on the other bank, as it was on this one, and there was a wide stretch where it was wet. Frank saw droplets of water glistening in the sunlight as it played across the bank.

The grass would be wet like that if a number of horses had forded the creek here and emerged on the other side, he thought. That was further proof that the incident had taken place very recently. The water splashed onto the bank by the horses hadn't had time to dry.

Frank looked at the horse Salty had been riding. The lame animal just stared back at him, uncomprehending.

"I wish you could talk, old fella," Frank muttered. "Wish you weren't lame, too."

If the horse hadn't been injured, they wouldn't have stopped here, and whatever had happened wouldn't have had the chance to take place.

Frank couldn't use the horse that had been left behind to go after Salty and Meg, either. The animal couldn't carry his weight, not without being ruined permanently. Frank wasn't going to do that.

He patted the horse on the shoulder and said, "I'll be back for you if I can."

Then he waded out into the creek, feeling the tug of the current as the knee-deep water swirled around his legs.

When he reached the other side, he spotted a few hoofprints in the mud at the very edge of the stream. He couldn't tell from them how many horses had crossed over here, but he estimated half a dozen or more.

Those were formidable odds, especially for a man who had no supplies and no extra ammunition except for the rounds in the loops on his shell belt and another handful of bullets stuffed in a pants pocket.

Frank didn't hesitate, though. He picked up the trail, using bent and broken branches in the undergrowth to tell him which way the riders had gone.

Too bad he didn't have Dog with him, he mused. The big cur's keen senses would have led him right to his quarry.

Palmer could have doubled back, Frank supposed, and met up with some allies. That thought had crossed his mind earlier while he was looking for the men he and Meg had heard.

Those men had turned out to be the smugglers he had spied on. They didn't have anything to do with kidnapping Salty and Meg.

Which meant there were two groups of strangers out here in this wilderness . . . three if you counted him and his two companions. Plus Joe Palmer, Frank reminded himself.

Damned if these Canadian Rockies weren't getting as crowded as some of the cities back east, he thought grimly.

The brush was so thick that one man on foot could move just about as fast — or faster — than several men on horseback. Frank was counting on that.

But at the same time, he had to be careful not to rush. He didn't want to go charging right up the backsides of these kidnappers without any warning. That might get him shot, and more importantly, it might get Salty and Meg shot.

From time to time he stopped to listen, and the third or fourth time he did that, he heard noises ahead of him. Horses moving through the brush, he judged. That meant he was close.

He picked up his pace. He wanted to get ahead of them if he could. Outnumbered like he was, an ambush was his best chance to free the prisoners. Hit the men before they knew what was going on.

The slope grew steeper as he circled to get ahead of the riders. That was good, Frank told himself. It would slow down the horses more than it would him.

He paused again to listen, heard them off to his right, maybe fifty yards away. Like a ghost, he started through the woods again.

The ground leveled off into a shoulder about a hundred yards deep. An almost sheer cliff rose on the far side of the open ground. The riders would have to go around it to one side or the other. From where he was, Frank couldn't see a trail leading on up the mountainside, but there probably was one somewhere around here. A game trail, if nothing else.

There were several boulders clustered at the base of the cliff, but if he holed up in those to challenge the kidnappers, he would be in effect pinning himself down. They could turn and flee, and he couldn't do anything to stop them.

Instead he abandoned the idea of getting in front of them and dropped behind a large deadfall at the edge of the slope instead. The fallen tree would make good cover, and he could see the whole stretch of open ground from here.

He waited.

But not for long. Only a few minutes had passed when the riders reached the top of the slope and emerged from the trees.

Frank's mouth tightened in anger as he spotted Salty and Meg. The old-timer was riding double with the man in the lead, who was a big hombre with a black beard. The man wore buckskins and a wide-brimmed slouch hat.

Salty was in front of him on the horse, draped over the animal's back like a sack of grain. That had to be a mighty uncomfortable position for the old-timer.

One of the other men had Meg in front of him on his horse. She was sitting up, but the man had an arm held tightly around her. She had lost her hat, and Frank could see that her face was pale with anger and strain. She seemed to be unharmed, though, and that was a relief.

The men were dressed like trappers or hunters, but Frank didn't see any of the gear they would have had with them if they were after furs. They were leading the horses and the pack mules they had brought from the camp along with Salty and Meg, and they had another pack horse that was loaded down with what looked like a couple of small chests. Frank had no idea what was in those chests.

All he knew for sure was that his friends were prisoners, and he didn't like that one damned bit. He waited until all seven of the riders had emerged from the trees and started across the open ground toward the cliff.

Then he laid the Winchester's barrel across the thick log behind which he lay and sent a bullet whip-cracking over the heads of the riders. As they reined to a startled halt and the echoes of the shot rebounded from the surrounding mountains, Frank shouted, "Hold it right there! The next man who moves, I'll blow him out of the saddle!"

CHAPTER 12

The big, bearded man in the lead wheeled his horse toward Frank. He hauled Salty up in front of him to use as a human shield. For a split second, Frank still had a shot past the old-timer, but he didn't take it. The odds of hitting Salty were too high.

"Hold your fire!" the man shouted. Frank didn't know if the man was talking to him or to the other riders. Either way, no more shots rang out.

"Frank!" Meg cried. "Get out of here while you can!"

"I'm not going anywhere," Frank said as he squinted over the barrel of his Winchester. "Not without you and Salty."

"Take it easy, *mon ami,*" the bearded man said, his accent and the French words giving away the fact that he was a French-Canadian. Frank didn't know much about Canada's politics, but he knew that some of the country's population was descended from the French trappers who had been the first to explore its interior.

This man's high cheekbones and the faintly coppery shade of his skin indicated that he might have some Indian blood as well. His companions appeared to share that ancestry.

"Who are you?" the bearded man went on.

"That's my business," Frank snapped. Palmer wasn't part of this group, and they didn't appear to be the sort of men that Palmer would throw in with.

That realization increased Frank's puzzlement, but this wasn't the time to ponder the matter. Salty and Meg were prisoners, and that was the only important thing.

"We have business here as well," the bearded man said, "and we cannot afford for anyone to interfere with it."

"My friends and I have no interest in you," Frank replied. "Set them on the ground, leave our animals and supplies, and ride on. We'll forget about this."

"I regret to say we cannot. Throw down your gun and come out, or I will snap this old man's neck."

The coldness of the man's voice told Frank that he probably meant the threat. Frank wasn't used to letting himself be bluffed, though, and there was a chance of that.

Of course, it was Salty's life he was betting. . . .

"If you do that, you'll have a bullet through your brain before the old-timer hits the ground," Frank said.

Salty yelled, "Shoot him anyway, Frank! Shoot me! A Winchester round'll go right through me and get him!"

"It appears to be your play, Frank," the bearded man said with grim amusement.

Frank didn't like what he had to do next, but he called, "Yeah, that's right."

Then he shot the bearded man's horse.

He had a clear shot. The bullet drove deep into the animal's chest. The horse screamed and went down, its front legs collapsing so abruptly that Salty and the bearded man were thrown forward over its head.

The collision with the ground broke loose the man's grip on Salty. The old-timer reacted with surprising swiftness for his age, rolling away from his captor.

Frank saw the other men reaching for their guns and sent another shot whistling over their heads.

At the same time, Meg acted, driving an elbow backward into the belly of the man holding her. That must have taken him by surprise. His grip slipped, as well, and Meg dived off the horse. No sooner had she hit the ground than Salty was there beside her, reaching down to grab her arm and haul her to her feet.

"Kill him!" the bearded man bellowed, adding a spate of French words that had to be curses.

That order put things on a different footing where Frank was concerned. Before, he had been willing to give the men a little benefit of the doubt.

No longer. He worked the Winchester's lever and fired again at the man he had just set afoot.

The bearded man flung himself to the ground, making Frank's shot miss by a hair. Frank swung the Winchester and fired again. This time his target was the man who had been leading their horses and pack mules. The man howled in pain and let go of the reins as he clutched at a bullet-busted shoulder.

Meg and Salty ran for the trees. One of the men swung his rifle toward them. Frank drilled the man through the body, knocking him out of the saddle. A second later, Meg and Salty reached the shelter of the pines.

The other men concentrated their fire on the deadfall behind which Frank crouched.

He had to duck lower as slugs slammed into the log and sent splinters and chunks of dead bark flying.

When he risked a look again, he saw that one of the other men had spurred over to the bearded hombre. He reached down, grasped the bearded man's wrist, and hauled him up.

"Let's get out of here!" the bearded man shouted.

The men who were still mounted wheeled their horses and galloped toward the cliff, turning still more to race along parallel to the rocky face. They must have known where a trail was, because moments later they vanished into the trees that grew almost to the base of the cliff.

Frank kept his rifle trained on the spot where they had disappeared as he listened to the hoofbeats fade. It sounded like they were really lighting a shuck out of here, but he suspected a trick.

"Frank!" Salty called.

"Stay where you are!" Frank replied. "Don't come out until we're sure they're not doubling back! Are the two of you all right?"

"We're not hurt," Meg called back. "How about you?"

"I'm fine," Frank told her.

137

After a moment he couldn't hear the horses anymore. He waited another fifteen minutes just to be sure before he stood up behind the deadfall.

"All right," he told Salty and Meg. "I'm pretty sure they're gone now."

The two of them emerged from their hiding places in the pines. Salty went to gather up the horses and mules while Meg hurried over to join Frank as he went to check on the man he had shot off one of the horses.

The man was dead, his eyes staring lifelessly at the sky. Frank had never seen him before.

"I'm sorry," Meg said. She pointedly avoided looking at the corpse. "They were on top of us before we knew what was happening. We tried to convince them to go on about their business, but they jumped us."

"What is their business?" Frank asked as he reloaded the cartridges he had burned in the Winchester. "Did they say?"

Meg shook her head. "No. They seemed to have some idea that Salty might be a lawman, though. That's what it sounded like from some of the talk I overheard."

"I used to be, you know," the old-timer said as he came up leading the horses and the mules. "Range detective, anyway, and unofficial deputy a time or two."

Frank said, "If they were worried about star packers, that means they were likely up to no good."

Salty nodded. "I reckon you could bet a hat on that."

"Do you think they have anything to do with Palmer?" Meg asked.

Frank frowned as he thought about it. After a moment, he said, "I don't see how they could. But there are things going on out here that we obviously don't know anything about."

"Dang mountains is downright crowded," Salty said.

"The same thought occurred to me. And it's worse than you think, because I found those men you and I heard earlier, Meg."

She looked confused. "It couldn't have been the same bunch. They came from opposite directions along the creek."

"That's right. The men I saw appeared to be some sort of smugglers." Frank thought about the chests he had seen strapped to the pack animals of the bearded man's gang. "I don't suppose this bunch said anything about what they were carrying?"

"Not a word," Meg replied. "What in the world is going on here, Frank?"

"I don't know," he said, "but I reckon it would be a good idea for us to find out."

Salty said, "I figured we'd stay on Palmer's trail and keep headin' for Calgary."

"The problem with that is, we don't know whether or not Palmer has run into those smugglers. He could have even joined up with them."

Salty raked his fingers through his beard. "So we got to find them so-called smugglers, dodge that other bunch o' killers, and look for Palmer all at the same time?"

"That's about the size of it," Frank admitted with a shrug.

"You don't never do nothin' simple, do you, Frank?"

"Well, sooner or later it usually comes down to killing." Frank's mouth tightened into a grim line. "Can't get much more simple than that."

Anton Mirabeau seethed with anger. He and his companions had climbed to a rocky promontory where they could look back down the mountainside. One of his men had a pair of field glasses in his saddle bags. Mirabeau took them and scanned the rugged landscape that fell away in front of him, searching for any sign of the two men and the blond girl.

He didn't see them. Scowling in disgust,

he handed the glasses back to the other man.

"What do we do now, Anton? We're short a horse."

"We'll go back and get Pierre's horse," Mirabeau said. "From the way he fell, he won't be needing it anymore."

Another rider spoke up. "I don't like losing a man."

Mirabeau turned angrily toward him. "You think I do? Pierre was like a brother to me!" He made a curt gesture. "You all are. We are a band of brothers, are we not?"

A couple of the men shrugged. The others just regarded him sullenly. They had started out on this journey with such high hopes, and now one of their number was dead.

"The plan will proceed," Mirabeau declared. He couldn't allow their resolve to weaken. "Pierre will not be there to see us triumph, but triumph we will. Come. We'll fetch his horse."

Mirabeau rode double with one of the other men this time as they headed back toward the meadow where the fight had taken place. He was confident that the man called Frank and the other two would be long gone by now.

That turned out to be true. The three of them were gone . . . but they had taken Pierre's horse with them. Pierre still lay there lifeless on the ground.

Mirabeau ground his teeth together for a moment before he got control of his surging emotions. "We will bury him," he declared. "Then we push on. We will take turns riding double. Our horses are strong. They will be all right."

This was a setback, though. There was no doubt about that. At least they still had the money for the guns. Soon, Joseph and Charlotte would make contact with the Americans and arrange the transaction. Soon, the Métis would have what they needed to win their freedom. That was the most important thing.

But once that goal was accomplished, Mirabeau intended to turn his attention elsewhere. He would find out who Frank was. More importantly, he would find out where Frank was.

And once he did, Mirabeau would settle the score.

The man called Frank would die.

CHAPTER 13

They took the dead man's horse with them. That would allow them to push on without having to wait for the animal that had gone lame to heal completely.

Frank thought about trying to bury the man, but they didn't have a shovel and it would be a difficult chore scratching out a grave in this rocky ground.

Anyway, the hombre had tried to kill them, so Frank didn't feel too bad about leaving him. Maybe the rest of the gang would come back and lay him to rest properly.

The three of them mounted up and headed back to the creek where Frank had left the other horse.

"I think it would be a good idea to find some other place to hole up for a while," he commented as they were making their way down the heavily wooded slope.

"Yeah, that bunch knows where we were

campin', so we ought to move," Salty agreed.

Meg put in, "Whatever errand they were on, it seemed to be important to them. Maybe they won't take the time to bother coming after us."

"Maybe not," Frank said, "but we can't afford to take that chance."

The lame horse had wandered a short distance down the creek while grazing on the thick grass, but it wasn't hard to find him. Once they had taken him in tow, they left the stream and headed for the far side of the valley.

Frank hoped he could find some place over there where they could fort up. He planned to go scouting for the smugglers and also for the gang of French-Canadian mixed-bloods, but he wasn't going to set out on that mission until he had a safe place to leave Salty and Meg.

"Métis," he said suddenly.

"What?" Meg asked.

"Those fellas who grabbed the two of you, that's what they're called," Frank said. "Métis. I don't know exactly where it comes from, but I've heard the word. They're the descendants of the early-day French fur trappers and the Indians who lived here when the white men first came to this part of the world."

He recalled hearing something else about them, too, something that nagged at him as if it was important, but he couldn't quite remember what it was.

They came to a ridge that jutted up abruptly from the relatively flat ground of the valley. It was too steep for the horses to climb, so they turned and rode along the ridge until Frank spotted a wide crevice that ran back into the rock, as if someone had taken a giant knife and tried to hack the ridge into two pieces.

The crevice's opening was screened somewhat by trees and brush. Frank reined in and studied it for a while, deciding that with a little work they could conceal the opening even more than it already was.

"That's it," he said, pointing. "We'll put the animals in there, then drag enough brush into the mouth of the crevice that nobody'll be likely to notice it if they ride past."

Salty nodded. "I reckon that might work, all right. Be a good place to fight off an attack, too. They couldn't come at you from but one direction."

"That's what I was thinking. Come on."

Once they were through the screen of brush at the mouth of the crevice, they found that it formed a box canyon extending about fifty yards into the ridge. The canyon was approximately twenty yards wide at its widest point, narrowing down to nothing at the far end.

A man could probably climb up and down the walls inside the canyon. A horse definitely couldn't negotiate them.

"We'll have to have somebody standin' guard all the time," Salty said, "but we can hold this place if we have to."

Frank nodded. "I agree. You and Meg can stay here while I try to find out why these mountains are so blasted crowded all of a sudden."

"Don't you think it would be better if we all went looking for those smugglers and that gang of Métis, or whatever you called them?"

"It's a one-man job," Frank said firmly.

Salty chuckled. "Danged if you don't sound like all the other fellas I ever partnered up with. Always so dadburned stubborn and determined to go it alone."

"Don't worry, I'll come back for you," Frank told the old-timer with a grin.

"Oh, I ain't worried. I know you'll come back." Salty paused. "We got the grub."

Frank laughed. "Let's drag some more brush up to hide that entrance."

They spent the rest of the afternoon working to conceal and fortify the box canyon. Frank used the pack mules to drag some logs into the canyon; then he and Salty stacked them three deep and five high to form a barricade of sorts, behind which they could kneel to fire their rifles if they needed to.

By the time that was done, it was too late for Frank to venture out in search of either of the groups they had encountered earlier in the day. He would start his search in the morning.

Salty built a small fire to boil coffee, fry bacon, and cook biscuits. While he was doing that, Frank and Meg made sure that all the horses were taken care of.

After supper, they put out the fire. It would be chilly without the warming flames, but night was falling and they didn't want to announce their presence here in the canyon.

"I'll take the first watch," Frank said. "Salty, are you all right with the second turn?"

"Sure. When you get to be my age, you don't sleep much, anyway."

Frank knew what he meant. He wasn't that far behind Salty in years.

"I can take a turn, too," Meg offered.

Frank shook his head. "You'll be responsible for keeping an eye open during the day tomorrow while I'm gone, so you'll need to be alert then."

"All right," she said with a grudging shrug. "I just want to do my share."

"Don't worry, you will."

Salty and Meg turned in, rolling in their blankets near the glowing ashes of the fire, which would continue to give off a little heat for a while. At this latitude, the nights cooled off quickly once the sun was down.

Frank took his rifle and walked to the mouth of the canyon, where he sat on the log barricade and listened to the small, stealthy sounds of nocturnal life carrying on around him. Everything seemed peaceful.

He wished once again that he had Dog with him, as well as Stormy. The big cur and the rangy gray stallion could be counted on to warn him if anybody came sneaking around.

They were hundreds of miles away in Seattle, though. Knowing that made Frank feel a mite lonely.

So did the fact that he had no idea where his son was at this moment. Conrad had been through hell in the past year or so, losing his wife that way and then abandoning the life he had been living to roam the

148

Southwest as a gun-toting loner, always getting in one scrape or another.

Like father, like son, Frank thought wryly. That was how the old saying went, wasn't it? When he and Conrad had first met, the younger man had been determined to have nothing to do with him and to be as little like him as possible.

Fate, though, had had other ideas.

Some men would have been glad that their sons were following in their footsteps. For Conrad's sake, Frank would have given anything for that not to be true in their case.

Unfortunately, the clock couldn't be turned back. The tragedies of the past couldn't be erased.

This time, even in his musing, he heard the rustle of footsteps behind him. Turning, he saw Meg coming toward him. Enough starlight filtered down into the canyon for him to recognize her slender figure.

"What are you doing here?" he asked quietly. "You're supposed to be asleep."

"That's easier said than done."

Even from here, Frank could hear Salty sawing logs. He laughed and said, "Yeah, I reckon you're right. He'll quiet down after a while, though."

She sat down on the piled-up logs beside him. "I was thinking about what happened earlier today, Frank."

"You mean when those fellas grabbed you and Salty?"

"Before that. I'm talking about when you and I walked up the creek from camp."

Frank had thought that might be what she meant, although he'd hoped that it wasn't.

He wasn't going to waste time pretending that he didn't understand. He said, "We came mighty close to making a mistake there."

"Would it really have been a mistake, Frank?"

"I think it would have been. Some things, it's just hard to get past."

"Like the difference in our ages?"

"Yeah, that and the fact that I'm too blasted old and set in my ways to ever settle down again. At least, not until I get too decrepit to ride a horse, and you wouldn't want me then."

"I'm not so sure about that," Meg said. "Anyway, you haven't heard me say anything about settling down, have you?"

Gruffly, Frank said, "Well, that's what you deserve. A gal as young and pretty as you ought to have a husband and a home. A passel of kids, too."

"That sounds good . . . if I ever met the right man."

"You will," he said. "That is, if you ever stop gallivanting around and getting into all these shooting scrapes with a couple of old mossbacks like Salty and me."

She laughed. "I've had more fun the last year than all the rest of my life put together."

"Well, then, you've got a mighty odd notion of fun, that's all I can say. I seem to recall nearly drowning in the ocean, and being half frozen to death, and getting shot at a lot."

"I guess it's the company I was keeping while that was going on that made it enjoyable."

"Maybe so. But it's no life for a young woman."

Meg sighed and leaned her head against his shoulder. "Don't worry, Frank. I'm done. I'm not going to throw myself at you anymore." She paused. "One of these days you're liable to regret not taking me up on it, though."

"I don't doubt it for a second."

They sat there in companionable silence for a while. Back at the camp, Salty snorted loudly, then grew quiet.

"Hear that?" Frank asked. "He rolled over."

"Yeah. I guess I'd better go back and try to get some sleep." Meg stood up. She rested a hand on Frank's shoulder and bent over to brush against his cheek. "Good night . . . Uncle Frank."

"Get on with you," he growled in response to her mocking tone. She laughed lightly as she turned to walk back to the bedrolls.

She was wrong about one thing, despite what he'd told her. He wouldn't regret this, because he knew he was doing the right thing.

But sometimes being an honorable fella was damned inconvenient, he thought with a sigh.

CHAPTER 14

Palmer had been following Joseph and Charlotte Marat all day without them being aware that he was anywhere around. Their Indian ancestors would have been ashamed of them for being so unobservant, Palmer thought.

For one thing, they didn't appear to know what they were doing or where they were going. They roamed back and forth among the little valleys between the mountains, seemingly aimlessly.

Maybe there was some method to their madness, but Palmer was damned if he could see it.

Sometime during the afternoon, he heard a single shot. Then, an hour or so later, another shot was followed by a whole flurry of gunfire that echoed through the mountains, sounding like a small-scale battle.

It was hard to be sure, but Palmer thought the shots were at least a mile west of the area where he was following Joseph and Charlotte.

They heard the guns, too, and seemed to be quite agitated by the shooting, reining in their horses and looking around wildly. Palmer, watching them from the top of a wooded knoll about a quarter of a mile away, wondered if they were going to turn around and ride back the other way to see what all the shooting was about. He supposed that if they did, he would have to follow them.

But the shots stopped after a few minutes, and after a few more minutes during which Joseph and Charlotte talked animatedly, the two of them resumed their wandering. Palmer continued spying on them, staying out of sight.

That went on the rest of the day. As dusk began to settle down over the rugged landscape, the Marats made camp again. Palmer climbed to a ridge where he could watch them.

As he settled down to a cold supper, he told himself, not for the first time on this long day, that he was acting crazy. He should have been twenty miles closer to Calgary by now. Somebody, either his former partner Yeah Mow Hopkins or that vengeful old-timer Stevens, would be on his trail, and lingering around here was just giving them a chance to catch up to him.

But the mystery of those guns Marat had mentioned was an intriguing one, and Charlotte's beauty was intriguing as well. Often, guns were worth their weight in gold on the frontier, and if that was the case here, Palmer wanted to get his hands on some of that loot.

Marat and Charlotte had stopped where the ground swelled up into a thick stand of pine trees on top of the ridge. Palmer's horses were on the far side of those pines, picketed so they could graze but not wander off.

The shadows were already thick enough to hide him, so after he had eaten, he crawled over to a spot where he could look down the hill at the camp. He placed his rifle on the ground beside him as he lay on his belly.

They had built a big fire again, just as they had the night before. They *wanted* to be found, Palmer realized as he avidly watched Charlotte prepare supper.

That was why they had been wandering around all day. Someone was supposed to meet them in this area, but they didn't know exactly where.

So they just drifted, thinking that sooner

or later they were bound to run into whoever was searching for them.

They had built the fire for the same
reason, to guide whoever was supposed to
rendezvous with them to the camp. That
would be the person, or persons, who had
the guns, Palmer speculated. The situation
made sense now, even though he didn't
know all the details yet.

So all he had to do was sit back and wait,
he told himself. When the right moment
came, he would make his move.

In the meantime, he had to suffer the
torture of watching Charlotte Marat walk
around down there. Her long dark hair, the
curves of her body in the tight-fitting shirt
and jeans, the sensuous grace with which
she moved . . . those were maddening
reminders of just how long it had been since
he'd been with a woman.

The smell of coffee and bacon didn't help
matters, either. He was hungry for more
than Charlotte.

Guns, he told himself. *Gold.* He tried to
keep his thoughts focused on the things that
were truly important.

Under the circumstances, he couldn't help
but be distracted. So he didn't know anyone
else was around until the cold, unyielding
ring of a gun muzzle suddenly pressed

against the back of his neck and a harsh voice ordered in a whisper, "Don't move, you son of a bitch, or I'll kill you."

Palmer's breath froze in his throat, and his heart seemed to stop dead in his chest. He knew how dangerous it was not to pay close attention to everything around him, and yet he had done that anyway, had let his brain be consumed by thoughts of the woman, the guns, and the gold.

Now he might pay for that mistake with his life.

"Take it easy." He forced the words out between suddenly dry lips. "There's no need to shoot."

"We'll decide about that," the man holding the gun against his neck said.

From the corner of his eye, Palmer saw a hand pick up his rifle. At the same time, somebody else plucked the revolver from the holster on his hip.

He still had a knife and a small hideout gun on him, but they wouldn't do much good if he was outnumbered, as he seemed to be. He put the number of his captors at three, maybe more.

The gun muzzle went away from his neck. He heard men moving around and figured they had stepped back so they could cover him better.

He was thinking about flipping over and reaching for that hideout gun, even though he knew it was a foolish move and would just get him killed, when the man who had spoken before went on in his gravelly voice. "All right, get on your feet."

Suddenly, something about that voice struck Palmer as familiar. He knew he had heard it before, although not any time recently. As he climbed awkwardly to his feet, well aware that guns were pointing at him while he did so, he wracked his brain in an attempt to figure out who the voice belonged.

The memory burst on his brain like an exploding shell. He started to turn around to see if he was right, but the voice snapped, "Hold it! Don't try anything funny."

"I wasn't going to," Palmer said. "Owen? Owen Lundy? Is that you?"

He heard air hiss between a man's teeth in surprise. "What the hell? Who are you?"

Convinced now that he was right, Palmer said, "It's me, Owen, Joe Palmer. I haven't seen you since Chicago, but I heard you were up here in this part of the world."

"Joe Palmer?" The gravelly voice was confused. "Can't be. I heard Palmer got hisself hanged over in Alaska."

Palmer laughed. "You heard wrong. It's

me, all right. Let me turn around, and you can see for yourself."

A moment of hesitation went by before the man said, "All right, but take it slow and easy. Keep your hands where I can see 'em, and no tricks."

Palmer kept his open hands elevated to shoulder height and swung around so he could look at the men who had snuck up on him. Three of them stood close by, covering him with pistols and rifles, while farther back, dim blurs in the shadows, several more men waited.

The moon had risen and provided enough light for Palmer to see the man who took a step toward him holding a leveled revolver. The man had a craggy face, along with white hair and bushy side whiskers, under a black Stetson. Palmer knew him without any doubt as Owen Lundy.

"Last time I saw you, you weren't dressed like a cowboy, Owen," Palmer said with a smile. "It was in a dive on State Street in Chicago, and you looked like a real swell."

"Well, as I live and breathe," Lundy said. "By God, it really is you!" He lowered the hammer on his gun and holstered the weapon. With a motion to the men with him, he went on, "Take it easy, boys. This is Joe Palmer, an old friend of mine."

Lundy stepped forward and held out his hand. Palmer clasped it firmly.

"It's good to see a familiar face out here in the middle of nowhere, Owen," he said. A thought occurred to him. "I'll bet you've got something to do with that pair camped down there, don't you?"

One of the other men grated a curse and started to raise his rifle again, saying, "He knows what's going on, Lundy. We can't take any chances —"

"Put that gun down," Lundy ordered harshly. "I told you, this man can be trusted."

"Maybe so," another man put in coolly, "but I ain't fond of the idea of carving another share out of the payoff."

"Nobody said anything about that," Palmer responded before Lundy could say anything. "Whatever you fellas have going on, I don't want to horn in on it."

That was a bald-faced lie, of course. If there was money involved, Palmer damn sure wanted to dip his fingers in the pie. But it would be unwise to let these men know that right now.

"You let me worry about the shares, Radford," Lundy said. "Unless you think you'd rather start runnin' things around here."

The threat in Lundy's voice was unmistakable.

"I never said that, Owen," the man called Radford replied. "This job's gone all right so far with you in charge."

"Yeah," the other man said, "except for that business with Blake."

"Jericho?" Palmer said, remembering Lundy's old partner. "Is he here, too, Owen?"

"No," Lundy said with a grim edge in his voice. "He didn't make it."

"The soldiers killed him," Radford said.

Lundy's head turned. "That's enough." He looked again at Palmer, who sensed the tension in the air, and went on, "You'd better tell me what you're doing here, Joe. It's one hell of a coincidence that two fellas who know each other from the old days in Chicago wind up bumpin' noses in the Canadian Rockies."

"Not so much of a coincidence," Palmer said. "I was on my way to Calgary to look for you. I'd heard that you and Jericho were operating around there now."

Lundy considered that. "What's your connection with those two 'breeds?"

"There's not any, except that I met them last night. We just talked and then went our separate ways, though."

"Did they tell you what they're doing up here?"

"Not a word."

"But you've been trailing 'em, haven't you?" Lundy's words held a cunning tone. "You think you're on to something that might wind up with a big payoff."

Palmer didn't bother denying it. "They mentioned something about guns." His brain made the connections between everything he had heard. "And you're supplying them, aren't you, Owen? What did you do, slip down across the border and steal a shipment of rifles from the U.S. Army? Is that how Jericho got killed?" His excitement grew, but he tried not to let it show. "Those two kids are carrying the money to buy those guns from you, aren't they?"

"You always were a smart son of a bitch," Lundy said. "You think you've got it all figured out."

"I don't?"

"Not all of it. We didn't steal a shipment of rifles from the Army."

"No? Then what did you steal?"

"Just four guns," Lundy said. "Four very special guns."

CHAPTER 15

Meg already had a small fire going and the coffee brewing when Frank rolled out of his blankets the next morning. His muscles were painfully stiff as he climbed to his feet. He tried to tell himself that was because he'd slept on the cold, hard ground.

But that wasn't completely true, and he knew it. Sleeping on the ground might have made it worse, all right, but at his age, his muscles would be stiff and slow to loosen even if he'd spent the night in a four-poster feather bed.

Meg poured a cup of coffee and handed it to him with a smile. He thanked her, sipped the hot, strong brew, and asked, "Where's Salty?"

"Taking a look around outside the canyon."

Frank frowned. "I'm not sure that's a good idea. We don't want to draw attention to this place."

"He said he'd be careful not to be noticed."

Frank knew the old-timer meant well. And Salty was an experienced frontiersman who knew how to not be seen when he didn't want to be.

But it still seemed like an unnecessary chance to Frank. He was about to go looking for his friend when he saw Salty slipping into the canyon through the brush barrier across its mouth.

"Nothin' stirrin' out there this mornin'," Salty reported when he came up to the small, almost smokeless fire that Meg had built.

"You didn't see anybody?" Frank asked.

"Nope, and nobody saw me, neither, if you were worryin' about that," Salty replied. "It's plumb peaceful in these parts."

Just then, as if Fate were enjoying having a horse laugh at the old-timer's expense, the sound of shots suddenly racketed through the early morning air. They blasted out with incredible swiftness.

Frank and Salty stiffened. Meg came to her feet in alarm. The gunfire sounded as if it was no more than half a mile from their campsite.

"That'll teach me to open my dadblasted mouth," Salty said during a lull in the firing. They waited to see whether the fight was over or if it would resume again.

After a couple of minutes, another round of firing began. Again, the shots pounded out with breathtaking speed.

Salty looked at Frank and said, "Them ain't regular guns goin' off."

Frank had already figured out what was going on. He shook his head and said, "Not guns. Gun. Just one. I've heard that sound before. The last time was at Yuma Prison."

"It's one of them devil guns," Salty said.

"Devil guns," Meg repeated. "What's that?"

"A Gatling gun," Frank said. "A rapid-firer. It has revolving barrels and can spit out about three hundred rounds a minute."

The distant hammering sound of the shots stopped again.

"Somebody's trying it out or demonstrating it for somebody else," Frank continued.

Salty said, "I thought the soldier boys were the only ones who had them guns."

Frank shook his head. "No, other people can get their hands on them, too. Like I said, the guards at Yuma had one mounted on a wagon."

Salty and Meg didn't ask how he came to know about the arms possessed by the guards at the infamous territorial prison down in Arizona, and Frank didn't offer an explanation. He had put that trip to Ambush Valley behind him.

"What do you reckon is goin' on?" Salty asked. "Why would somebody have a Gatlin' gun up here in the middle o' nowhere? Ain't no Injun fights in these parts anymore, are there?"

"No, the Indian threat is over. Anyway, the Mounties are responsible for law and order in this part of Canada, and I'm not sure if they have any Gatling guns." Frank rubbed his jaw as he frowned in thought. "Those smugglers I saw had some heavily loaded pack mules with them. Those crates could have had some broken-down Gatling guns in them."

Salty pounded a knobby fist into a callused palm. "Dadgum it, I'll bet a hat you're right, Frank! Those varmints could'a stole them devil guns somewhere, and they've come up here to sell 'em."

That sounded like a reasonable explanation to Frank. Another idea occurred to him as well, but before he could say anything about it, Meg spoke up.

"Could this have anything to do with those men who grabbed us yesterday, Frank?" she asked. "Those . . . what did you call them? Métis?"

"I think that's exactly what's going on here," he said. This morning's developments had jogged his memory. "The Métis have always had trouble with the Canadian government. Their leader, a man named Louis Riel, led two rebellions in hopes of gaining a separate country for the Métis, or at least more power for them in the Canadian government. Neither war amounted to much, though. Canadian troops put down the first rebellion, and the North West Mounted Police took care of the second one. Riel was arrested, tried, and hanged. I remember reading about it in the newspapers." He frowned. "But that was more than a dozen years ago. I haven't heard anything more about the Métis since then."

"Some folks have mighty long memories," Salty pointed out. "Maybe some o' the ones who followed that Riel fella want to try again to break away from Canada."

Frank took up the thought. "In which case, they would need arms. Like some Gatling guns."

The three of them stood there looking at each other for a long, silent moment. Finally Meg said, "I think you're probably right, Frank. But if all that's true, it doesn't have anything to do with us. There's nothing stopping us from heading for Calgary as fast as we can and trying to find Joe Palmer so we can get Salty's money back."

Frank nodded slowly. "You're right," he said.

But despite that, the situation nagged at him. He was convinced the theory they had come up with was correct: The smugglers had stolen some Gatling guns, probably from the U.S. Army, and brought them north into Canada to sell to rebellious Métis.

The question remained, what were the Métis going to do with them?

The answer couldn't be anything good. The more Frank thought about, the more his gut told him that innocent people would die if those Gatlings fell into the wrong hands.

His instincts told him he ought to look into this, but did he have any right to drag Salty and Meg into what was potentially a very dangerous mess?

He pondered on this while they ate their breakfast and then tended to the horses. After the second burst of shooting, the Gatling guns were silent, which meant the deal had been concluded, Frank thought. In the end, he decided that he didn't have any right to ask his companions to risk their lives.

Besides, he didn't know for sure that what was going on in this stretch of mountains had anything to do with a budding rebellion by the Métis.

There were practical matters to consider, too, and Frank addressed those after breakfast.

"I think we ought to hole up here for the day like we planned," he said. "That'll give those folks, whoever they are and whatever they're up to, time to move on out of these parts."

"You're not gonna go lookin' for 'em?" Salty asked.

Frank shook his head. "I reckon not. There's no reason for us to get mixed up in their business."

Salty frowned as he raked his fingers through his beard. "Well, I, uh, been thinkin' about that, Frank. You know I used to do some range detectin', and I helped out the law more'n once, and it sorta rubs me the wrong way to stand aside when there's somethin' shady goin' on."

"We don't know that there is," Frank pointed out.

"No, but there's one thing you can be dang sure about. . . . Anybody who wants to get his hands on one o' them devil guns is plannin' on doin' a whole heap of killin'."

That was exactly the thought that had gone through Frank's mind earlier.

Meg spoke up, saying, "I think Salty's right, Frank. Now that I've thought about it, I'm not sure we ought to just ride away from here. What if those people are planning to use those guns to ambush a bunch of Mounties or even attack a town full of innocent people?"

"It's not our job to stop them," Frank said, playing devil's advocate even though he leaned toward agreeing with both of his friends.

"Maybe not," Salty said, "but when a fella sees somethin' wrong happenin', sometimes he's got to step in."

"Or she," Meg added.

Frank didn't argue any more. Instead he grinned and said, "I'm glad you two feel that way. I don't reckon we can turn our backs on this, either. But we've got to be smart about what we do next. I think the two of you should stay here while I go take a look around. If I can find the bunch that has the guns now, we can follow them and try to find out what their plan is."

"You better be careful, Frank," Salty advised. "I don't figure they'd take kindly to bein' spied on. You saw how quick they was to grab me an' Meg yesterday, and

170

they're gonna be even proddier now that you killed one of 'em."

"I plan on being careful," Frank assured him. "Let's get one of those horses saddled up."

When he had the animal ready to ride, he took hold of the reins and led the horse toward the mouth of the canyon. Salty and Meg came along with him.

"The two of you lie low and stay alert," Frank said. "I'll be back later."

"It's a shame we can't do nothin' about them smugglers," Salty said. "I reckon it's better if we follow the guns, though."

Frank nodded. "There's nothing we can do about the guns being stolen. That's already happened. But maybe we can stop them from being used to slaughter innocent folks."

He pushed some of the brush far enough aside to lead the horse through the gap he created. When he was gone, Salty and Meg could pull the brush back into place and make sure the canyon mouth was concealed again.

Frank had just stepped out into the open when the morning erupted in noise. The terrible hammering of shots filled the air, and a veritable storm of lead pelted around him.

CHAPTER 16

Earlier that morning, just as the sun was about to creep up over the horizon to the east, Joseph Marat had opened his eyes and found himself staring down the barrel of a pistol.

He started to jerk upright and reach for the revolver on his hip or the rifle lying on the ground beside him, but the gun muzzle suddenly pressed hard against his head and a gravelly voice ordered, "Don't try it, boy. I don't want to blow your brains out, but I will if I have to." The man holding the gun chuckled. "Reckon I can always do business with your sister, if you're not around anymore."

"Don't . . ." Joseph had to stop and swallow hard before he could go on. "Don't shoot," he said. "I won't give you any trouble."

"Didn't think so." The man lifted the gun away from Joseph's forehead and straightened from where he had crouched beside the sleeping man.

He was big and dressed like an American cowboy, with a black hat and denim trousers and jacket. He had bushy white side whiskers, and his face looked as if it had been carved out of a particularly rugged piece of sandstone.

Nor was he alone. Several other men clustered around the camp, and Joseph felt a sudden surge of fear for his sister. He jerked his head from side to side, looking for her as he exclaimed, "Charlotte!"

She cried out briefly, and a voice that was vaguely familiar to Joseph said, "Take it easy, Joe. Your sis is fine. Nobody's going to hurt her."

In the weak light, Joseph saw a man in a derby hat holding Charlotte's arm. The man's other arm was around her waist, pinning her to him. To his surprise, Joseph recognized the man holding Charlotte as Joe Palmer, the American who had been spying on their camp two nights earlier.

"I should have known you were with them," Joseph said bitterly to Palmer. "You didn't just stumble over us."

"That's where you're wrong," Palmer insisted. "It was just a coincidence, sure as shooting." He grinned. "The woods are full

173

of 'em these days, seems like."

The white-haired, craggy-faced man said, "He's right. Stand up, boy. We got business to conduct." He added, "Keep your hands away from your guns, though."

Joseph obeyed the order, climbing stiffly to his feet and scowling at the strangers as he did so. He could see now that there were seven or eight of them, and they were all hard-faced, roughly dressed men who held their guns with an air of long and frequent use.

He and Charlotte were a pair of sheep in the company of ravenous wolves, Joseph thought.

But they had one advantage over sheep. They were the key to something these wolves wanted.

Gold.

"Let go of my sister," he said to Palmer in a cold voice.

"I'm not hurting her," Palmer insisted. "I just grabbed hold of her to keep her from running around and getting in trouble."

The white-haired man made a curt gesture to Palmer. "Let her go."

Clearly, Palmer didn't like the order, but he followed it. He took his hands off of Charlotte and stepped away from her.

"Hope I didn't offend you, Miss Marat,"

he said as he reached up and touched the brim of his derby.

She looked away from him pointedly and didn't acknowledge what he'd said.

The white-haired man faced Joseph and said, "Palmer tells me your name is Marat."

"Joseph Marat. This is my sister Charlotte."

"I'm pleased to make your acquaintance," the man said with an attempt at gruff courtesy. Just then he seemed to realize that he was still holding his revolver. He slid the heavy, blued-steel gun back into its holster. "My name's Lundy. Owen Lundy."

"You are the one we came here to these mountains to meet?" Joseph asked. "We were not given any names."

"We're the fellas you came to meet, all right. We've got what you want."

Joseph looked around. "I see no pack animals."

A humorless grin etched even more lines into Lundy's face. "You don't reckon we'd bring the guns with us to the rendezvous, do you? That's not the way we do business, Marat. Where's the gold?"

Joseph was scared, but he forced himself to look and sound calm and cool-headed as he said, "That is not the way *we* do business. First we see the guns."

175

Lundy's features darkened with anger. He took a step closer to Joseph and snapped, "You didn't bring the gold?"

Joseph steeled himself not to retreat in the face of the American outlaw's wrath. "We can get the gold whenever we need it," he said. "But not until we have examined the guns and found them to be everything you promised."

"Oh, they're everything I promised, all right," Lundy said savagely. "They'll spit out more slugs in the blink of an eye than you can count!"

"Show me," Joseph said.

For a long moment, the two of them stared at each other. Finally, Lundy shrugged and motioned to a couple of his men.

"Bring up the mules."

They hurried to obey his command. Within minutes, they returned through the thick woods leading several mules with long wooden crates lashed onto them by thick leather straps that ran over the backs of the animals. Other mules had what appeared to be wagon wheels strapped to their flanks.

"Break out one of the guns and set it up," Lundy ordered.

Joseph watched with rapt attention as the men took down a couple of the crates and pried the lids off of them. From the packing straw inside, they lifted out bundles wrapped in oilcloth. When they folded back the oilcloth on one of the bundles, the gleaming barrels of a Gatling gun came into view. The barrels, arranged in a circle, had an aura of death and destruction about them, Joseph thought . . . or perhaps he was being too poetic.

"These weapons are mounted on wheeled carriages," Lundy explained as the men began assembling the component parts of the Gatling gun. "The Army's been experimenting with making them a little lighter in weight and easier to move around. They've taken out the cotton packing from around the barrels that had to be soaked in water to keep the gun from overheating. Turns out the air cools it enough."

The men took a couple of wheels from one of the mules and mounted a metal crosspiece between them. Two men held the wheels upright while another man fastened a curved wooden beam to the crosspiece. It extended out several feet to the back and the other end rested on the ground to form a brace that supported the wheeled carriage. Then two more men lifted the body of the Gatling gun out of the crate and bolted it into place on the carriage.

"Once it's set up, it's pretty mobile," Lundy said. "A couple of men can pick up that tongue in the back to turn it around or wheel it from place to place. You don't have to have horses to pull it or even to transport it. Several men can do the job if they have to, once the gun's broken down, and you can see for yourself that it doesn't take all that long to set it up again." The man shrugged. "Anyway, if you set it up where you want to do your shooting, you shouldn't have to move it much."

Joseph frowned. "You brought ammunition?"

Lundy pointed to one of his men and ordered, "Get those sticks of bullets."

The man brought out a pair of long, narrow metal magazines that fit into loading slots on the top of the weapon. The magazines held bullets that fed into the chambers as the barrels revolved and the gun fired.

"Once your loaders get the hang of it, the thing'll fire four hundred rounds a minute without much problem," Lundy said. "The gun can actually handle close to a thousand rounds a minute without jamming or overheating, but men can't reload that fast. You'll need three men on each gun, a couple to load and one to turn the firing crank."

Lundy pointed out the wooden-handled crank attached to the body of the weapon.

"Set up four of them around a target, and you can pour more than fifteen hundred rounds a minute into it," he went on. "That'll shoot holes in just about anything and blow it to hell in a hurry. And it'll mow down the Mounties like wheat in a field."

Joseph's voice was grim as he said, "They used a Gatling gun against my people the last time we tried to fight for our rights. It's only fair that we use such weapons against them."

"That's none of my business," Lundy said. He waved a hand at the gun. "Well, there it is. How about that gold?"

"Does it work? I have to see how it works."

Lundy smiled. "Try it yourself."

"You mean it?"

Lundy motioned Joseph toward the gun. "It's loaded and ready to go. Just turn that crank, like I said."

Joseph couldn't resist the temptation. He glanced over at Charlotte. She looked apprehensive, as if she didn't like this at all, but she didn't shake her head to tell him he shouldn't. Joseph approached the Gatling gun carefully, as if it were a wild animal that might attack viciously without any warning.

As he grasped the crank's handle, he bent

down and squinted along the barrels to see where the gun was pointing. It was aimed across the valley at a stand of pines. There might be some small animals and birds in those trees, he thought, but that was their misfortune.

He took a deep breath and turned the crank, hard and fast.

The noise was incredible, slamming against his ears again and again. The shots roared out, coming so close together that it was hard to tell them apart. The rear brace shuddered from the recoil. The rate of fire slowed slightly and then picked up again, depending on how fast Joseph turned the crank. Across the valley, branches jerked and chunks of bark flew as the bullets chewed into the trees with ferocious power.

Abruptly, the gun fell silent. The quiet sounded odd after that terrible racket. Lundy said, "You're empty."

Joseph turned toward the outlaw in amazement. He had heard stories about these weapons, of course, but he had never seen one in action until now. It was awe-inspiring in its devastation. He peered across the valley and saw the scattered branches and the huge holes that the bullets had gouged into the tree trunks.

If those trees were men, they would be lying dead on the ground now in bloody heaps, shot to pieces.

Joseph turned to his sister. Charlotte still had her hands over her ears, where she had clapped them when the shooting started.

"Do you want to try it?" he asked her.

She lowered her hands and shook her head. She was pale and looked a little sick.

"No. I don't mind guns, but this . . . this is . . . evil."

"Nonsense," Joseph said. "This is exactly what we need." He looked at Lundy. "Can we reload it and shoot it again?"

The outlaw grinned. "Sure. This time, my boys'll show you how to load it, and you can do it yourself."

Joseph spent a while familiarizing himself with every part of the gun's apparatus. He found himself fascinated by it. He thought not so much about the bloody havoc it was capable of wreaking, but more about what a mechanical marvel it was. He had to learn all he could about it so he would be able to teach his comrades among the Métis how to use the weapons.

"We brought plenty of ammunition, but you don't need to be wasting it," Lundy cautioned.

"One more magazine," Joseph said eagerly. He cranked through those shells as well, watching with avid interest as several large branches fell off the pines. The hail of bullets had sawed them loose.

When the Gatling gun fell silent again, Lundy said, "All right. You've seen what this thing can do. It's time for you to keep your part of the bargain, Marat. Where's our gold?"

Before Joseph could answer, Palmer said, "That fella you sent out to scout the area is coming back, Owen."

Joseph looked around and saw a man riding up the valley toward them. When the man reached the camp, he reined in and swung down from his horse. He wore an excited look on his face.

"What is it?" Lundy asked.

"We've got some spies up the valley a ways, holed up in a little box canyon," the man reported. "They've pulled some brush up in front of the canyon mouth to hide it, and I might not have even seen it if I hadn't spotted some old pelican wanderin' around. I watched him go back through the brush and slipped up to take a closer look. I think there's several people in there."

Lundy frowned at Joseph. "Is that some of your bunch? You got the gold stashed in that canyon?"

"I don't know anything about this," Joseph answered honestly. He looked at the scout. "You say this was an old man?"

"Yeah, with a white beard and an old hat with the front pushed up."

Joseph shook his head. "These people are not part of our group."

Palmer spoke up, saying to the scout, "An old man with a white beard?"

"That's right. He had on a cowhide vest, too, if that means anything to you."

"Stevens!" Palmer said under his breath, adding a muttered curse.

"You know these folks, Joe?" Lundy asked sharply. "I was willing to let you throw in with us, but if you're trying to pull some sort of double cross, you'll be damned sorry you did."

Palmer shook his head. "No double cross, Owen, I swear. But that old man's an enemy of mine. He tried to kill me a while back, and I guess he's followed up here into the mountains, the son of a bitch."

Lundy rasped fingertips over his beard-stubbled jaw as he thought. "Then I reckon you don't really care what happens to this fella, do you?"

"Not hardly. In fact, if you were to get rid of him, I'd consider it a mighty big favor."

Lundy nodded as he reached a decision. "Come on, then. Grab hold of that gun, boys." He gave Joseph a savage grin. "You're about to get a real demonstration of what a Gatling can do, Marat."

CHAPTER 17

Frank's instincts, honed to a razor's edge by decades of the dangerous life he had led, were the only thing that saved him. Nerves and muscles galvanized into action and sent him diving backward.

The horse reared up, screaming in agony as slugs pounded into its body. The animal shielded Frank as he rolled across the ground into the brush.

Then one of the bullets struck the horse in the head, ending its pain and sending it toppling over backward. Frank had to scramble to keep the horse from falling on him.

The Gatling gun still hammered out its lethal rhythm. Slugs tore through the brush.

"Get down!" Frank yelled to Salty and Meg as he broke free of the brushy barrier into the canyon.

He saw that they had already dived behind the log barricade. He joined them, vaulting over the logs and landing hard on the ground behind them. The jolt went all the way through him as his hat went flying.

A stream of profanity from Salty's lips threatened to turn the air blue around them. He got the torrent under control and asked over the racket of the Gatling gun, "What in blazes is goin' on? Did we wander into the middle of a dadblamed war?"

"It sure sounds like it," Frank said.

Slugs thudded into the log barricade and whipped through the air over their heads. The one thing they had on their side was that the brush across the canyon mouth concealed their position from the attackers. Whoever was using the Gatling gun was sweeping the fire back and forth across the canyon mouth, rather than concentrating his shots on the barricade.

That was good, because at the rate those bullets were coming, after a while they might begin to penetrate the barricade if they were all aimed straight at it.

"Blast it, this is all my fault!" Salty said bitterly. "Somebody must'a spotted me when I was out scoutin' around earlier."

Frank had already figured out the same thing, although he hadn't seen any point in bringing it up.

"Shoot, we wouldn't even be here if I

hadn't wanted to come after that varmint Palmer," Salty went on.

"Nobody forced us to come with you," Meg said. "We're here because we wanted to be." She flinched and ducked as more slugs slammed into the logs. "Well, maybe we don't want to be in this exact spot. . . ."

Frank risked a look around the end of the barricade. The dead horse lay about thirty feet away. The animal had fallen so that the side of the saddle where the rifle sheath was strapped was turned up. Frank could see the Winchester's stock protruding from the sheath.

"I need to get my rifle," he said.

"Have you gone loco?" Salty demanded. "These logs are the only things keepin' us from gettin' shot to pieces!"

"They won't last forever," Frank pointed out. "We need to be able to put up a fight, otherwise whoever is out there can take their time about killing us."

"Let me go get the rifle," Meg suggested. "I'm thinner than you, Frank. I can stay closer to the ground."

"Forget it," he answered curtly. "You're not going out there and risking your life."

She glared at him. "You think I'll be a lot better off in the long run if *you* get your head shot off? You know I have the best chance of succeeding, Frank. You're just too damned stubborn to admit it!"

Frank frowned as he considered what she'd said. He couldn't deny that, in a way, she was right. Her chances of survival would drop considerably if he was dead, and those chances weren't all that high to begin with.

But it went deeply against the grain for him to stay behind cover while a woman risked her life. He didn't know if he could allow that.

"Look," Meg said. "Most of the bullets are going above us, about waist-high to a man. I can stay lower than that, and if they dip a little, I'll still have a better chance of avoiding them than you would, Frank."

He couldn't argue with that. Instead he said, "You get down as flat on the ground as you can and keep your face in the dirt. Try to crawl straight toward the horse. If I see that you're veering off to the side, I'll call out to you and let you know."

A grin flashed across her face, but it couldn't completely conceal the fear in her eyes as she took off her hat and said, "Now you're being sensible."

Pressing herself to the ground, she slithered out from behind the logs. Frank's heart slugged with worry for her as he watched her crawl toward the fallen horse.

Meg couldn't move very fast. She had to inch herself along with fingers and toes. The seconds seemed like minutes, the minutes like hours.

Salty said, "Frank, they ain't gonna just keep on shootin' with that devil gun. After a while, they're gonna come in here to see what damage it did."

"I know," Frank said with a nod.

"We'll have a real fight on our hands then. Why do you reckon they want us dead?"

"Well, neither bunch probably wants any witnesses left alive." Frank's mouth twisted grimly. "I reckon the main thing, though, is that those smugglers are demonstrating just how effective a Gatling gun can be."

"They'd kill us just to make a point?"

"That's what I'm guessing," Frank said.

"Well, if that don't beat all. Them sorry buzzards —"

Salty stopped the tirade he was about to launch when Frank stiffened suddenly and caught his breath.

"What is it?" the old-timer asked anxiously. "Did Meg get hit?"

"No. She made it to the horse."

Meg had to lift herself up now to reach the rifle, but the horse's body served as protection for her. She snaked her arm over the animal's motionless flank and wrapped her fingers around the Winchester's stock. Slowly, she began to ease the rifle from the saddle boot.

The Gatling fell silent.

"Uh-oh," Salty said to Frank. "You reckon they're fixin' to come chargin' in here?"

"Could be. Or they might just be letting the gun cool off for a few minutes."

Meg pulled the Winchester the rest of the way from its sheath.

Then, to Frank's surprise, she rolled over, surged to her feet, and started running back toward the log barricade.

He knew what was going through her mind. She thought she could get back to the logs before the Gatling gun opened up again.

And maybe she could, but if she didn't —

In the eerie silence that now hung over the canyon, Frank heard a faint metallic clatter from outside. More ammunition magazines were being racked in the rapid-firer.

Meg was only halfway back to the logs.

Frank sprang up and dashed out to meet her. Her eyes widened in surprise. He left his feet in a long dive that carried him to her. His arms went around her calves and jerked her legs out from under her. She fell with a startled cry.

A split-second later, the devil gun started singing its unholy song again.

The slugs whined through the air above them. Frank rolled Meg onto her belly and pushed her toward the barricade. She had dropped the Winchester when she fell. He picked it up and crawled after her, staying as low as he could.

Luck was with them. They made it back behind the logs to join a grim-faced Salty.

"I thought you two was goners for sure," the old-timer said.

"I'm sorry, Frank," Meg said. She was pale, probably from knowing how close she had come to being cut in two by that deadly barrage. "I thought maybe I could get back before they started shooting again."

He nodded. "It wasn't a bad gamble. But I heard them reloading and knew you didn't have time."

"You saved my life. Not for the first time, either."

"Don't worry about that," he told her. "We're still in a mighty bad fix."

The Gatling gun stopped firing again. Frank figured that this time, the men who'd been using it would venture into the canyon for sure, to find out if anyone was left alive in here.

He looked back over his shoulder. He

191

already knew there was no real cover in the canyon; that was why he and Salty had built the log barricade.

But while the logs would do a fine job of stopping rifle fire, they wouldn't stand up to an all-out assault from the Gatling gun.

Frank knew that, but he also knew they had no choice but to play the hand they were dealt.

He would try to keep the attackers out of the canyon as long as he could. As long as they couldn't get a good look at the setup in here, they wouldn't know what bad shape the defenders were in.

Frank rested the Winchester on top of the logs and nestled his check against the smooth wood of the stock as he peered over the sights. He trained the rifle on the brush they had dragged up in front of the canyon mouth and waited.

Several tense minutes ticked by.

A rifle barrel appeared, pushing some of the branches aside. The rifle's owner was being cautious. Frank held his fire. He wanted the man to show himself.

A coarse, unshaven face appeared under a floppy-brimmed felt hat. The man started to step through the gap he had made in the brush.

Frank shot him in the head.

The .44-40 slug from the Winchester took the man just above his left eye, bored on through his brain, and exploded out the back of his head. Frank saw the pink spray of blood in the air as the man jerked backward and disappeared.

"Get him?" Salty asked.

Frank worked the Winchester's lever. "I did."

He heard angry cursing; then the Gatling gun started up again.

Salty ducked his head and said, "At this rate, them varmints are gonna burn up a thousand bullets before sundown."

"More than that," Frank said. "With one of those contraptions, it only takes a few minutes to fire a thousand rounds."

"That's a lot o' lead and gunpowder to spend on just three folks," Salty pointed out.

Frank nodded. "You're right. It's almost like they've got a personal grudge against us, whoever they are. Like they're bound and determined to root us out of here."

But that didn't make any sense, he thought. They didn't know anybody in Canada except . . .

"Palmer," he said under his breath.

Salty looked over sharply at him. "What's that you say, Frank?"

"I was just wondering if maybe Joe Palmer

is out there with that bunch. We know from what Hopkins told us that Palmer has friends up here on this side of the border. Maybe he didn't have to go all the way to Calgary to meet up with them."

Salty took off his hat and scrubbed a hand over his face. "Dad*gum* it!" he said. "That'd explain why they're comin' after us so fierce-like. If Palmer's with 'em and knows I'm in here, he'd dang sure want me dead, and anybody who was with me. That's just one more reason I'm to blame for this whole blasted mess —"

The Gatling gun fell silent yet again.

"Do you think they'll try to get in here again?" Meg asked.

"Maybe," Frank said. He started to lift his head to take a look over the logs.

But as he did so, a rifle cracked and a bullet whipped past his ear to smash into the logs.

They were under attack again . . . but from a different direction this time.

CHAPTER 18

Frank spun around, lifting the Winchester. He spotted a man on the rimrock, above the canyon. The man had a rifle in his hands and had already levered another shell into the chamber. Flame spurted from the weapon's muzzle as he fired a second shot.

Frank's Winchester blasted a split second later, the sound of the rifle's report blending with a yelp of pain from Salty. The man on the rimrock doubled over as Frank's bullet punched into his guts. He dropped his rifle, staggered to the side, and lost his balance.

With a scream, he toppled off the edge and plunged toward the canyon floor. The soggy thud of his body striking the rocky ground silenced the scream.

Gut-shot as he was, he would have died anyway.

The fall had just hurried things along.

Frank turned toward his friend, saying

urgently, "Salty, are you all right?"

Salty was clutching his left arm, where blood stained the sleeve of his faded flannel shirt. "I'm fine," he said. "Dang buzzard just nicked me."

"Let me see —" Frank began.

Meg interrupted him. "Frank, there's another one!"

Frank's head jerked up. Meg was right. A second rifleman had appeared on the rimrock. Frank knew that the men with the Gatling gun must have sent them up there to see what the situation was inside the canyon and ambush anyone who was still alive.

Frank reacted instantly, lifting his rifle to draw a bead on the bushwhacker, but he knew he was going to be too late.

The whipcrack of a shot split the air, but it didn't come from the man on the rimrock. Instead, a bullet hit him from behind and drove him forward. Frank could tell that much by the way the man arched his back and threw his arms in the air. The rifle flew from his hands, unfired.

This man fell into the canyon, too, but he didn't scream on the way down. He plummeted in silence, a grim silence that told Frank the man was probably dead already.

A figure appeared on the rimrock holding

a rifle. Frank was about to snap a shot at him when the man lifted the Winchester over his head one-handed and waved it back and forth in a signal of some sort. With the way the light was, Frank couldn't tell much about the man. He was mostly just a silhouette.

But he disappeared without firing again, fading back out of sight.

"What in Hades just happened?" Salty asked.

"I'm not sure," Frank said, "but I think we've got a friend up there."

"A friend? You just said we didn't know nobody in Canada except Palmer, and he dang sure ain't our friend!"

"Anybody who wants to keep those rascals from killing us is a pard as far as I'm concerned," Frank said drily.

"Huh. Well, I can't argue with that, I reckon."

The Gatling gun started its fearsome pounding again, but after a moment, Frank heard a rifle bark and the rapid-firer stopped short.

Frank lifted his head. The rifle shot had come from somewhere up on the ridge, to the left of the canyon mouth.

"He's up there somewhere," Frank said. "He can see the Gatling gun, and he

197

plugged the man turning the crank."

"They'll try to roust him out in a minute," Salty predicted.

Frank's grip on the Winchester tightened. "More than likely. When they do, I'm going to get up on the other rimrock."

He nodded toward the right side of the canyon. The wall was steep, but a man could climb it if he was careful.

"Frank, you can't do that," Meg protested. "If they start shooting in here again while you're halfway up there, you won't have a chance!"

"I'll have to move fast," he said. "Anyway, once you've got one of those Gatlings set up, you can't change the aim as quick as you can with a rifle or a handgun. You have to pick up the back of the carriage and turn the whole thing."

The rifleman on the rimrock fired again; then two more shots cracked out from him.

"They're probably trying to get the gun adjusted now, and he's trying to pick them off while they're doing it," Frank said. He surged to his feet. "I'm going."

Meg called after him to be careful as he ran toward the right side of the canyon. It took only a moment to reach the steep wall. He took his belt off and ran it through the rifle's lever to make a crude sling that went around his neck.

Reaching up, he grabbed a projecting rock, found a toehold, and began to climb.

With every passing moment, he was aware that the Gatling gun could start up again at any time. If that storm of lead filled the canyon once more, the odds were that some of the screaming, ricocheting bullets would find him, would rake him off the canyon wall like a bug.

He didn't let himself think about that. And when the hellish hammering of the Gatling gun filled the air again, he kept climbing, pausing only long enough to glance over his shoulder and catch a glimpse of the slugs throwing up dust and grit as they smashed into the rimrock on the other side of the canyon.

Just as Frank had expected, the attackers had swung the weapon's revolving barrels toward their mysterious benefactor. In the face of that onslaught, the rifleman would have to withdraw if he could.

That gave Frank time to reach the top, though. He pulled himself up the last few feet and rolled over the edge into the boulders that littered the top of the ridge.

From there he could look across the narrow canyon and see that the other side was just as rocky. He caught a glimpse of a figure huddled in the lee of a rock slab that protected him from the hail of lead. A ricochet might still find the man, but he was relatively safe where he was.

Frank could see Salty and Meg from where he was, too. Meg was tying a bandana around Salty's wounded arm as a crude bandage. The old-timer gestured up toward Frank with his other arm. Meg turned her head to look, and Frank gave them a wave and a grin to let them know he was all right.

Then he crawled forward, searching for a spot where he could look out into the valley and maybe get a shot at the murderous bastards manning the Gatling gun.

A few moments later, he spotted the rapid-firer. It was set up at the edge of a clump of trees. Flame licked from its muzzle as each of the revolving barrels lined up with it in turn and fired its cartridge. Frank pulled his rifle up where he could use it and tried to draw a bead on the man turning the gun's crank. The wheels of the carriage and the body of the weapon itself gave him some cover . . . but there weren't many better shots on the frontier than Frank Morgan. He lined his sights on an exposed shoulder and squeezed the Winchester's trigger.

The man flopped backward, howling from

the pain of a broken shoulder as the Gatling gun stopped firing. Frank saw another man dart forward. He had already worked the rifle's lever and fired again. The second man staggered back into the shadows under the trees.

Angry shouts drifted up to the top of the ridge. The attackers were arguing among themselves now, and that was always a good thing, Frank thought with a grim smile.

Their options were limited. They could turn the Gatling gun toward him and try to kill him . . . but if they did that, the rifleman on the other side of the canyon could open up on them again. They would be right back in the same spot they were in now.

Frank held his fire and waited to see what they were going to do.

After a few minutes, rifle shots began to crack. Bullets whistled and whined around the rimrock, forcing Frank to duck lower behind the rocks. He suspected the same thing was happening on the other side of the canyon, but he didn't risk a look.

The men down in the valley were throwing a lot of lead up here, but nothing compared to what they had been doing with the Gatling. Frank figured this was just covering fire so they could move the rapid-firer. When he edged his head up for a look during a lull in the shooting, he saw that he was right.

The Gatling gun was gone.

A few more shots blasted, but they trailed away, to be replaced by the sound of horses moving off through the trees. The attackers were cutting their losses and lighting a shuck before they lost too many men to the unexpected resistance they had encountered.

Unless they were pulling some sort of trick, Frank reminded himself. He would have to give it some time before he decided about that.

The sun had climbed high in the sky by now, although it was still morning. The temperature had risen as well. It was actually getting hot up here on the rimrock. Frank sleeved sweat off his forehead, then leaned forward suddenly as he squinted into the distance.

Movement had caught his eye. As he watched, a whole line of men on horseback came into view heading east, away from the canyon. They were probably half a mile down the valley, Frank judged. Some of the men were leading what appeared to be pack mules.

His earlier hunch was right. They were leaving.

"Salty! Meg!" he called down to his friends. "The two of you all right?"

"We're fine!" Meg shouted up to him. "What about you?"

"Yeah. I'm coming down. They're gone!"

Before he started the descent, he looked across the canyon at the other side of the rimrock. The man he had seen there earlier was gone. Frank had never gotten a good look at him, and he couldn't help but wonder where the hombre was now.

He could try to figure that out later. Right now, he wanted to get down from this rocky perch.

Climbing down was harder than getting up there, and by the time he reached the ground he was winded. Carrying the rifle, he walked across the canyon toward Salty and Meg, who were standing beside the log barricade. The logs had suffered a lot of damage during the attack, but they had done their job.

"What happened to that other fella?" Salty asked as Frank came up to them.

"Don't know," Frank replied with a shake of his head. "I lost sight of him, but he's got to still be around somewhere close by." He nodded toward Salty's wounded limb. "How's the arm?"

"Aches a mite, but it'll be fine."

"How about you?" Frank asked Meg. "Are you hurt?"

"Well, my ears are still ringing a little from all that racket, but other than that I don't have any complaints," she told him, returning his smile.

Salty asked, "What're we gonna do now?"

Frank grew solemn. "I'd like to go after that bunch. I don't much cotton to being shot at, so I reckon they've got a whole heap of marks chalked up against them right now."

"Dang right," Salty agreed with an emphatic nod. "Besides, if what we was sayin' earlier is right, there's a chance Palmer is with 'em, and I still got a score to settle with that polecat."

Frank looked at Meg. "What do you say?"

"I say I don't like being shot at, either," she answered.

"You know the odds are against us. We downed a few of them, but they still outnumber us."

"And they got them devil guns," Salty said. "But I vote we go after 'em anyway."

Meg nodded again, and Frank said, "I reckon it's settled then —"

The sound of hoofbeats nearby made him turn toward the brush piled in front of the canyon. It had been shot up so much by the

Gatling gun that it wasn't much of a barrier anymore. They could see the rider reining in there. Frank covered the man as he swung down from the saddle and pushed through the branches into the canyon.

"Howdy," the stranger said with a friendly grin. "Looks like you folks are all right. I'm glad to see that."

"Well, I'll swan," Salty said in surprise. "What circus did you escape from, mister?"

CHAPTER 19

Charlotte looked like she was going to be sick, and Joseph Marat felt that way himself. He had not expected the sort of wanton slaughter that he had witnessed.

And yet, he told himself, the change that he and his friends wanted so fervently could not come without violence. The oppressive representatives of the British Empire understood only one thing — deadly force.

But despite the firepower they possessed, things hadn't worked out exactly like Owen Lundy and Joe Palmer thought they would. Those people in the canyon, Palmer's enemies, had put up more of a fight than they expected.

So now, as they retreated, the only ones who had died were some of Lundy's men. Three of the outlaws had failed to come back: the one who had ventured through the brush barrier, and the two men Lundy had sent up onto the rimrock to ambush the people inside the canyon.

Lundy was angry about it, too.

"You cost me three men with that wild scheme," the white-haired man complained to Palmer as they rode along at the head of the little column. Joseph and Charlotte were right behind them, then the other outlaws strung out in a line, leading the pack mules that were loaded down with the disassembled Gatling guns.

The rapid-firer they had put together earlier was still on its wheeled carriage. It had been turned around and the rear brace had been lifted so it could be tied to one of the mules. The stolid animal pulled the gun behind it.

"They must have had some place to fort up in there," Palmer responded bitterly. "Otherwise we would've gotten them. We poured enough lead into that canyon to wipe out anybody in it."

"Yeah, well, that ain't the way things worked out, is it?" Lundy snapped. "From now on, Joe, I'll be doing all the thinking around here."

Palmer bristled. "Damn it, going after Stevens and his friends was *your* idea, Owen." He waved a hand behind him at Joseph and Charlotte. "You wanted to show off for these two."

For a second, Joseph thought Lundy was going to reach for his gun. He was ready to grab Charlotte and hustle her away from the line of fire if gunplay broke out between Lundy and Palmer.

Instead, after a moment Lundy grunted and said, "I guess that's three less shares we'll have to take out of the gold."

Palmer gave him a curt nod. "That's the best way to look at it, all right."

Lundy didn't rein in, but he turned halfway around in the saddle to look at Joseph. "Speakin' of gold, where are those friends of yours? I'd like to get this over with."

"They should be along soon," Joseph said, hoping that nothing had happened to Anton and the other members of the group.

The plan had been that Anton and the others would keep the gold with them while Joseph and Charlotte met the men who were bringing the guns across the border and would examine the merchandise. When Joseph was satisfied that the guns were what they had been promised, he would signal Anton and they would rendezvous to make the payment and take delivery of the Gatlings.

A short time after riding away from the canyon, Joseph had given the signal: three quick shots, a pause, then two more shots.

Anton should have been alert for it. He had to know that something was going on. The noise of the Gatling gun had been so loud it seemed to Joseph that it could have been heard as far away as Calgary.

Anton Mirabeau was a cautious man, though. That was why he had been entrusted with the safekeeping of the gold. He was probably watching them right now, Joseph thought, waiting to make sure that everything was all right before he showed up with the payoff.

Joseph hoped that was the case, because Lundy was getting impatient. He had seen with his own eyes how ruthless the American could be, and he was worried about what might happen to him and Charlotte if everything didn't go as planned. Lundy might seek vengeance if he didn't get his hands on that gold soon.

"Who do you reckon was in that canyon with the old man?" Lundy asked Palmer, putting aside the matter of the gold for the moment.

Palmer shook his head. "I don't know for sure. The last time I saw Stevens before I ran into him in Powderkeg Bay was over in Skagway, and then he was hanging around with a fella named Morgan. I don't know if the two of them are still pards or not."

"Not Frank Morgan, I hope," Lundy said.

"Well . . . yeah."

That was enough to make Lundy haul back on his reins and bring his horse to a stop. He turned angrily toward Palmer and demanded, "Frank Morgan the gunfighter? The one they call the Drifter?"

Palmer looked distinctly uncomfortable as he nodded and said, "Yeah, that's him."

"You loco son of a bitch!" Lundy burst out. "Frank Morgan's one of the most dangerous men west of the Mississippi. Don't you think it might've been a good idea to tell us exactly who we were goin' up against?"

"I don't know for sure that Morgan is still traveling with the old man," Palmer argued. "Morgan wasn't with him in that saloon in Powderkeg Bay."

"That doesn't mean he wasn't somewhere close by."

Palmer shrugged and tried to sound un-concerned as he said, "Frank Morgan'll die just as quick as any other man if he goes up against one of those Gatling guns."

"Maybe, maybe not. If he was back there in that canyon with Stevens, he's probably still alive." Lundy swore. "I never bargained on having Frank Morgan on my trail."

"Don't worry about it," Palmer said.

"Pretty soon you'll have the gold those half-breeds promised you, and you can get out of this part of the country."

Joseph felt a surge of anger at the contemptuous way Palmer referred to him and his people, including his sister. But he suppressed the urge to say something. There was already enough tension in the air without adding to it.

"Jericho and me had a pretty good setup in Calgary," Lundy said with a frown. "I'm not sure I want to leave it behind just like that."

"You'll be rich enough to go wherever you want," Palmer argued. "Hell, the two of us could go back to Chicago. We'd be big men there now, Owen. We'd be running all the gangs on the south side within a year."

Lundy didn't look convinced of that at all. He said, "We'll see. First we've got to get our hands on that gold we've been promised."

He turned in the saddle again to give Joseph a hard, meaningful look.

"The gold is coming," Joseph said. He lifted a hand to point at the riders he had just spotted emerging from a thick growth of trees up ahead. "There."

Beside him, Charlotte said excitedly, "It is Anton and the others."

It was accepted by many who knew them that Charlotte and Anton would be married someday. Joseph wasn't so certain that was a good idea. Anton Mirabeau was a good man to have as an ally, brave and devoted to the Métis cause, but he was also reckless and could be brutal at times. Joseph wasn't sure he wanted his sister to be married to a man like that.

Charlotte had a mind of her own, though, and a stubborn streak a mile wide. Joseph was content to bide his time, hoping that eventually Charlotte would come to realize Anton wasn't the right man for her.

Since the party led by Lundy and Palmer had already halted, they waited where they were and let Mirabeau and the others come to them. Joseph counted the riders and realized with a shock that one man was missing. Joseph hoped the man was just out scouting and that nothing had happened to him.

Mirabeau and the others reined in when they were about twenty yards away. The big, black-bearded man raised a hand in greeting and smiled.

"Joseph! Charlotte! It is good to see you again. You are all right?"

Joseph nodded. "We're fine, Anton. You heard our signal?"

"Yes. We heard what sounded like a little war, too. What happened?"

Lundy said, "We were just demonstrating the Gatling guns for your friends."

"Burning up ammunition that we will be paying for," Mirabeau said with a frown.

"You're still getting a damned good deal," Lundy snapped.

"Perhaps in light of these developments, the deal should be changed," Mirabeau suggested.

Joseph stiffened with worry. This was just like Anton, he thought, going off on some wild tangent that would just wind up causing trouble.

Lundy didn't like it, either. Joseph could tell that from the way the outlaw straightened in the saddle and moved his hand slightly toward the butt of the gun on his hip.

The Métis outnumbered the Americans, six to five. Eight to five if he and Charlotte were counted, Joseph thought.

But Lundy, Palmer, and the other men were all hardened criminals, well-versed in the art of killing. Mirabeau might succeed in refusing to hand over the gold and take the Gatling guns anyway, but it would be at a high cost in human life. In fact, they might all die, which would do nothing to help the cause.

"Anton," Joseph said sharply. "There will be no change in our arrangements with these men. Mr. Lundy has kept his part of the bargain, and we will keep ours."

Mirabeau frowned at him. He didn't like being spoken to that way, and Joseph knew it. Joseph felt that he had no choice but to put a stop to this trouble before it blew up into violence.

After a moment, Mirabeau shrugged brawny shoulders and said sullenly, "Fine. If you want to pay for bullets that have already been fired, it's your decision, Joseph. You're our leader, after all. You're the *educated* one."

The scorn in Mirabeau's voice was plain for all of them to hear, including Charlotte. Anger and resentment burned inside Joseph, but he forced it down. More important things than his pride were at stake here.

"If your men will open the other crates, Mr. Lundy," he said, "we will unload the gold."

"You don't trust us that those other crates have Gatling guns in them?" Lundy asked with a tight, humorless smile.

"As much as you trust us that we brought the right amount of gold," Joseph said.

Lundy grunted. "Fair enough." He gestured toward the pack mules. "Break 'em out, boys."

During the next ten minutes, Lundy's men took down the crates from the pack mules, pried off the lids, and unwrapped the other Gatling guns. They opened the crates that contained thousands and thousands of rounds of ammunition, as well.

"Well?" Lundy asked when they were finished. "Are you satisfied?"

Mirabeau had dismounted. So had Joseph. Together they examined the guns.

"You know more about these things than I do," Mirabeau admitted grudgingly. "Does everything look as it should to you, Joseph?"

He nodded. "Yes. We have what we need here to assemble four Gatling guns, as agreed."

"Then let's see that gold," Lundy rasped. "We've been patient long enough."

Joseph didn't think Lundy had been all that patient, but he kept that opinion to himself. He and Mirabeau went over to the pack horse the other Métis had brought with them and lifted down the chests, using the leather straps on their ends.

Joseph knelt beside one of them and unfastened the catches that held the lid down. He opened it, revealing the gold bars stacked within.

Palmer let out a low whistle. "That's mighty nice," he said. "Where'd you get those bars?"

"That's none of your business," Joseph said.

As a matter of fact, it had taken a number of train holdups and bank robberies in various Canadian cities to assemble this much gold. In the eyes of the North West Mounted Police, he and his comrades were simply outlaws, common thieves out for themselves.

The Mounties had no idea that the men who had taken these gold bars were revolutionaries, men who would forge a new nation for their people.

"Open the other chest," Lundy said.

Mirabeau opened it. Lundy nodded in satisfaction when he saw the gold bars in it.

"Looks like we've got a deal. We'll throw in the pack mules. You'll need 'em to carry those Gatlings around."

Joseph closed the chests and fastened the catches.

"What are you gonna do with those guns, anyway?" Palmer asked.

"That is our business," Joseph said.

Palmer shrugged. "Sure. I was just curious, that's all."

With the transaction complete, there was no need for the two groups to stay together. As soon as everything was loaded up again, they could go their separate ways.

Lundy and his men were ready to leave first, since they only had the two chests of gold to deal with. They mounted up and set off without looking back. They continued heading east, toward the edge of the mountains and Calgary on the plains beyond.

"We will let them get ahead of us," Mirabeau said. "But not too far ahead."

Joseph looked at the man and frowned. "What are you talking about? Our business with them is done."

Slowly, Mirabeau shook his head and smiled. The expression was without warmth.

"Now, Joseph," he said with a cold chuckle, "you didn't really think we were going to let them ride off and keep all that gold we worked so hard to steal, did you?"

CHAPTER 20

The last person Frank had seen dressed in such a gaudy outfit was Buffalo Bill Cody, when he had stopped in Chicago on his way to Boston a couple of years earlier. The old scout and buffalo hunter's Wild West show and extravaganza had been putting on performances at the Columbian Exposition there.

They were a long way from Chicago now, but the cream-colored Stetson, fringed jacket, tight trousers with fancy stitching, and high-topped boots looked like something Bill Cody might have worn.

Instead, the owner of the duds was a young man with a smiling, friendly face and wavy brown hair under the thumbed-back Stetson. In his left hand he held a Winchester with a gleaming barrel tipped back on his shoulder. An ivory-handled Colt rode in a holster on his right hip.

He didn't seem offended by Salty's question. "No circus," he said. "I was just passin' through these parts and heard what sounded like a mighty interestin' ruckus." His voice held the soft drawl of a Southerner, possibly from Virginia. "Name's Russell. Reb Russell, they call me."

"You're too young to have been in the war," Frank said.

"Yes, sir. Fact is, I wasn't even born until a few years after it was over. But my pa, he was an officer in the Confederate cavalry, rode with Jeb Stuart, in fact, so I was sort of brought up in the tradition, you could say." Russell's smile widened as he turned to Meg and took his hat off. "We haven't been introduced, ma'am, but I'm mighty pleased to meet you. Reb Russell, at your service."

"I'm Meg Goodwin," she said, looking a little flustered.

"It's an honor."

"You ain't gonna kiss her hand, are you?" Salty asked.

"Not unless the lady asks me to," Russell said.

Frank stepped forward and introduced himself. "Frank Morgan," he said as he stuck out his hand. "I reckon that was you up on the rimrock, taking a hand in that fight?"

Russell shook with him. The young man's grip was surprisingly strong.

"Yes, sir. I was ridin' back a ways behind this ridge when all the commotion started, so I thought I ought to see what was goin' on."

"How did you know which side you ought to take?"

"Well, it's true I don't really know who you folks are or why those other folks were tryin' to kill you, but I just naturally sort of stick up for the underdog." Russell's voice hardened slightly as he added, "I guess that comes from growin' up in the South while the Yankees were havin' everything their way durin' Reconstruction."

As a Texan, Frank had fought for the Confederacy during the Civil War, but he had long since put that conflict behind him. As far as he was concerned, both sides had been so damned stubborn that war was inevitable, and then to make things even worse, the Yankees had proved to be mighty poor winners. Nothing was going to be gained by dredging all that up now, on either side.

"Anyway," Russell went on, "I saw they had you outnumbered and outgunned, and then those bushwhackers climbed up on the ridge and tried to get you in a cross fire.

Didn't seem like a very sportin' thing to do."

"Well, we appreciate the help," Frank said. "We can offer you some coffee and something to eat, if you're hungry."

"That sounds mighty fine." Russell leaned his head toward the canyon mouth. "You don't think those varmints are liable to come back?"

"I'll stand watch," Salty volunteered. "Y'all go ahead."

He muttered something about circus cowboys as he walked off.

As the others started back toward the fire, which had burned down and gone out during the battle, Frank told Meg and Russell, "You two go on. I'd better do something about those bodies."

The two dead men lying on the canyon floor where they had fallen, plus the one lying sprawled just outside the brush barrier, were grim reminders of what had happened here. Frank still couldn't be certain *why* the men with the Gatling gun had tried to kill him and his friends, but there was no doubt about their deadly intentions.

He walked over to the corpses, retrieving his hat along the way. The first man he came to lay face down. That was the one Frank had shot in the belly.

221

Frank rested his hand on the butt of his Colt as he got a toe under the man's shoulder and rolled him over. The chances of the bushwhacker still being alive were practically nonexistent, but it never paid to take chances.

Sure enough, the man's beard-stubbled face had the lax looseness that came with death. Frank hunkered next to him and went through his pockets, but the search didn't turn up anything except a plug of tobacco, a few coins, and a harmonica.

Frank held the harmonica in his fingers and looked at it for a long moment, wondering what songs the man had played on it around a lonely campfire at night. His mouth tightened into a grim line. He tossed the harmonica on the man's chest. Thinking about such things didn't do any good. They were just reminders of what a waste it was when a man took a wrong turn in life and went down a trail that ended with him dying by the gun.

Frank had taken his own wrong turns, some by choice and some he'd been forced into by circumstances, and someday his own trail would end the same way.

He stood up and walked over to the other man who had fallen from the rimrock. This one had turned over as he plummeted and landed on his back, splitting his skull like a watermelon. His face was unmarked, though.

Frank didn't recognize him, either, although he knew the type. This one, like the other man, was a hardcase, an outlaw, the sort of man who would steal a Gatling gun from the Army and smuggle it across the border into Canada for God knew what reason . . . although money was bound to be involved somewhere. The dead man didn't have anything in his pockets except the makin's and some folded, greasy greenbacks.

Frank went back to the first man, took hold of his legs, and dragged him over next to the other corpse. After he fetched the body outside the canyon, he and Salty could put the corpses next to the canyon wall and collapse part of it over them in a makeshift burial. Maybe Reb Russell would give them a hand, if he didn't mind getting his fancy duds a mite dirty.

Thinking of Russell made Frank glance toward the camp. Meg had gotten the fire going again and was heating up the coffee. He saw her and Russell talking.

Frank didn't trust the stranger. Why was someone dressed like Russell wandering through these rugged Canadian Rockies by himself? That didn't make a lick of sense as far as Frank was concerned.

But there was no denying that Russell had helped them out of a bad spot. If he hadn't given them a hand, they might not have been able to drive off the attackers.

Maybe after he'd had his coffee and something to eat, Russell would go on his way, leaving them in the canyon. Frank wasn't going to count on that, though.

And he wasn't going to take his eye off the man who called himself Reb Russell for very long, either.

He walked back to the brush across the mouth of the canyon. Salty stood there looking up and down the valley.

"Nobody movin' as far as I can see," the old-timer said. "Frank, I want to tell you again how sorry I am for gettin' you and Meg into this mess."

"Don't worry about it, Salty. Like we told you, nobody forced us to come along." Frank nodded toward the dead outlaw who lay out here. "Ever see him before?"

"Nope. Looks like a typical hardcase, all gun and no brain."

Frank nodded. "Same as the two inside the canyon. You still think Palmer was with this bunch?"

"I got no earthly idea. It makes sense,

though, and these are just the sort of ornery, no-good varmints he'd throw in with. He worked for Soapy Smith, after all, and Soapy was about as bad as they come."

"You want to roll some rocks down on these three?"

Salty scratched at his beard. "I'd rather leave 'em for the wolves." He sighed. "But I reckon that wouldn't be fittin'. We already left that fella you had to kill yesterday."

Frank took the dead man's shoulders while Salty got his feet. They carried the corpse into the canyon and placed him with the other two.

"Give us a hand, Russell?" Frank called over to the man.

Russell joined them right away. "Are you going to bury them?" he asked.

Frank shook his head. "No shovel." He pointed to some loose talus rock on the slope above the dead men. "We'll start a little rock slide and cover them up that way."

"Sure, I'll help you." Russell started to climb, with apparent disregard for his clothes.

He and Frank took their rifles up the slope and used the Winchesters to pry loose some of the rocks. Salty and Meg stayed on the canyon floor. Once the rocks began to move, they picked up speed and dislodged more stones and dirt. Almost immediately, Frank and Russell had a small-scale avalanche going that swept down and raised a cloud of dust as it covered the bodies of the dead men.

They slid back down to the ground and joined Salty and Meg. The old-timer took his hat off, and the others followed suit.

"Lord, I ain't much for speechifyin'," Salty said, "and I reckon it's more'n likely these fellas went the other way instead of up yonder to your homestead, but wherever they wind up, we're puttin' that in your hands. It ain't for us to judge. Amen."

"Amen," Frank repeated.

Salty clapped his hat back on his head. "Now that's done, let's get after them skunks. I sure don't take it kindly when somebody shoots at me."

"You're going after them?" Russell asked.

"Dang right we are. I got a suspicion there's a fella with 'em who owes me money."

"Do you even know why they tried to kill you?"

"We've got some ideas," Frank said without going into what those ideas were.

"Well, if you don't mind the company, I'd be glad to come along with you," Russell said. "I've got my horse right outside the canyon, and I left my pack animal with my supplies not far from here when all the shooting started. I won't be a burden to you."

"You don't have any business of your own to tend to?" Frank asked, trying not to sound too suspicious.

"Yeah, but those fellows headed east when they left here, didn't they? That's the way I was going anyway. I'm bound for Calgary."

Frank decided to be blunt. "What for, if you don't mind me asking?"

Russell grinned. "Sure, it's no secret. There's talk that some of the cattlemen in those parts are fixin' to put on a big rodeo there. I plan to take part in it."

"A ro-day-o?" Salty said. "I been to the one down in Pecos a bunch o' times. You mean to say they have such things up here in Canada?"

"They have rodeos anywhere there's a bunch of cowboys gettin' together," Russell said. "There are ranches here in Canada just like there are down in the States. Say, Mr. Stevens, if you've been to the rodeo in Pecos, you might've seen me. I won the saddle-bronc ridin' there, three years runnin'."

Salty's eyes widened in recognition. "Why, fry me for a gopher!" he exclaimed. "I

227

knowed there was somethin' familiar about you. You rode that dang Razor horse four or five years ago, the one ever'body said was a killer and couldn't ever be rode!"

Russell nodded. "That's right. The purse was a mighty good one that year."

Salty turned to Frank. "I know this boy now, Frank. He'll do to ride the river with."

"I'm glad to hear it," Frank said. He had long since stopped being surprised when people ran into folks they knew out here on the frontier. The West, and that included this part of Canada, too, he supposed, was a vast place, but at the same time it was possible to encounter someone you might not have seen for years. The network of mutual acquaintances stretched over hundreds, even thousands, of miles.

Frank went on, "You're welcome to ride with us, Russell, but I warn you . . . we're liable to run into more trouble."

"That's fine. Nothin' I like better than a good scrape, Mr. Morgan. And call me Reb."

Frank nodded. "All right, Reb. Just as long as you know what you're getting into."

He wished he could say the same thing for himself.

And despite the opinion of Reb Russell that Salty had expressed, Frank didn't fully trust the young man. There was something about him that still didn't ring true.

As they headed back to the fire, Salty said, "They let you wear that kind of getup to the ro-day-o these days?"

CHAPTER 21

"What are you talking about?" Joseph asked as he stared at Anton Mirabeau in surprise.

"Those men have no right to that gold," Mirabeau replied with a confidence that bordered on arrogance. He thumped a fist against his buckskin-clad chest. "It belongs to the Métis!"

Joseph waved a hand toward the crated weapons. "We gave it to them in return for those Gatling guns. You know that, Anton."

"And *you* know how hard we worked for it. You know the price that was paid."

Joseph scowled. He knew, all right. Shooting had broken out during several of those robberies. Friends of his had died, gunned down by the law. Almost as bad, he had to live with the fact that innocent people also had been killed.

But such tragedies had happened before and no doubt would happen again before his people finally achieved their freedom, he reminded himself. There was always a price to be paid for everything in this world.

"What are you suggesting?" he asked coldly. "That we go after them and steal the gold back from them?"

An eager grin stretched across Mirabeau's bearded face. "Exactly!"

"What about honor?"

Mirabeau shrugged and said, "They are Americans," as if that excused anything he and his friends might do.

Joseph looked over at his sister. Charlotte was chewing her bottom lip worriedly. He knew the prospect of more violence bothered her, too, but he also knew she didn't like to go against what Mirabeau wanted.

Like everyone else, she still had the idea in her head that one day he would be her husband.

Though his jaw was tight with anger, Joseph said, "There is nothing I can do to stop you, is there?"

Mirabeau shook his head. "No." He turned to the other men. "Mount up. They will have gotten far enough ahead of us by now. We'll circle around in front of them and set up an ambush. Wolverine Rock would be a good place."

Several of the men nodded in agreement. They swung up into their saddles.

Mirabeau turned back to Joseph and Charlotte. "The two of you can follow us and bring the mules and the guns."

From the sound of Mirabeau's voice, Joseph was no longer in charge of this mission. Injured pride welled up inside him, but he forced it down.

"You don't want us to come with you?"

"Someone has to bring the guns along," Mirabeau said. He was trying to sound reasonable, but Joseph knew the real reason for the decision. Mirabeau no longer fully trusted him. He was afraid that Joseph would do something to ruin his plan.

"Fine," Joseph said. *Go get more blood on your hands,* he thought. *It won't be the last, will it?*

Mirabeau nodded and waved his companions into motion. They headed down the valley, riding hard. They would have to set a fast pace in order to reach Wolverine Rock ahead of the American outlaws. Fortunately for the Métis, this was their homeland. Mirabeau had hunted and trapped all over these mountains. He knew all the shortcuts.

"This could turn out badly, Joseph," Charlotte said. "I wish Anton were not so stubborn."

"But he is, and we cannot change him."

Joseph began gathering up the reins of the

pack mules. The Gatling gun that had been used earlier had been disassembled and returned to its crate. All the crates had been closed up and lashed to the animals again. He waited until Charlotte had climbed into the saddle of her horse and then handed some of the reins to her. He took the others.

They started down the valley, leading the mules. Their pace was much slower than that of Mirabeau and the other men. Joseph supposed that when they were done with their ambush — when they had finished killing the Americans and stealing back the chests of gold — they would either wait at Wolverine Rock or return for him and Charlotte.

There was nothing to say, so they rode in silence. The sun moved toward its zenith. It was almost midday, Joseph judged, when the sound of gunshots in the distance came to his ears.

Charlotte heard them, too. She caught her breath, stiffened in the saddle, and said, "I pray that Anton is all right."

Sadly, Joseph was no longer certain he shared that sentiment.

Joe Palmer gave in to his curiosity and asked, "Say, exactly how much are those gold bars worth, anyway?"

Lundy grinned over at him as they rode side by side. "Tryin' to figure out what your share's gonna be, Joe?"

Palmer shrugged. "Seems like that would be an important thing to know."

"Well, you know the same as I do that it all depends on how much you get for it. There's not a set price."

"You're bound to have a pretty good idea, though," Palmer insisted.

"It ought to be in the neighborhood of fifty thousand dollars," Lundy said.

Palmer let out a low whistle. "That's a lot of money. Ten grand apiece since there's only five of us left."

"Hold on a minute," Lundy said, his voice hardening. "You're not figuring the same way I am."

"What do you mean?"

"Jericho and I were taking thirty percent."

"Jericho's dead," Palmer pointed out.

Lundy shook his head. "That don't change anything. I'm still taking fifteen thousand."

The tone of his voice made it clear that Palmer, or anyone else, was going to have plenty of trouble on his hands if that decision was challenged.

"All right," Palmer said. "So that leaves thirty-five grand to split four ways."

"You weren't in on the whole deal. Five for you, ten each for the other fellas."

Palmer had to swallow an angry curse. He glanced over his shoulder at the other three outlaws. He didn't know any of them personally, but he recognized the wolflike intensity with which they were watching him. They were listening to the conversation with great interest.

"You know what?" Palmer said, recognizing the razor-thin line he was walking. "That sounds mighty fair to me, Owen. I'll be just fine with that split."

Lundy grunted. "Good. Because that's the way it's gonna be."

The valley had narrowed down as they headed east. Rugged, snow-capped peaks still loomed to the north and south, but ahead of them, Palmer could see a gap where the trail sloped down to the flats. They would still have to ride through some foothills, but they were about to leave the mountains at last.

A large rock squatted on the left side of the trail. Something about it struck Palmer as familiar, and after a moment he realized what it was.

The rock generally had a rounded shape, but it thrust out sharply toward the trail like an animal's snout and on top of it were two knobs that looked like ears. Most of the rock was dark in color, but a lighter band encircled it.

"It looks like a wolverine," Palmer said with a grin.

"What?" Lundy sounded confused.

"That big rock up yonder." Palmer pointed. "It looks like a wolverine's head."

Lundy began, "Yeah, I guess it —"

He stopped short when smoke puffed from behind one of those earlike knobs and a bullet made a flat *whap!* as it passed through the air between them, near their heads.

A fraction of a second later, one of the men riding behind them let out a pained grunt. Palmer whipped his head around in time to see the man topple out of the saddle with a black, red-rimmed hole in the center of his forehead where the bullet had struck him.

"Move!" Lundy yelled as he kicked his horse into a run. "Somebody's shootin' at us!"

That seemed pretty obvious to Palmer. He heard the wind-rip of another bullet past his ear as he leaned forward to make himself a smaller target.

"Hyaaaahh!" he shouted at his horse as he urged the animal into a gallop. Lundy had gone to the left, so Palmer went to the right. When you were under attack, it wasn't smart to bunch up. Make your enemies split their fire.

The other two outlaws were scattering as well. Palmer heard the flat *crack-crack-crack* of rifle fire now and saw a cloud of powder smoke rising over the odd-shaped rock. Some bastards had gotten up there and set up an ambush for them.

Palmer had a pretty good idea who they were, too. Those damn half-breeds were trying a double cross, he thought as he rode swiftly toward some trees.

His horse suddenly lurched underneath him. Palmer cursed bitterly as he felt the animal going down. He kicked his feet out of the stirrups and let go of the reins. He was thrown clear as the horse fell, but after sailing through the air for a few feet, he slammed into the ground so hard that he was stunned and all the breath was knocked out of his body.

He lay there gasping, unable to get any air in his lungs. He knew he needed to get up and make a run for the trees. Out here in the open, he was an easy target.

His muscles wouldn't obey him, though. He tried to force himself up but slumped back down, helpless.

A few feet away, his horse lay bleeding to death from the terrible wound a bullet had ripped in its throat. Its hooves thrashed madly in agonized panic.

The horse's body would give him a little cover, Palmer thought, if he could just get behind it. Gritting his teeth, he finally succeeded in forcing his body into motion. He began to crawl toward his stricken mount.

Palmer had to circle around the wildly flailing hooves. The horse's movements were less urgent now as death approached rapidly, but those slashing hooves were still dangerous.

The horrible bubbling sounds the horse was making came to an end. The hooves stilled. Palmer pulled himself behind the carcass just as bullets began to thump into it.

He huddled as low to the ground as he could and hoped that would be enough to protect him. What felt like a burning brand raked along his leg. He realized that one of the bullets had just grazed him. He pressed himself closer to the dead horse.

From where he lay, he couldn't see Lundy anymore, but he saw that one of the other men was down, knocked from his saddle by bushwhacker's lead.

Where was the pack horse with the two

chests full of gold bars?

That question suddenly filled Palmer's mind. He desperately wanted to lift his head so he could take a better look around, but he knew that doing so would invite the bushwhackers to put a bullet through his brain. He clenched his teeth together and made himself keep his head down.

The first man who'd been hit had been leading the pack horse, Palmer recalled. Shot in the head like that, he would have let go of the reins.

A horse wasn't like a mule. It would spook a lot easier when the shooting started. The pack horse could have bolted.

Which meant that it — and its valuable cargo — could be anywhere by now.

The ambushers continued firing from the rock for what seemed like an eternity to Palmer as he hunkered behind the dead horse. In reality, it was probably only a few minutes.

Then the shots died away, leaving an eerie, echoing silence in their wake.

Palmer knew better than to move. He stayed right where he was, convinced that if he popped up from behind his bloody cover, he'd be dead a second later.

He heard horses moving down the valley, from the vicinity of the gap that the funny-looking rock guarded. The hoofbeats faded into the distance, but still Palmer didn't move. This could be a trick. The others could have pulled out but left behind a sharpshooter to finish him off when he showed himself.

But more time dragged past, and flies started to buzz around the horse's carcass. The coppery stink from the pool of blood in which he sprawled filled Palmer's nostrils and sickened him.

"Owen?" he called. "Owen, can you hear me?"

There was no response.

"Anybody else? Anybody alive out here?"

Nothing. Palmer's teeth ground together as he tried to figure out what to do.

When he judged that at least an hour had passed, he muttered, "The hell with it," and heaved himself up from behind the carcass. Nobody shot at him. He climbed laboriously to his feet and staggered toward the two bodies he could see. They belonged to a couple of Lundy's men.

Palmer had never learned their names. He didn't give a damn about that, either.

He spotted another body lying at the edge of the trees. When he hurried over to it, he saw it was the third member of Lundy's gang. This man was as dead as the other two.

And sure enough, there was no sign of the pack horse as far as the eye could see. The saddle horses had stampeded and were gone, too.

In utter disgust, Palmer asked aloud, "Now what the hell am I gonna do?"

Somewhere not far off, somebody moaned.

CHAPTER 22

The sound made Palmer twist around and reach for his gun. His fingers found only empty air where the butt of the revolver should have been.

Shocked, he looked down and saw that the holster was empty. The gun must have fallen out when he was thrown from the falling horse, he realized.

His rifle was still in the saddle boot strapped to the carcass. He had been so stunned by crashing to the ground that he hadn't been thinking straight. Otherwise he never would have gone wandering around this killing ground without any weapons except for a small knife hidden under his coat.

The moan sounded again from somewhere in the trees. The timber grew so thickly that Palmer couldn't see very far into the woods. He glanced at the horse and wondered if he could run out there and get his rifle.

If he did, he would be turning his back to whoever was hidden in the trees, making him a perfect target.

But there was only one logical person it could be, he told himself. When he heard a strangled cough, he knew he had to risk it.

"Owen?" Palmer called. "Owen, is that you? Are you hurt?"

The voice that responded was so low and weak that at first Palmer wasn't even sure if he had heard anything. Then it came again, and he knew.

"J-Joe . . . ? Joe, I need . . . help . . . I . . . I b-been shot. . . ."

"I'm coming," Palmer said. "Speak up. Where are you?"

"H-here . . ."

Palmer followed the voice into the shadows under the trees. A moment later he found Lundy propped up against one of the trunks. His hat was gone. Lundy had a gun in his hand, but that hand lay in his lap as if it was too heavy for him to lift.

Palmer supposed it was, and he could see why. Lundy was weak from all the blood he'd lost. The right side of his shirt was soaked with it.

Palmer knelt beside him and asked, "How bad are you hit, Owen?"

"I . . . don't know. Just know it . . . hurts

like hell."

"I thought you'd gotten away clean," Palmer said as he carefully moved aside the blood-soaked shirt in an attempt to see the wound in Lundy's side.

"I thought . . . I had, too. . . . One of the . . . sons o' bitches . . . winged me . . . just as I got to the trees. . . . I fell off . . . my horse. . . . Don't know where the bastard . . . ran off to."

"Neither do I. All the horses are gone except for mine, and he's dead."

"What about . . . the pack horse?"

"Gone, too. I'd be willing to bet those bushwhackers took it."

Lundy groaned. "The gold . . ."

"Yeah," Palmer said grimly.

He had the hole in Lundy's side uncovered by now. The bullet had torn through the outlaw's flesh, but the wound didn't appear to be too deep. Palmer reached around behind Lundy and brought his hand back with crimson smeared on the fingers.

Lundy cursed in pain. "What'n blazes . . . are you doin'?"

"Checking for an exit wound," Palmer explained. "It's there. The bullet went clear through, Owen. That's good."

"Yeah," Lundy said wearily. "It is."

"You've lost quite a bit of blood, and the

244

shock of being hit by that bullet has knocked you for a loop. But I reckon you'll be all right. I'll clean the wound and bandage it up, and you'll be fine."

As long as he didn't get blood poisoning and fester to death, Palmer thought. He didn't mention that possibility. All he could do was patch up the wound the best he could.

"Fine . . . hell," Lundy said. "We're out here . . . set afoot . . . and our gold's . . . gone."

"Yeah, but as long as we're alive, we've still got a chance of finding the sons of bitches who stole it and getting it back," Palmer said. "And that's exactly what we're gonna do."

Reb Russell's horse was a big, good-looking sorrel, and he rode well, not surprising since he had won saddle-bronc-riding competitions. At least, according to Reb, he had won those contests. They had no way of knowing if that was actually true, Frank mused as he rode along with the others, heading east toward the edge of the mountains.

They rode four abreast, with him and Salty on the ends and Meg and Reb in the middle. Meg seemed quite interested in what Reb had to say and prompted him to talk more about his rodeo experiences.

As it happened, Frank had been down in Pecos, Texas, a number of years earlier when the first official rodeo had taken place there. It had been quite a spectacle, with cowboys riding in from ranches all over West Texas to test their skills against each other. The contests were the same sort of things they did in their everyday work — roping, riding, throwing steers so they could be branded — but when you added spectators and an air of competition, it became something quite different from a chore.

The practice had spread, and now there were rodeos all over the place, some fancy and some just simple get-togethers. But Reb Russell evidently made a practice of traveling from one to the next, earning his living from the prize money he won rather than working as a regular hand on any of the ranches.

Something about that didn't seem right to Frank. He had a hunch that Russell could have been a top hand if he'd wanted to, only the young man didn't have any appetite for that much hard work.

But how Reb Russell lived his life was none of his business, Frank reminded himself.

Reb changed the subject from himself by asking, "Those fellas who had the Gatling gun, you didn't get a good look at them?"

Frank shook his head. "No, we were too busy ducking all those bullets that were flying around."

"And there was a whole heap of 'em," Salty added. "I never heard so many shots so close together."

"Yeah, a Gatling gun'll spit out a lot of bullets in a hurry," Reb agreed. "Or at least that's what I've heard. I never actually saw one of the contraptions until today."

"You probably saw the men who had it better than we did," Frank said. "You were up on the rimrock taking potshots at the ones trying to shoot it at the canyon."

Reb shrugged. "Just looked like reg'lar hardcases to me. Well, except for an hombre who was wearin' one of those eastern dude hats."

"Dude hats?" Frank repeated.

"Yeah, you know." Reb made a circular motion over his head. "One of those derbies."

"Palmer," Salty said with an angry vehemence in his voice.

"So you *do* know one of the varmints."

"Maybe," Frank said. "We've been on the trail of an hombre who started out as a crook somewhere back east before coming to Colorado and throwing in with an owl-hoot named Soapy Smith. They wound up going to Alaska and taking over a town there called Skagway. They stole some of Salty's money."

"No, they stole *all* my money, the dad-blasted skunks," Salty corrected. "Palmer's likely the only one of the bunch left. We're gonna try to get the dinero back from him if we can ever catch up to him. Seems like we've already chased him halfway across Canada and back."

Reb looked confused. "If Palmer's the only one left, who're those other fellas he's with, the ones with the Gatling gun?"

"Now that we don't know," Salty said. "But a former pard of his told us that Palmer's acquainted with some bad men who've been raisin' hell up here north of the border. Could be he met up with them."

"Must be," Reb said with a nod. "Seems like there's a lot goin' on up here in these mountains."

"Yeah," Frank said drily. "It does."

Late in the morning, they heard shots up ahead somewhere. Frank reined in, and the others followed suit. Most of the reports were the sharp whip cracks of rifles, but there were a few heavier booms from handguns as well.

"Some sort of fracas goin' on," Salty said.

"No Gatling gun, though," Reb said. "Maybe it's not the same bunch."

Meg looked over at Frank. "We're going to find out what it's about, aren't we?"

"It may mean riding right into trouble," he said.

She gave him a cocksure grin. "Wouldn't be the first time, would it?"

She had a point there . . . but he was getting tired of risking her life over and over again.

"You and Salty stay here," he said as he reached a decision. "Reb, come with me. We'll see what we can find out."

Reb looked a little surprised that Frank was giving him orders, but he didn't argue the point. He just said, "Sure, Frank."

Salty looked as if *he* was going to argue, and so did Meg. Frank forestalled their protests with a hard look. He nodded to Reb and said, "Come on."

They heeled their mounts into a fast trot that left Salty and Meg behind. Once Salty thought about it, he would realize that Frank hadn't wanted to drag Meg along into danger yet again, and he also didn't want to leave her there alone with Reb Russell, even though they had known him for only a few hours.

The shooting died away before they had covered half a mile. "Sounds like the battle's over," Reb commented.

"For now," Frank said.

"That usually means one side or the other's had all the fight knocked out of it and has given up."

Frank nodded. "Or else everybody on one side is dead. You sure you want to get mixed up in this?"

"You bet I do," Reb said. "This whole mess has got me plumb curious."

A short time later, Frank spotted something on the ground up ahead and reined in as he realized that the dark shape was a fallen horse.

"Somebody over there, too," Reb said, pointing.

Frank looked and saw the bodies sprawled on the ground. Victims of the shooting they had heard, no doubt.

He drew his Colt and sent his horse ahead at a careful walk. Reb slid his ivory-handled revolver from its holster as well. The way the young man handled the gun told Frank that he probably knew how to use it, too.

When they came to the first body, Frank said, "Cover me while I take a look at him."

"Sure, Frank," Reb replied easily. His eyes

squinted slightly as he looked at the trees, searching for any signs of danger.

Frank swung down from the saddle and hunkered next to the dead man. He appeared to be a hard-faced gunman of the same sort that had attacked them back at the canyon. In fact, Frank considered it pretty likely that this man was part of the same gang.

"Ever seen him before?" he asked Reb.

"Me?" The young man sounded surprised. "Why would I have seen him?"

"I don't know. There's no telling who you might run into out here on the frontier."

Reb looked down at the dead man. "Well, I don't reckon I've ever laid eyes on him until just now . . . unless he was one of those hombres I was shootin' at earlier, at the canyon. I never saw any of them close up."

Frank straightened. "All right. Let's take a gander at the others."

It quickly became obvious that the other two dead men were the same sort of hard-cases. If these men had been part of the gang with the Gatling gun, they were getting whittled down in a hurry.

Frank looked toward the far end of the valley at a big rock that sat there, then considered the positions of the dead men.

"Looks to me like somebody ambushed

251

them," he said. "Put a few riflemen up on that rock, and they'd have clear shots back up the valley."

"The rock that looks like some sort of animal, you mean?" Reb asked.

Frank saw the resemblance now and nodded. "Yeah. I figure these men were riding toward that gap when the men on the rock opened up on them. They tried to scatter, but the odds were against them."

"Where are their horses?"

"Got spooked by all the shooting and ran off, I expect." Frank rubbed his chin as he frowned. "I wonder if this is all of them."

"There might be more bodies, you mean?"

"No. More men who escaped the ambush and are still out there somewhere, still alive and ready to cause more trouble."

CHAPTER 23

"Who . . . who are they?" Lundy asked weakly. "Can you tell?"

Palmer hesitated before answering. When he and Lundy had heard the hoofbeats, he had moved carefully to the edge of the trees so he could see who was coming, staying far enough back that he wasn't likely to be spotted.

He could see well enough that he recognized one of the men, though. He hadn't seen Frank Morgan since they'd both been in Skagway the previous winter, but it would be hard to forget *that* son of a bitch.

Lundy was already upset about the possibility of Morgan being mixed up in this, and even though the outlaw was wounded, Palmer was going to need him.

"Two men," he said. Then he lied, "I don't know them."

Well, it was a *half* lie, anyway. He had never seen the gent who dressed like some

Wild West show cowboy. Which meant it was a half-truth, too.

"Stay away from that horse, damn you," he muttered as Morgan and the other man took a closer look at the dead animal. What was left of the loot Palmer had brought with him when he and Yeah Mow Hopkins fled from Skagway was still in the saddlebags, and he didn't want to lose it.

"What'd you say?" Lundy asked from behind him.

"Nothing," Palmer said. He wanted Lundy to shut up. Right now they couldn't afford to draw Morgan's attention. Lundy was still too weak to be any use in a gunfight. "Just be quiet, all right? We'll let them go on their way."

"They got horses," Lundy said, ignoring Palmer's request. "We need horses."

"And we'll get 'em," Palmer said as he tried to control the irritation he felt. "To-night when you're feeling better, we'll find their camp, kill them, and take their horses so we can get after that other bunch."

He had cleaned the wound in Lundy's side, which started the bullet holes bleeding again, so he'd had to stop the bleeding before tightly wrapping strips of cloth cut from his own shirt around Lundy's torso as makeshift bandages. Now Lundy needed to rest for a while before he started moving around much.

"What if we can't find their camp?"

"We'll find it, all right. Don't worry about that."

"Wish we had one of those Gatling guns," Lundy said. "Wouldn't have to worry about anything then."

Palmer wished he had one of the rapid-firers, too. He would have gladly cut Frank Morgan and that other man into little pieces if he did.

But the Gatlings were gone, God knows where, he thought, and the only weapon he had other than a knife was his cunning.

That had been enough in the past, Palmer told himself, and it would be again.

To his great relief, Morgan and the other man mounted up without searching the saddlebags on the dead horse. An ugly smile tugged at Palmer's mouth. Morgan was probably helping Stevens try to recover the money Soapy had stolen from him.

Dumb son of a bitch didn't have any idea how close he'd been to what was left of that loot.

Instead of heading east, as Palmer expected them to, Morgan and the other man turned around and rode west, back up the valley in the direction they had come from.

They must have left the old-timer behind and were going back to get him now, Palmer figured. In the long run, it wouldn't really matter.

"You just take it easy now, Owen. We'll make our move tonight."

"Good . . ." Lundy sounded as if he was about to doze off. "I want to get that gold back."

"We'll get it back," Palmer promised. "This thing is a long way from over."

"Can you tell who they are?" Charlotte asked.

"A woman and an old man," Joseph said as he peered around the edge of one of the rocks where he and Charlotte had hidden with the pack mules. "I've never seen them before."

"What about the two men who left?"

Joseph shook his head. "Strangers."

His nerves were pulled as tight as a barbed-wire fence. The two people who sat their horses out there in the open didn't look particularly dangerous, but it was difficult to tell about such things. Joseph was acutely aware that the four Gatling guns were loaded on the mules behind him.

If anything happened to those guns, the rebellion was probably doomed to failure.

Joseph wished that Mirabeau and the others hadn't ridden off and left him and Charlotte responsible for the safety of the weapons.

The two men who had ridden off earlier had gone in the direction of Wolverine Rock. They might run right into Mirabeau's party. Joseph listened for the sound of more shots but didn't hear any.

Two men wouldn't be any match for Mirabeau and the others, he told himself. Everything would be all right. All he and Charlotte had to do was be patient.

And hope that none of the mules decided to let out a loud bray. If that happened, the old man and the woman were bound to ride over to the boulders and investigate.

Joseph's hands sweated on the Winchester he clutched as he considered that possibility. One by one, he wiped them off on his trousers. Maybe he wasn't cut out to be a revolutionary after all, he thought.

Frank was relieved when he and Reb came in sight of Salty and Meg. He hadn't heard any more shooting and figured they were all right, but it was always good to see that with his own eyes.

"Any problems?" he asked as he and Reb rode up and reined in.

"Nary a one," Salty replied with a shake of his head. "What'd you two find up yonder?"

"Three dead men," Frank said.

Salty didn't look surprised by the news. "Any idea who they were?" he asked.

"Not really, but from the looks of them, I figure it's likely they were part of the same bunch that attacked us earlier."

"Palmer's bunch, you mean."

"I doubt if Palmer's the leader of the gang. I think he probably just joined up because he knew some of them."

"I'm just glad he wasn't one o' them corpses you found. I'd like to see to it my own self that the varmint gets what's comin' to him."

Reb smiled. "You sound a mite bloodthirsty, amigo."

Salty snorted and said, "You'd be bloodthirsty, too, if a bunch of polecats stole ever'thing you had and dang near ruined you."

"I suppose you're right about that."

Meg asked, "What do we do now?"

"This doesn't really change anything," Frank said. "Palmer's still somewhere ahead of us, as far as we know. We stay on his trail."

With that settled, the four of them set out again. By late afternoon, they had passed the spot where the three dead men lay and ridden past the giant boulder that was shaped something like the head of a predatory animal.

Frank kept a close eye on the rock as they approached it — if it had been used for an ambush once, it could be again, he reasoned — but nothing happened.

He called a halt when they were past the rock and said, "Salty, let's go take a look around over there and see if we can find any tracks. I'd like to know how many bushwhackers there were."

"Good idea," the old-timer agreed. "We're liable to run into the varmints ourselves sooner or later."

Frank nodded. "That's what I was thinking."

He didn't mind leaving Meg with Reb Russell this time, since he and Salty would be close by, but as it turned out, Reb said, "Meg and I will ride along with you, Frank. I'd sorta like to know the odds we might be facin', too."

Frank didn't object. The four of them scouted around behind the huge boulder until Frank spied some hoofprints. He dismounted and hunkered on his heels to study the marks on the ground.

"Looks like half a dozen riders," he announced. "One man stayed here to hold the horses." He looked up at the rugged rock looming above them. "I figure the rest climbed up there and waited for those dead men to come in range."

"You reckon anybody escaped that ambush?" Reb asked.

"I don't know. They could have, I suppose."

Salty said, "What I can't figure out is who this bunch is. They ain't the hombres who had the Gatlin' gun with 'em. That gang is the bunch that got bushwhacked."

"Maybe the ambushers stole the Gatling gun," Meg suggested. "That could have been the reason for the ambush in the first place."

Frank considered the theory and nodded slowly. "Yeah, it could've happened like that," he said. "The only way to find out is keep trailing them."

"Why do you care about that Gatling gun?" Reb asked bluntly. "I thought you were just after this fella Palmer who helped steal Salty's money."

"I don't know how they plan to use the Gatling gun, but it can't be anything good," Frank said. "I don't want to see a bunch of innocent blood spilled if there's anything I can do about it."

"That's sort of an odd way for a notorious gunfighter to feel, ain't it?"

Frank regarded Reb coolly. "So you *do* know who I am," he said.

The young man shrugged. "I recognized the name. Shoot, anybody who's lived in the West for very long has heard of Frank Morgan. To tell you the truth, if anybody had asked me before today, I would have said it was likely you were dead by now."

"Not hardly," Frank said.

"Yeah, I can see that." Reb smiled. "I don't mean any offense, Frank. It's just that gunfighters are usually pretty good at killin'."

"I don't care what you've heard about me. I've never killed anybody who wasn't trying to kill me, or somebody else who didn't deserve it. I'm not a hired gun and never have been, no matter what the law thinks of me."

Reb nodded. "Fine. Like I said, I meant no offense. I just didn't know. Now I do."

"That's right," Frank said in a flat voice. "You do."

Probably in an attempt to change the subject, Salty said, "I don't see no blood on the ground or up on that rock. I reckon none o' the bushwhackers got winged."

"Those fellas tried to scatter before they

were gunned down. They may not have even gotten any shots off of their own."

"That's just plain murder," Meg said.

Frank nodded. "It sure is."

"And those are the people we're trailing now." Meg paused. "But I don't understand. If Palmer was with the men who were ambushed, he wouldn't be with this gang now. So where is he?"

Frank didn't have an answer for that, except to say, "He's not here. Maybe he's trailing the same bunch we are."

"Which would put us on the same side?"

"Nope," Salty said. "There ain't but two sides . . . us and ever'body else. We got no friends out here."

Frank couldn't argue with that. He had a feeling that whoever they might run into between here and Calgary would just as soon see them all dead.

CHAPTER 24

They rode on, leaving the bodies behind them. That bothered Frank, but they still didn't have a shovel and there were no handy canyon walls to collapse on the dead men.

Even though the gap through which they rode marked the end of the really rugged mountains, they were still miles from the actual plains. In between were foothills, many of which were almost as tall and rocky as the peaks behind them.

As the sun lowered toward the Canadian Rockies, the four riders found a place to camp at the foot of a ridge. Frank and Reb tended to the horses while Salty and Meg gathered wood for a fire and got started on supper.

Sensing that they were still in hostile territory, Frank suggested to Salty that they keep the fire small tonight. The old-timer agreed and used a flat rock to scrape out a small depression where he arranged the wood. More rocks piled around the shallow pit would serve to shield the flames from easy view. Once they had boiled up some coffee and cooked bacon and biscuits, the fire could be allowed to burn down.

While they were eating supper, Frank indulged his curiosity and said to Reb, "You sound like you're from Virginia. Is that right?"

The young man shook his head. "No, but my ma and pa were, and they raised me, of course." He grinned. "My pa had a farm near a little place in Virginia called Culpeper, not far from Bull Run. He fought in the war, fought all over the place, in fact, and when it was finally over and he got back home at last, he found that the farm was ruined. The Yanks had burned down everything and tore up the fields. He might've tried to rebuild the place, but some carpetbagger judge took the land away from him on account of taxes."

Frank nodded. "That happened a lot. Same thing went on in Texas, where I'm from."

"I know. It was all over the Confederacy, I reckon. Anyway, my pa had himself a sweetheart, a gal who lived on one of the farms close by, and when he decided to leave

Virginia and light out for some place where he could make a fresh start, he asked her to marry him and come with him. Her daddy didn't like the idea, but they ran off and got hitched anyway."

"That's very romantic," Meg said.

"Maybe so, but it was a hard life for 'em, for a while, anyway. They wound up in Arkansas and eventually moved on to Texas. Settled in a place called Cross Plains."

Frank nodded. "I've been there."

"That's where I was born," Reb said. "I saw plenty of carpetbaggers there while I was growin' up, but Pa said it wasn't as bad as it was back in Virginia. He worked on a ranch and saved up his money until he could afford a place of his own. I was ridin' a horse before I could walk, so naturally I helped him out as much as I could. Had a handful of little brothers who pitched in, too, as soon as they were old enough. We got by. More than that, really. The Russell spread wound up bein' one of the best ranches in that part of Texas."

"That's a nice story," Meg said. "I'm glad your mother and father finally had a happy ending."

"Yeah. When they didn't really need me around anymore, I decided to do some travelin'. I was always a mite fiddle-footed.

That's how I wound up goin' around to all the rodeos."

Reb Russell clearly didn't mind the sound of his own voice, Frank mused. But the talkative young man seemed friendly enough.

The problem was that Frank's instincts still told him Reb was lying about something, or at least not telling the whole truth. But when he tried to figure out how Reb might be connected to that Gatling gun, or to Joe Palmer for that matter, he couldn't make the pieces of the picture fit.

He would just stay on his guard, he decided. He would be doing that anyway, as a matter of habit.

When it came time to turn in, Frank said, "Salty and I will take turns standing watch."

"You really think we need to do that?" Reb asked.

"You saw those bodies back there. This can be dangerous country."

"Yeah, I reckon you're right about that. I can take my turn."

Frank shook his head. "Salty and I can handle it."

"You'd get more sleep if you let me help out." Reb paused, and when he went on, his voice had taken on a harder edge. "That is, unless you don't trust me, Frank."

"Nobody said that," Meg put in. "You trust Reb, don't you, Frank?"

"He hasn't given me any reason not to," Frank replied, which didn't really answer the question.

"We can share a turn," Meg suggested.

Reb smiled in the fading light of the fire. "I never turn down the company of a pretty gal," he said.

Frank was uneasy about the arrangement, but he didn't want to press the issue. He nodded and said, "All right. I'll stand the first watch, Salty the middle one, and the two of you can finish out the night. That agreeable to everybody?"

The others all nodded.

"Better roll up in your blankets and get some sleep, then," Frank went on. He reached for the coffeepot. "I'll just finish off this Arbuckle's."

If it hadn't been for the faint smell of wood smoke lingering in the air, Palmer might have missed the camp. He was alert for that very thing, though, and when he caught a whiff of the smoke, he followed it to a long, low ridge. Owen Lundy limped along behind him, grunting now and then from the pain in his wounded side.

It had been a long walk out of the mountains from the spot of the ambush. They'd had to hide once when a group of riders too large for them to attack had ridden past, heading west. A short time later, what could have been the same bunch rode past again, this time going east.

Damned mountains were turning out to be as busy as State Street back in Chicago, Palmer thought disgustedly.

Now, Palmer put a hand on Lundy's arm to stop him and whispered, "I smell a campfire, or what's left of one, anyway."

His eyes searched the darkness along the base of the ridge for flames but didn't see any. The fire must have burned down to embers. It might have gone out entirely by now, even with the faint scent of smoke lingering in the air.

"If it's the bunch that rode past us earlier, there are too many of 'em," Lundy said. His voice was drawn thin and tight with pain and weariness. "We can't jump 'em."

"Maybe it's Morgan and the old man."

"The shape I'm in, the two of us ain't any match for Frank Morgan."

Palmer was afraid Lundy was right about that. Morgan was hell on wheels all by himself. Throw in the old-timer Stevens, the young woman, and the kid Palmer didn't know, and those odds were just too blasted steep.

Unless they could split the group up somehow.

At least he and Lundy were well armed again. Palmer had scavenged weapons and ammunition from the members of Lundy's gang who had been killed in the ambush. He had a rifle and two pistols, and so did Lundy. If it came to a fight, they wouldn't be lacking for firepower.

Palmer hoped he could figure out some way to avoid most of the gunplay, however. The fewer shots they had to exchange with Frank Morgan, the better their chances were of surviving the night.

As a matter of fact, most of the night was already gone. It wouldn't be long until morning. The two men had trudged along for hours in the darkness, guided only by light from the moon and stars. That was enough to keep them on the trail.

Palmer studied the situation for long minutes, then finally said, "I'm gonna get above them on that ridge. You'll draw Morgan out, Owen."

Palmer halfway expected Lundy to argue with him. Lundy was used to being in charge and might not like the idea of taking orders.

But he must have been too tired and hurt to care about such things now, because he said, "All right. How do I do that?"

"You see those dark shapes there at the base of the bluff? Those are their horses. I think their camp is there, too, just to the right."

Lundy squinted into the shadows and finally said, "All right, I see 'em."

Palmer didn't know whether Lundy really saw the camp or not. But that didn't matter, as long as he aimed in the right direction. Palmer knew Morgan and the others were there. There weren't enough horses for it to be the larger group camped here.

"You give me time to get up on the ridge above them," Palmer said. "Then you open fire on the camp, but aim high. We don't want to kill any of the horses. We may need them all."

"What are you gonna do?"

"Morgan will come out to see what's going on. I'll ambush him if I can, but if I can't get a shot at him, I'll slide down the ridge and grab the horses for us. They can't come after us if they're on foot."

Slowly, Lundy nodded. "Yeah, that sounds like it'll work."

The pain really did have his mind muddled, Palmer thought. He saw several big holes in the plan, but Lundy didn't seem suspicious.

Some part of Lundy's mind must have worked again for a second. He said, "You'll come back around and get me, right?"

"Sure. Then we'll go after those sons of bitches who stole our gold."

"Yeah," Lundy muttered. "Yeah, those sons o' bitches."

He was swaying slightly on his feet. Palmer put the back of his hand against Lundy's cheek. The outlaw was burning up with fever.

"What're you doin?" Lundy said.

"Checking to see if you have a fever. You're fine, Owen. Must not be any infection from that bullet hole."

"Good. I always was a quick healer."

Not this time, Palmer thought. Lundy was on his last legs. He might not make it even a few more hours until dawn. This was the best chance to get a little more use out of him and then leave him behind to his fate. Palmer knew that if he waited much longer, Lundy wasn't going to be any good to him.

"All right, there are some rocks right over here. We'll get you forted up in them."

Palmer led Lundy over to the rocks. Lundy knelt and rested his rifle on the top of one of the granite slabs. Palmer fished his pocket watch out of his trousers and opened it, placing it face up on the rock in front of Lundy. There was enough light for him to be able to make out that there were ten minutes until four o'clock in the morning.

"Can you see the watch, Owen?"

"Yeah, I can see it."

"Give me fifteen minutes to get in position. That'll be five minutes after four o'clock. Can you remember that?"

"Sure. Five minutes after . . . four o'clock."

"That's when you start shooting at the bluff over there. Remember, aim high, but not too high, because I'm gonna be on top of it. And when you see me start shooting from up there, you hold your fire, because I'll be coming down and you don't want to hit me."

"Sure," Lundy said.

Palmer knew he was taking a chance. Lundy might pass out before the fifteen minutes went by. He might even die before then.

But there was nothing else Palmer could do. He couldn't take on Frank Morgan and three other people alone.

Palmer squeezed Lundy's shoulder. "I'm leaving now, Owen. Don't forget, I'm counting on you. You start shooting, and I'll get the horses."

"Right . . ."

If Palmer had been a praying man, he would have sent a prayer heavenward as he stole away into the darkness. A prayer that Lundy would remain conscious and alert long enough to play out his final act in this drama.

But since the only god Joe Palmer really believed in was money in all its forms, he didn't waste the time and effort.

He just hurried in a very roundabout path toward the ridge that ran behind the camp-site.

He didn't climb to its top until he was a good quarter of a mile away from the camp. The ridge was rugged enough that by the time he made it to the top, he was out of breath and his heart pounded heavily in his chest. The life he'd led hadn't really prepared him for so much physical exertion. Mostly, the only exercise he got was with soiled doves.

But he was where he needed to be now. He started along the top of the ridge, heading back toward the spot where his quarry had made camp.

From up here, he could see the faintly glowing embers of the fire when he reached the right place. It was good to see proof with his own eyes that his hunch had been correct. Four people were down there, along with four saddle horses and a couple of pack animals. Palmer planned to grab all the horses he could and scatter the others.

Two of the people were asleep, rolled up in their blankets not far from the remains of the fire. The other two sat on a log. The blond hair shining in the moonlight told Palmer that one of them was the woman.

He couldn't tell who the man was, but as he watched and waited for Lundy to start the ball, he saw the two of them move closer on the log. The pair of shadows suddenly seemed to merge into one.

Whoever that fella was, he was kissing the girl. Had to be the kid, Palmer thought. Morgan and Stevens were both too old to be carrying on with her.

This would be a good time for Lundy to open fire, while the two people standing guard were more concerned with each other than with any dangers lurking in the darkness. But so far the night was quiet and peaceful. Palmer's frustration and impatience grew.

"Damn it, Owen," he muttered. "It's time. It's gotta be past time by —"

The whip crack of the shot came at the

same time as the bright spurt of flame from the rifle's muzzle.

CHAPTER 25

Frank never slept too deeply. The life he had led made sure of that.

So he was instantly alert when the sound of the shot jerked him out of slumber.

He came out of his bedroll reaching for the Winchester on the ground beside him. A bullet whined somewhere overhead and thudded into the rocky face of the ridge.

"Everybody down!" Frank called. "Stay down!"

He was already on one knee. He brought the rifle to his shoulder as he spotted a muzzle flash a couple of hundred yards away. The Winchester already had a round in the chamber. It kicked hard as he fired.

Frank worked the lever and threw himself forward, expecting return fire. He got it, but the shots continued to go high, smacking into the bluff.

Salty called, "Who in tarnation you reckon that is?"

"Don't know," Frank replied. "Are you all right?"

"Yeah, other than havin' my sleep disturbed!"

"Meg! How about you? Are you hit?"

She called back, "Reb and I are both fine, Frank!"

Shots continued to crack from the unseen rifleman. Frank considered the situation and said, "Salty, we're going to try to flush that varmint out. You go left and I'll go right."

"You bet," Salty replied eagerly. "I'm gettin' so dang frustrated, I'm just itchin' to shoot somebody."

"Let's take him alive if we can," Frank cautioned. "I'd like to find out who he is and why he wants us dead."

"Shoot, seems like *ever'body* wants us dead these days," Salty muttered as he started crawling off to the left.

Frank heard the comment. It brought a grim smile to his mouth. Salty was right. It seemed as if everyone they had run into in Canada was an enemy, with the lone exception of Reb Russell.

And Frank wasn't a hundred percent sure about *him* yet. . . .

On hands and knees, Frank moved away from the camp to the right. When he reached an area of taller grass, he came up into a crouching run but still stayed as low as he could.

The rifle continued to bang in the night. As Frank circled toward the bushwhacker's position, something began to nag at him. The light from the moon and stars was too dim for accurate shooting, but even so, it seemed that all the shots had been going too high for this to be a real ambush.

As soon as that thought crossed his mind, he stopped short and started to turn back. The shots were nothing but decoys, he realized, designed to draw him away from the camp.

But as he swung around, something smashed against the side of his head like a giant fist. The terrible impact made rockets go off in his brain. He felt himself falling and tried to catch his balance, but he couldn't stop.

He hit the ground, and that was the last thing he knew for a while.

Joe Palmer was pretty sure the man had just taken a shot at was Frank Morgan. His heart leaped as he saw Morgan fall.

Take that, gunfighter, he thought. *Not such a big man now, are you?*

Palmer didn't waste any time gloating. He

started down the slope, which was steep enough that part of the time he was bounding and the other part he was sliding.

He hoped Lundy remembered the plan and was holding his fire now. Otherwise Palmer might run smack-dab into a bullet from the outlaw's rifle.

The kid and the blonde were still at the camp. They must have heard the shot from the top of the bluff and they probably heard Palmer making his way down the ridge, so he was expecting trouble. He wasn't going to give them a chance to get oriented. He pulled one of his revolvers and emptied it in the direction he had last seen them.

He had barely reached level ground when a figure loomed up in front of him. The night was too dark for him to tell which one it was. Since he still had the empty gun in his hand, he lashed out with it.

At the same time, a gun went off practically in his face. The report slammed deafeningly against his ears. Burning bits of powder stung his left cheek. He felt a tearing pain in that ear, as if somebody had just tried to rip it off his head.

The gun in his hand crashed against his opponent's skull. The figure went down like a poleaxed steer.

Palmer didn't get any respite, though.

Somebody tackled him from behind. They both went to the ground.

As he rolled in the dirt, wrestling with his attacker, Palmer's hands told him he was fighting with the woman. He had dropped the empty pistol and the rifle when she knocked him down, but that meant he had both hands free. He drove a knee into her body, pinned her arms to the ground with one hand, and landed a punch to her jaw with the other fist. Her head bounced against the ground, and she went limp.

Palmer knew he had no time to waste. The way Morgan had gone down, he hoped the gunfighter was dead. But it was possible that Morgan was just wounded, and the old man was still unaccounted for, too. Palmer scrambled to his feet.

An idea occurred to him as he did so. He leaned down, and working by feel, he pulled the blonde's belt from the trousers she wore and rolled her onto her stomach while she was still stunned and helpless. He pulled her arms behind her back and used the belt to bind her wrists together.

The horses were picketed. He grabbed a blanket and saddle and threw them on one of the mounts, hurriedly cinching the saddle in place. He risked taking long enough to saddle one of the other horses. The blonde was starting to make angry noises now as her wits returned to her. Ignoring the burning pain in his wounded ear, Palmer scooped her up and put her on one of the saddled horses.

"Don't cause any fuss or I'll kill you," he warned.

She tried to kick him. Palmer dodged it and reached up to punch her in the belly. As the woman groaned and bent over, he used one of the picket ropes to tie her already-bound wrists to the saddle horn.

Now if she didn't cooperate, she would fall off the horse and probably get dragged to death. So if she knew what was good for her, she would do what she was told.

All too aware that he was working against time, Palmer slung some supplies onto the pack animals, then jerked the other ropes loose, freeing the rest of the horses. An eerie silence hung over the night now that the shooting had stopped.

Where was the old man?

That question was answered just as Palmer picked up his rifle. A shot roared from somewhere close by. Palmer heard the bullet sizzle past his head. He swung around and opened fire, cranking off three rounds from the Winchester as fast as he could work the lever.

Stevens, who had reared up in the grass after crawling back to the camp, went over backward as at least one of the bullets ripped into him. The gun in his hand went off again, but it was pointed toward the stars now as he fell.

Palmer didn't waste any more time. He leaped onto the other saddled horse, grabbed the reins of the horse carrying the blonde, and kicked his mount into a gallop. Together they thundered away from the campsite, scattering the other horses in the process. He rode close enough to one of the pack horses to reach over and grab its reins as well.

Palmer left the camp and his enemies behind him. He knew all three of the men were hurt, but he didn't know how badly. All of them might be dead. He hoped fervently that was the case.

But even if they weren't, they were set afoot now, while he had horses, supplies, guns . . . and a hostage, if he needed one.

Best of all, if he could get his hands on those chests of gold; now he wouldn't have to split that fortune with anybody.

A grin stretched across Palmer's face as he galloped through the night. Things were finally starting to go his way again.

Frank couldn't hold back a groan as awareness seeped back into his brain. Thundering pain filled his skull.

If anybody was watching him, he had already betrayed the fact that he was regaining consciousness. He managed to lift a hand and touched the side of his head where the pain seemed to be centered. The sticky wetness he felt there was unmistakably blood.

But he was alive, and this was hardly the first time he'd been shot. He realized that the bullet that had come out of the night had barely creased him. Just a little hot lead kiss on the side of the head that had knocked him down and out for a while.

How long? he wondered.

Probably not that long, judging by the smell of burned powder that still hung in the air. The fight seemed to be over, though. No shots rang out, no angry yells. Instead everything was quiet and peaceful.

But so was a grave, Frank reminded himself.

He pushed himself up in a sitting position and looked around. A wave of dizziness went through him as the world seemed to spin in the wrong direction for a moment.

That feeling subsided. He was able to orient himself. He saw the ridge about a hundred yards away.

The shot that had felled him had come from the ridge, confirming his hunch that there were at least two bushwhackers. Both of them were probably gone now.

Cold fear for Salty and Meg gripped him. To a lesser extent, he was worried about Reb Russell, too. He looked around, spotted his rifle lying on the ground, and reached over to pick it up. He used the weapon to help lever himself to his feet.

Frank's iron constitution helped him throw off the effects of being shot, at least for a while. Feeling stronger by the moment, he walked back toward the camp, his face hardening into a grim mask as he thought about what he might find there.

The moon was almost down and the eastern sky was turning gray, heralding the approach of dawn. As Frank came up to the camp, his keen eyes noted that the horses were gone. That came as no surprise to him. The horses could have been what the bushwhackers were after.

He heard a groan, followed by a muttered curse. That led him to a sprawled figure. As the man started to sit up, Frank drew the

Colt and leveled it at him.

"Hold it right there, mister."

"Wha—" The man sounded confused. "Frank?"

The voice belonged to Reb Russell. Not completely sure that Reb hadn't had something to do with the attack, Frank didn't lower his gun as he asked, "What happened here?"

"I . . . I don't know. Somebody let off a shot from the top of the ridge. I heard him slidin' down the slope and tried to jump him, but it felt like a mountain landed on my head." Reb paused. "I've got a lump the size of a goose egg on my head! Son of a bitch must've pistol-whipped me."

Frank's instincts told him Reb was telling the truth, but he was still cautious. "Where's Meg and Salty?"

Reb looked around. "Meg was with me. . . . I don't know about Salty. . . ." Alarm was in his voice as he called, "Meg!" He scrambled to his feet, ignoring the threat of the gun in Frank's hand. "Meg, where are you?"

Frank was looking around, too. He said, "I don't think she's here."

Reb let out a bitter curse. "The varmint must've grabbed her and taken her with him! Where are those damn horses? We

285

gotta get after 'em!"

"The horses are gone. The bushwhackers either took them or ran them off."

"But . . . but . . . blast it! It's hard to think straight with my head hurtin' so much."

Frank knew the feeling. Despite the pain in his skull, he started walking around the campsite, ranging farther out as he searched for Salty.

He almost tripped over the old-timer. Salty was lying on his side in the tall grass. For a second, Frank was afraid that his friend was dead. Then he heard the strained rasp of Salty's breath.

Frank holstered his gun and knelt beside Salty. He rolled the old-timer onto his back. Salty groaned.

"Can you hear me, Salty?" Frank groaned. "How bad are you hit?"

"Did you find him?" Reb called. He hurried toward Frank and Salty.

Before Reb could get there, a figure loomed out of the shadows, gun in hand. "Where is he?" the man shouted hoarsely, but he didn't wait for an answer.

Instead he jerked the trigger, and flame spouted from the revolver's muzzle.

CHAPTER 26

Frank's instincts took over. He twisted around and the gun that rested in his holster seemed to leap into his hand as if by magic. The Colt roared.

At the same time, almost equally as fast on the draw, Reb Russell drew and fired his ivory-handled revolver. His aim was just as true as Frank's.

The attacker staggered as both bullets punched into his body. The gun he held sagged toward the ground as it went off again, his finger jerking the trigger spasmodically. The slug smacked harmlessly into the dirt.

The revolver slipped out of the man's fingers and thudded to the ground at his feet. He swayed as he clutched at himself. Blood welled between his fingers.

"Palmer!" he gasped. "My . . . gold . . . !"

He pitched forward onto his face.

"Reb, did his first shot hit you?" Frank

asked sharply.

"No, it went wild," Reb replied. Smoke curled from the barrel of the revolver in his fist. The ivory-handled gun might be fancier than the Colt that Frank carried, but obviously it was just as deadly. "I reckon you're all right, too?"

"Yeah, I'm fine. Keep him covered while I see how bad Salty's hurt."

Frank turned back to the old-timer. Salty was unconscious but still breathing. Frank ran his hands over Salty's body and found that his shirt was wet with blood.

"Got to have some light," Frank muttered. He fished a lucifer out of his pocket and snapped it to life with his thumbnail.

The glare from the match showed him that Salty was wounded in the side. Frank ripped the old-timer's shirt aside to get a better look at the wound. Relief went through him when he saw that a bullet had plowed a fairly deep furrow in Salty's flesh but hadn't penetrated to anything vital.

As Frank shook the match out, Reb asked, "Is he gonna be all right?"

"I think so. I'll get him back over to the fire and see if I can patch him up. You keep an eye on that one."

Frank slid his arms under Salty's body and straightened to his feet, lifting the old-timer and cradling him as if Salty was a baby. Salty didn't really weigh all that much. He wasn't much more than bones and skin like whang leather.

Gently, Frank placed him on top of one of the bedrolls and then put some more wood on the ashes of the burned-down fire. He kindled a small blaze so he'd have enough light to see what he was doing.

It would have been good to clean the wound with whiskey or some other disinfectant, but Frank didn't have anything like that on hand. Instead he drew his knife from its sheath and heated the blade in the flames until it glowed red from the heat.

He hated to do this, but he didn't want that bullet crease in Salty's side to fester. Without hesitation, he pressed the red-hot knife to the wound.

The steel sizzled as it burned into the flesh. Even unconscious, Salty howled in pain and tried to arch up off the ground, but Frank's other hand held him down.

Salty sagged back when Frank took the knife away. His breath rasped strongly in and out. Frank thought the old-timer would be all right now, once he'd had a chance to rest.

Frank stood up and went back over to where Reb stood next to the other man, gun in hand.

"Is this one still alive?"

"Not sure. I think so."

Frank knelt and took hold of the man's shoulders to roll him onto his back. The man gasped and cursed. His eyes fluttered open. The whole front of his shirt was sodden with blood. The thatch of white hair on his head was wildly askew.

"What's your name, hombre?" Frank asked. He could tell that the man didn't have long to live, and he wanted to find out as much as he could.

"G-go . . . to hell!"

Frank shrugged. "Fine. I just thought you'd like to have your name on the marker we'll put up after we bury you."

"D-damn you. You've k-killed me."

"You come into a place with a gun in your hand and start blazing away, folks are going to shoot back at you. You look like you've been around enough to know that."

The man hesitated, air hissing between his teeth as his ruined body struggled to draw breath. Finally he said, "It's . . . Lundy. Owen . . . Lundy."

Frank didn't recognize the name, but he hadn't heard of every owlhoot west of the Mississippi, either.

"You said something about Joe Palmer."

"He was supposed to . . . come back for me . . . after he stole . . . the horses."

"But he rode off and left you behind, didn't he?"

"I was . . . already wounded. . . . Guess he thought . . . I couldn't keep up." What might have been a strangled laugh came from Owen Lundy's lips. "What he really wanted . . . was to go after that gold . . . all for . . . himself."

"Your gold?" Frank said.

"Y-yeah. B-bastards . . . stole it back . . . from us."

The wheels of Frank's brain turned rapidly as he made connections between the facts he knew and the things he had guessed.

"They paid you in gold for the Gatling gun you smuggled in from the States, then double-crossed you."

"Yeah . . . but it was . . . guns . . . four Gatling guns."

Frank's jaw tightened. One Gatling gun could do a hell of a lot of damage. Four could wipe out a small town.

"Who are they?" he asked, urgency creeping into his voice. "Who has the guns?"

"Bunch of . . . breeds. Half-breeds . . ."

"Métis," Reb said.

Frank didn't look around, didn't waste time right now worrying how come this

291

rodeo cowboy knew about the mixed-bloods who had tried twice to rise in rebellion against the Canadian government.

"Yeah," Lundy said. "Didn't . . . trust 'em. . . . Didn't really think they'd . . . bushwhack us . . . though. Sons of . . . bitches."

"So Palmer's going after them?"

"I . . . I reckon. He wants that . . . gold. Never should've . . . trusted him . . . either. Somebody always . . . double-cross —"

Lundy's head tipped back. The cords in his neck stood out as a shudder went through him. When he relaxed a second later, a long sigh came from him, and Frank knew the outlaw was dead.

The whole thing was a lot clearer now. The theories that Frank had put together concerning the Gatling guns had been confirmed. Somewhere out there in the night, a group of Métis revolutionaries had four Gatling guns and a couple of chests full of gold. There was no telling what kind of hell they meant to raise with those guns, but it couldn't be anything good.

Joe Palmer was trailing them, intent on getting his hands on that gold, but Palmer wasn't alone. He had Meg with him as a prisoner and a hostage if he needed one.

And Frank and Reb were left behind with

a wounded Salty and no horses.

Any way you looked at it, they had been dealt a bad hand.

"You told him we'd bury him," Reb said.

"I lied," Frank snapped as he straightened from kneeling next to Lundy's body. The sky was light enough now that they could see. Frank went on, "I don't like doing that, especially to a dying man, but I wanted to know what was going on here so we could figure out what to do next."

"What *can* we do next?" Reb asked. "We don't have any horses."

"That's true. But there's one thing I can take care of." Frank faced Reb and gave him a cool, level stare. "Just who the hell *are* you, anyway?"

Joseph Marat was exhausted, but he had no choice except to keep up as the group of riders made its way eastward toward the dawn.

He glanced over at his sister. Charlotte swayed wearily in the saddle. She was just as tired as he was. Anton Mirabeau kept pushing them through the foothills, though.

There was no longer any doubt who was in charge here. Mirabeau had shoved Joseph aside as the leader of the rebellion. Joseph had been relieved when Mirabeau and a couple of the other men had shown up to rendezvous with him and Charlotte and lead them back to join the others, but in weak moments he was no longer so sure it was a good thing.

"When can we rest, Anton?" Charlotte asked. "We've been riding all night."

"Soon," Mirabeau told her. "We can't be sure that Lundy and all of his men are dead. I want to be well ahead of them before we stop. There are too few of us to take un-necessary chances."

That was true, Joseph thought. Only eight of them remained to protect the gold and transport the Gatling guns to Calgary.

The gold was important, Joseph supposed, but the guns were everything. Without them, the plan would fail, and if the plan failed, the rebellion would fall apart before it ever truly began. They were counting on the conflagration they would ignite with the Gatlings to spread quickly across the entire western half of Canada.

Mirabeau was true to his word. He called a halt a short time later, next to a creek that twisted and turned through a narrow gap between a couple of hills.

"We'll rest here for a couple of hours," he said. "Gabriel, ride up to the top of that hill and keep an eye on the trail behind us. If you see anyone following us, let me know immediately."

The man Mirabeau had addressed nodded and set off to carry out the order.

Mirabeau went on, "The rest of you unsaddle your horses. We'll fill up all our canteens before we push on, too."

Joseph swung down from his saddle. As Charlotte dismounted, he told her, "I'll take care of your horse."

"No," she said with a stubborn shake of her head. "I can do it." She leaned tiredly against the horse's flank. "Just let me rest for a moment first."

Joseph took hold of her shoulders and gently moved her aside. "Go sit down somewhere." His tone made it clear that he wouldn't put up with any argument. "I can handle this."

Obviously reluctant, she said, "Well . . . if you're sure . . ."

"I'm sure —" Joseph began.

Mirabeau shouldered him aside. "Tend to your own horse, Joseph," he said. "I'll take care of Charlotte, and her mount."

Anger flared inside Joseph, and for once he was too tired to suppress it for the good of their shared cause. "You'll do no such thing," he snapped. "In fact, I think you should stay away from Charlotte."

Mirabeau frowned at him in surprise. "What are you saying? She and I are going to be married."

"I don't think so. I can no longer give my blessing to such a union."

Charlotte acted surprised, too. "Joseph, what are you saying?" she asked. "You know that Anton and I have an . . . an understanding."

"Perhaps you shouldn't," Joseph said. "I don't think he's the right man for you, Charlotte."

A booming laugh came from Mirabeau, but the sound had an undercurrent of anger in it. "You're tired and not thinking straight, my friend. These are personal matters and should not be discussed in public."

"Public?" Joseph repeated. He laughed, too, and waved an arm at their surroundings. "We're in the middle of a wilderness! There probably aren't fifty people within a hundred miles of here."

Mirabeau's eyes narrowed and glanced toward the other men. Joseph understood then. Mirabeau didn't want to appear weak in front of them, now that he had taken over command of the group. It was a matter of honor and pride.

"We will talk about this later, once we have finished our mission."

"You mean our attack on the North West Mounted Police barracks at Calgary?"

He might as well be blunt about it, Joseph thought. Their actions would amount to a declaration of war against the Crown. It was highly likely that none of them would survive except for Charlotte. Joseph didn't intend to let her anywhere near the scene of the attack. So this argument with Mirabeau might well be pointless. He should have held his tongue.

But it was too late for that now.

He realized that Mirabeau was giving him an odd look. Joseph suddenly felt a chill go down his back. Something else was going on here, something he didn't even know about.

"I've been meaning to talk to you about that," Mirabeau said. "I don't think it would be a good idea to attack the Mounties."

Joseph tried not to sneer. "You're afraid of them?"

Mirabeau shook his head. "Not at all. But that's what the Crown would expect us to do. We need to do something to surprise them, something that will leave no doubt as to how serious we are about winning freedom for our people."

"What are you talking about, Anton?" Charlotte asked. She seemed to be as baffled by this turn of events as Joseph was.

"In a few days, they're going to be holding a competition in Calgary for the cowboys who work on the ranches," Mirabeau said. "A rodeo, they call it. Hundreds of people will be there, and no one will be expecting trouble."

A feeling of horror washed through Joseph as his eyes widened in amazement. He said, "You can't mean —"

Mirabeau nodded. "We're going to set up those Gatling guns and wipe out the crowd before anyone knows what's happening. Then the damned English will have no choice but to give us what we want."

CHAPTER 27

Reb Russell gave Frank a friendly smile in the strengthening dawn light.

"What are you talkin' about, Frank?" he asked. "I told you who I am. Reb Russell. Just a cowpoke from Texas headin' for the rodeo."

"A cowpoke who knows about the Métis and their troubles with the Canadian government?"

Reb shrugged. "It was in all the papers. How do *you* know about it?"

Reb had a point there, Frank supposed. It was true that he had read newspaper stories about the previous rebellions up here north of the border.

That wasn't enough to get rid of all of Frank's suspicions, though.

"That was a fast draw you made a few minutes ago."

"I have a lot of time to practice," Reb said. "And I won't lie to you. I've run into my share of trouble in my time. Too many hombres still seem to think the best way to settle an argument is with a gun."

"Funny I haven't heard of you, then."

"I've been lucky. I never had to kill anybody until I came up here to Canada." Reb gave a rueful chuckle. "Maybe I should've stayed home." He grew more serious as he hooked his thumbs in his gunbelt. "Look, Frank, if you and me are gonna have a problem here . . ."

Frank shook his head. "No problem. Just forget I said anything, Reb. With everything that's happened, I'm just naturally a mite leery, I guess."

"Well, yeah, I can understand that." Reb grinned again. "I'm glad you understand that you and I are on the same side, Frank. Seems to me that right now, you and me are all we got."

"And Salty," Frank pointed out.

"Yeah, sure, Salty, too, when he gets back on his feet."

Frank looked around for his hat. He found it, picked it up, and put it on.

"I'm going to take a look around. Maybe some of those horses didn't run off too far. If we can round up even one or two of them, it'll help."

"You bet it will," Reb said. "We're goin'

after Meg, aren't we?"

Frank nodded. "Of course we are. And the sooner we get on Palmer's trail, the better. Take care of Salty, will you?"

"Sure. If he wakes up and needs anything, I'll be right here."

Reb was right about one thing: Frank had no choice but to trust him. They would have to work together if they were going to get out of here and rescue Meg.

As he walked through the hills looking for the horses, Frank tried not to think about the fact that Meg was Palmer's prisoner. He knew she was good at taking care of herself, and he told himself that she would be all right until they could catch up to her and her captor.

If she wasn't, he would kill Palmer himself, even if it took him the rest of his life to track the man down.

A feeling of frustration grew stronger in Frank as he continued to search without finding any of the horses. Palmer might have taken several of the animals with him, but he couldn't have led all of them away. Some of them had bolted in panic from all the shooting after Palmer turned them loose. They ought to still be around here somewhere.

But he didn't see any, and when he

stopped and turned around to scan the hills around him, he realized that he was out of sight of the camp, too. He didn't want to go too much farther. Like most Westerners, he wasn't used to walking when he could ride. His feet already hurt.

Disgusted, he turned around and started back toward the camp. He could search again later. In the meantime, it was possible that some of the horses would wander up on their own and save him from having to look for them.

When he reached the camp, he saw that Salty was awake and propped up against a log. Reb knelt beside him, holding a canteen. The young man looked back over his shoulder at Frank and asked, "Any luck?"

Frank shook his head. "Nope."

"I was afraid that was what you were gonna say, when you didn't bring any of the horses back with you."

Frank sat down on the log. "How are you feeling, Salty?"

"Like I been shot," the old-timer replied. "Hurts like Hades, too. How bad am I hit, Frank? Am I gonna die?"

"Not from that bullet crease in your side," Frank said with a smile. "You're weak because you lost some blood, but you'll be all right."

Salty took the canteen from Reb and swigged down a long drink of water. He wiped the back of his hand across his mouth and said, "I sure wish I had a drink right about now. Danged if I don't."

"Reckon that'll have to wait until we get back to civilization," Frank told him.

"Civilization . . . bah! Civilization's full o' crooked varmints like Palmer and fiendish contraptions like them devil guns and a bunch o' skunks who ain't got nothin' better to do than stir up a whole heap o' trouble. Why, for a nickel I'd chuck the whole blamed thing and go live in a cave somewheres like a danged ol' hermit!"

"Then you'd never get a drink," Reb pointed out.

Salty scratched at his beard. "Well, that's true," he allowed. "I reckon there's a few good things about civilization . . . but mighty dang few!"

By now the sun was well up. Frank said, "We need to get some breakfast going."

"I'll handle that," Reb offered. He patted Salty on the shoulder. "You just sit there and rest, old-timer."

Reb bustled off to gather more wood and prepare a meal. While he was doing that, Salty said quietly, "The boy tells me Palmer ran off with Meg. Is that true, Frank?"

"I'm afraid so."

"Dadgum it! You got to get after 'em. You and Reb just leave me here and get on the trail. I'll be all right. I can take care o' myself."

"I'm sure you can," Frank said, "but we don't have any horses."

"Well, then, you're just gonna have to go after 'em on foot. You can't leave Meg in that bastard's hands, Frank. You just can't."

"I'm not going to," Frank promised. "But we'll never catch up on foot. We've got to find some horses somewhere. Maybe there's a trapper's cabin or a little ranch around here. I'll have a look again later."

"I don't like it. That son of a bitch could be doin' 'most anything."

Frank nodded. "I know. That's why I'm trying not to think about it right now, until I can actually do something about it."

"One thing we can count on," Salty mused. "Ol' Meg ain't gonna cooperate with him. If there's one thing that gal knows how to do, it's put up a fight!"

The blonde took Palmer by surprise, kicking him in the chest as soon as he untied her wrists from the saddle horn. He had thought she was only half-conscious after the long, hard ride and not really a threat.

304

But suddenly her boot thudded into him and the impact sent him staggering back a couple of steps. A rock rolled under his foot, and his balance deserted him. He went down, sprawling on the ground.

The wicked kick had thrown the woman off balance, too. She grabbed at the horn, and even in his pain Palmer knew that if she stayed in the saddle, she could gallop away from him and might succeed in escaping.

Her hands were still lashed together with her belt, though, and that made her grab an awkward one. Her fingers slipped off the horn, and she toppled to the ground with an angry cry.

Like a flash, she was up and running. Palmer struggled to his feet and went after her.

She was fast, and Palmer wasn't in the best shape in the world. She began to pull away from him.

He ought to just let her go, he thought. Out here alone and on foot, with no gun and no supplies, she wouldn't last long.

But she would be a loose end, and he didn't like those. He thought he might still be able to get some use out of her, too, even if it was just to warm his blankets. Looked like he wasn't ever going to get any comfort from Charlotte Marat, so he might as well take it where he could find it.

He ignored his pounding heart and summoned up some more speed. When he was close enough behind the blonde, he launched himself in a diving tackle that brought her down and sent both of them rolling in the grass.

The woman cried out in anger as she tried to get away from Palmer. He grabbed her and threw himself on top of her. The belt had come loose from her wrists. She flailed punches at him until he managed to grab her wrists and pin her arms to the ground. With him lying on top of her, she bucked and heaved but couldn't throw him off.

"Damn it, stop fighting!" he told her. "I don't want to hurt you."

"You son of a bitch! Let go of me! Oh!"

Palmer was well aware that he was lying on top of some nicely curved female flesh. He couldn't help but respond to that.

She must have felt his response, because she started struggling even harder. Palmer bore down on her and said, "Blast it, I'm gonna knock you out if you don't stop fightin'!"

"Try it, you bastard!" she yelled in defiance.

Palmer let go of her left wrist and tried to

use his right hand to clout her on the jaw. She was too fast for him, though. Her hand shot up. Her arm blocked his punch, and she reached across to grab his wounded ear and give it a vicious twist. Palmer howled in pain.

He hurt so bad that his grip on her loosened. She twisted away from him and tried to get up so she could run again. She had made it to hands and knees when he lunged after her and snagged her leg. He yanked it out from under her, which sent her plunging face first into the dirt.

Palmer tried not to think about how much his ear hurt or how he could feel the hot, wet trickle of blood down the side of his face. He scrambled on top of her again, and this time since she was face down she couldn't muster as much of a fight. He got hold of an arm and twisted it behind her, making her cry out.

He put his other hand on the back of her neck and held her down. "I oughta kill you, you little bitch!" he roared.

"Go ahead," she urged him through clenched teeth. "Go ahead, damn you!"

"Not hardly." He kept her arm trapped behind her and slid his other arm around her neck, tightening it into a choke hold that cut off her air. After a minute he got his legs underneath him and heaved to his feet, dragging her up with him. He marched her back toward the horses.

When they got there, Palmer threw her on the ground so hard that she rolled over a couple of times. She lay there struggling to catch her breath as she lifted her head and glared up at him.

Palmer's gun had stayed in its holster despite all the ruckus. He drew the weapon now and pointed it at the blonde.

"Listen to me," he said. "I don't want to hurt you, but I will if I have to. There's a lot more at stake here than just you."

"What are you . . . talking about?" she asked.

"Gold," he said. "And plenty of it. Does that interest you?"

"Not near as much . . . as killing you would," she managed to say with a sneer.

"Yeah, well, that's not gonna happen, so you might as well forget about it," he said. "But if you cooperate with me, you might come out ahead on this deal."

"You're trying to . . . buy me off?"

"I'd rather do that than shoot you." Palmer smiled. "Better gold than lead, right?"

She stared at him for a long moment before saying, "What's to stop me from tell-

308

ing you I'll cooperate and then double-crossing you?"

"The fact that you know I'll kill you if you try something like that. And the fact that your hands are going to be tied most of the time. But I can take it a little easier on you if you promise you won't try to get away again."

She appeared to consider what he was saying, then asked, "You'll stay away from me? You won't lay a hand on me?"

"Not like that, if that's the way you want it. You're pretty good-looking, but to tell you the truth, I'm more interested in that gold than in anything you've got."

She pushed herself up into a sitting position. "You're a vile son of a bitch."

"And the more you remember that, the better off we'll both be," Palmer said with a chuckle.

She sighed. "All right. I'll cooperate . . . for now."

"Good. You can get up, build a fire, and fix us some coffee and something to eat." Palmer paused. "I remember you from that bunch of mail-order brides in Skagway, but I don't recall your name."

She got up and brushed herself off, saying with obvious reluctance, "It's Meg."

"All right, Meg, get to work. You play

along with me and you'll come out of this all right. Maybe better than all right."

She gave him a narrow-eyed look. "You know Frank's going to come after you and kill you, don't you?"

"Frank Morgan?" Palmer smiled and shook his head. "I don't think so. Morgan's dead. I shot him myself and saw him go down."

Meg caught her breath as a stricken look appeared on her face.

"So are the other two who were with you," Palmer went on. "It's just you and me now, Meg, and that's the way it's gonna be from now on."

Even as he spoke, Palmer hoped he was right. He didn't know for sure that Frank Morgan was dead.

But even if the gunfighter was still alive, Palmer had himself an ace in the hole.

A blond ace in the hole, and he was going to hang on to her until the time was right.

CHAPTER 28

Later in the morning, Frank set out again to search for the horses. His frustration grew when he didn't see any sign of them. When they stampeded, they must not have stopped running for a long time.

It was impossible for him not to think about Meg being Joe Palmer's prisoner. Frank was worried about her, but he had learned over the years not to let himself be consumed by worry when he couldn't do anything about the situation.

Which meant he needed to do something. It might be a waste of time, but he and Reb and Salty were going to have to start after Palmer on foot. Taking Salty along would slow them down a little, but it couldn't be helped. Frank wasn't going to abandon the old-timer here in the wilderness.

When he got back to the camp, Reb and Salty watched him come striding up. They wore disappointed looks on their faces.

"Didn't find any o' them durned fool jugheads, did you?" Salty asked.

"No," Frank said. "We're going to have to hoof it out of here ourselves."

"Walk?" Salty said in the horrified disbelief of an old range rider. "All the way to Calgary?"

"Maybe not that far, if we're lucky," Reb said. "The countryside can't be completely empty between here and there. There's bound to be a ranch or even a small settlement where we can get our hands on some mounts."

Salty raked fingers through his beard. "Y'all go on," he said after a moment. "I ain't up to a long walk like that, not with this dang bullet hole in my side. I'd just hold you back."

Frank shook his head. "Forget it, Salty. We're not leaving you here. We'll just take it at a pace you can manage."

"Dadgum it! You can't do that. Meg's more important than me. An old pelican like me ain't got a lot of time left anyway, so if anything was to happen to me, it ain't no great loss to anybody. But Meg's got her whole life in front of her."

"Salty's got a point, Frank," Reb put in. "I don't like the idea of leaving him here, either, but if we're gonna save Meg —"

"If we're going to save Meg, we're going to do it together," Frank broke in with a tone of finality in his voice.

The other two men looked at him intently for a second; then Reb shrugged.

"I don't know about you, Salty, but I reckon it ain't safe to argue too much with a famous gunfighter like the Drifter."

Salty sighed. "Yeah, you're right about that. I've knowed him long enough to know how dadblamed stubborn he can be when he wants to."

Frank nodded and drew his knife from its sheath. "I'm going to cut a branch off one of those trees and make a walking stick out of it," he said. "That'll make things a mite easier for you, Salty. Reb, make a couple of packs out of our supplies. We'll have to travel pretty light, since we'll be carrying those packs."

"We're takin' along plenty of ammunition, though, right?" Reb said.

Frank nodded. "Yeah. Plenty of ammunition."

They set out about half an hour later, Frank and Reb with the packs of supplies slung on their backs, Salty clutching the pine branch that Frank had cut and shaped into a walking stick. Frank had wrapped more bandages around the old-timer's midsection, binding the dressing over the wound in place as tightly as he could.

"It's so tight I can't hardly breathe," Salty said. "But I can move around without it hurtin' too bad."

"As long as it doesn't start bleeding again, you ought to be all right," Frank said.

"I ain't worried about a little blood, as long as there ain't too much of it."

Everyone was ahead of them now: Palmer, Meg, and the Métis revolutionaries who had both the gold and the Gatling guns in their possession. At least, everyone that they knew of, Frank corrected himself as he thought about their situation. It might be a smart idea to keep an eye on their back trail anyway.

Out here on the frontier, you couldn't ever be sure about what might be coming up behind you.

Frank's feet already hurt, and it wasn't long before Reb and Salty were limping a little, too. They pushed on stoically, though, stopping to rest only occasionally.

By midday they had covered a couple of miles. When they stopped to rest and eat a sparse lunch, Salty sat down on a rock and started to take one of his boots off.

"Better not do that," Frank warned him.

"If you do, you're liable not to be able to put it on again because your foot would swell up. Then we really would have to leave you behind."

Salty grimaced. "Yeah, I didn't think about that. We're gonna have to wear these dang boots until we find ourselves some horses, ain't we?"

"That would be best."

Reb smiled and said, "Just think about how good it'll feel when you finally do get to take 'em off, Salty."

"Each foot'll be nothing but a big ol' blister by then," Salty groused. "But don't mind me. I'll make it."

"I know you will," Frank said. "You don't get to be as old as you are without being mighty stubborn."

"Speak for yourself," Salty muttered.

"I was."

After a while they started out again on their trek. Frank had been alert for droppings or any other sign of the horses. He hadn't completely given up on the chance of finding some of their mounts, even now.

Around the middle of the afternoon, he spotted some hoofprints and called a halt. He pointed them out, and Reb sounded a little excited as he asked, "Are those our horses?"

"Not unless they found some friends," Frank said with a slight frown. "At least a dozen horses left those prints."

It was true. A large group of riders had come through here sometime in the past couple of days, moving south to north through the foothills and cutting across the path of Frank and his companions, who were headed east.

"Who do you reckon they were?" Salty asked. "Them Metties, or however you say it?"

"Could be, but why would they be going north?" Frank mused. He tried to remember maps of Canada he had seen. "From here, there's not much in that direction except a big empty, all the way to Edmondton. We figured they were headed for Calgary."

"We figured, but we don't know that for sure," Reb pointed out. "Do you think we should follow these tracks?"

Frank pondered the question for a long moment before finally shaking his head. "I saw the hoofprints that the Métis's horses left back there where they bushwhacked Lundy's gang. I don't think these were made by the same animals."

Salty snatched his hat off and looked as if he was going to slam it to the ground in disgust, but he must have decided not to because picking it up would be difficult with those bandages wrapped so tightly around him.

"You mean there's *another* bunch o' varmints wanderin' around out here? For hell's sake, there weren't this many people in San Francisco the last time I was there!"

Frank had to smile. "Yeah, it's pretty crowded for the middle of nowhere," he agreed. "But these folks may not have anything to do with the ones we're after."

"Wish they'd left a few o' them horses behind," Salty muttered. "My feet ain't never gonna be the same. It's plumb unnatural for a man to have to walk so dang much, that's what it is!"

Reb said, "I can't argue with you there, old-timer."

"Come on," Frank said. "Whoever these fellas were, they're long gone."

By late afternoon they had covered several more miles. The hills around them were smaller now. The plains weren't too far off, and once they reached the plains Calgary would be relatively close.

But even so, that meant several more days of walking, and Frank wasn't sure any of them were up to that, especially Salty. The old-timer looked particularly haggard when Frank called a halt and said they would camp at the base of a wooded knoll.

Despite his obvious exhaustion, Salty said, "There's still some daylight left. Let me just catch my breath, and then I'll be able to keep goin' a while longer."

Frank shook his head. "No, we're staying here. I want to check that dressing and make sure the wound hasn't started bleeding again, and we all need some rest."

"Wish there was a nice icy stream somewhere close by, so I could soak these feet of mine," Reb said.

"That sounds good, but remember, keep your boots on."

Reb nodded. "Sure, Frank, I know."

Salty took his shirt off. Frank unwrapped the bandages. A little blood had oozed from the crease in the old-timer's side during the day, which made the dressing stick. Frank eased it off and studied the wound. It still looked raw and ugly, but the flesh around it wasn't red or swollen. That was his main concern.

"It looks like it's healing all right," he told Salty. "I'll just bind it up again."

"I reckon my feet probably look a lot worse. Dang, if the good Lord meant for man to walk, he wouldn't have given us critters to ride!"

They kept their fire small and put it out

318

before darkness settled down. The food and coffee made them feel better, but utter exhaustion was stealing over them quickly.

"I'll stand first watch," Frank said. "Then you, Reb, and you, Salty. That sound all right?"

The other two men nodded their agreement. Salty stretched out in his blankets while the western sky over the mountains still held a tinge of red from the sun. Within minutes, he was snoring.

Reb didn't doze off that quickly. He spread his blankets, then looked up at Frank, who sat nearby on a slab of rock holding his Winchester.

"You reckon Meg's all right tonight?" Reb asked quietly.

"I'm sure she is. Like Salty said earlier, if there's one thing she's good at, it's taking care of herself."

"This frontier is no place for a woman like her."

"That just shows that you don't know her very well," Frank said. "A woman like Meg, with the spirit she has, isn't going to be happy sitting in a parlor and knitting booties. She's got to be out and around, doing things and seeing whatever there is to see."

"Yeah, well, one of these days she's gonna want that parlor and those booties, I'll bet."

"Maybe, maybe not."

"She probably wishes she was in a parlor somewhere right now, instead of being Palmer's prisoner."

"You're not helping matters, Reb," Frank said flatly.

"Maybe not. But I can't help worryin' about her."

"Neither can I . . . and I've known her a lot longer than you have."

"You and her . . . I mean, the two of you ain't . . . you're not —"

"Meg and I are friends," Frank said, not wanting to sit there and listen to the young man stumble around what he was trying to say. "Good friends, but that's all."

"That's kind of what I figured." Reb sighed. "Guess I'd better get some shut-eye."

"That'd be a good idea," Frank said.

After a quiet, peaceful night, they were up again at first light in the morning. From the pained way Salty was hobbling around, Frank didn't know how far he would be able to go today. His own feet were in pretty bad shape, and Reb's probably were, too.

Salty tottered across the campsite and sank down on a log. "You're gonna have to leave me here today, Frank," he said. "I can't go on."

"Salty, I —"

"Damn it, listen to me. You owe it to Meg. You already wasted enough time takin' it easy on me yesterday. You got to go after her as fast as you can now."

Reb said, "That's not gonna be very fast. I'm not walkin' too good myself today."

Frank came to his feet. "Blast it, I'm not giving up, and neither are you two. Salty, we'll rig a travois and pull you."

"A travois? Frank, you've gone plumb loco —"

Frank held up a hand to stop Salty's argument.

"Blast it, I ain't gonna shut up —"

"Listen," Frank said.

Hoofbeats sounded through the early morning air. There were quite a few horses, Frank judged.

And they were coming closer, too.

CHAPTER 29

Frank lunged across the camp and took hold of Salty's arm. "Come on," he urged the old-timer. "We need to get up there in those trees."

Reb was already grabbing their packs and kicking dirt and rocks over the fire to put it out and hide the signs of it.

"Who do you reckon it is?" he asked.

"I don't know," Frank said, "but the way things have been going, chances are it's not anybody friendly."

He helped Salty up the slope into the trees that covered the top of the knoll. Reb came behind them, bringing both packs and his Winchester. They took cover behind the thick trunks of the pines and waited.

The riders were coming from the west, down the long, shallow valley between hills that Frank and his companions had been following. The sun had started to rise, casting its garish light over the landscape. That light was an explosion of red as the riders trotted around a bend in the trail and came into view.

The splash of color wasn't just from the early-morning sunlight. The riders wore scarlet coats, along with black trousers and tan, peaked, flat-brimmed hats. The brass buttons on the coats gleamed in the sunlight.

Frank recognized the uniforms, and so did Salty. They had encountered a number of North West Mounted Policemen at Whitehorse the year before.

"Tarnation!" Salty exclaimed. "It's the Mounties!"

Relief went through Frank, especially at the sight of the riderless horses being led by several of the red-coated men.

"It looks like they've got our horses, too. They must have stampeded back toward the mountains when Palmer and Lundy attacked us."

Frank had gone in that direction, as well as searching north, south, and east of the camp, but he hadn't found the horses. The Mounties had swept up the animals during their patrol, though.

"You two stay here," he went on. "I'll stop them."

He stepped out of the trees and pointed

his rifle skyward. Quickly, he squeezed off three shots, the universal frontier signal for somebody in trouble. Down below, the Mounties reined in their horses and wheeled toward the knoll.

Frank saw some of the red-coated constables draw rifles from saddle sheaths. He figured they had spotted him by now, so he waved his Winchester over his head in a sign that he was friendly. The Mounties came to a stop and waited.

Frank turned and waved for Salty and Reb to follow him. As he started down the slope, they came out of the trees behind him. Frank glanced over his shoulder and was glad to see that Reb had a hand on Salty's arm, helping the old-timer.

One of the Mounties walked his horse out ahead of the others. Frank recognized the insignia of a sergeant on the man's uniform. He had a ruddy face and watched Frank with narrow, suspicious eyes.

"We're sure glad to see you, Sergeant," Frank greeted him. "Are you in charge of this patrol?"

"That's as may be," the Mountie snapped. "Who am I addressing, sir?"

"My name's Frank Morgan." Frank nodded toward his companions as they came up to join him. "This is Reb Russell and

Salty Stevens. We've been set afoot out here. Been walking for a day, and our feet are mighty sore."

"Americans, aren't you?"

"That's right."

The sergeant's forehead creased in disapproval. "You American cowboys are too accustomed to riding. Even though we're mounted police, myself or any of these lads could walk halfway across Canada if need be."

Frank kept a tight rein on his impatience as he said, "I'm sure that's true, Sergeant. But those are our horses you've got there, and we're mighty glad to see them, too."

"I suppose you can prove that, as well as the identities you claim?"

Salty burst out, "Dadgum it, mister, why would we lie about such a thing?"

The sergeant regarded him coolly. "The men we seek are wanted for numerous crimes, including robbery and murder. I hardly think that they would shrink from telling a falsehood or two."

"You're after the gang that stole a bunch of gold," Frank said as he realized what was going on here.

His statement just made the Mounties more suspicious. The men holding rifles never took their eyes off of him, Salty, and Reb.

"What do you know about that?" the sergeant asked sharply.

"I know the men you're looking for are somewhere ahead of us to the east," Frank said, pointing in that direction even though it wasn't necessary. "While you were circling through the hills to the north yesterday on your patrol, they slipped past you and headed for Calgary."

He was only guessing that the Mounties' horses were responsible for the tracks he and his friends had found the day before, but the look of surprise on the sergeant's face told him that he was right.

"You *do* know something about this matter," the man said.

Frank nodded. "I sure do. More than you might think, because I also know they're Métis revolutionaries, and they have four Gatling guns as well as the gold."

Shocked muttering came from several of the Mounties. They fell silent abruptly as the red-faced sergeant twisted around in the saddle and gave them a stern look. He turned back to Frank and said, "I think you had better explain yourself, Mr. Morgan."

"I'd be glad to." Knowing that Meg was still Palmer's prisoner made any delay chafe at Frank, but he thought it would save time in the long run to lay his cards on the table for the Mountie sergeant. "Why don't you and your men get down off those horses? There's coffee in the pot, and we can always brew more."

The man hesitated for a moment, but then he nodded and said, "All right." He ordered his men to dismount and added, "At ease, lads."

The Mounties swung down from their saddles and fetched tin cups for coffee from their packs. The sergeant clasped his hands behind his stiffly held back and faced Frank.

"Now, then, Mr. Morgan," he said. "My name is McKendrick. What can you tell me about these Gatling guns?"

"I figure they were stolen from the U.S. Army. I know they were smuggled across the border by an outlaw named Owen Lundy and his gang. They delivered the guns to those Métis revolutionaries I mentioned, in return for a payment in gold . . . which the Métis turned right around and stole back from them a little later. They ambushed Lundy's bunch and killed all of them except a man named Palmer, who's gone after them. Palmer took a friend of ours, a woman named Meg Goodwin, with him as a prisoner. I figure he plans to use her as a hostage if the law catches up to him. Clear enough, Sergeant?"

McKendrick frowned at him. "Clear enough . . . but decidedly far-fetched."

Frank shrugged and said, "Maybe so, but that's what happened."

"What's your connection with the guns?"

"There isn't any, except that Lundy used one of them to try to kill us a couple of days ago. I think he was probably demonstrating it to the Métis, and we happened to be handy targets."

"Then what *are* you doing here on Canadian soil?" McKendrick demanded.

"We were on Palmer's trail. He stole some money from Salty a while back, and we hoped we could recover some of it."

"That's right, Sergeant," the old-timer put in. "Palmer was part o' Soapy Smith's bunch over at Skagway, if you heard about that."

"Skagway is in Alaska, out of our jurisdiction," McKendrick said. He added, "But I do recall hearing something about the rampant lawlessness that went on there before the vigilantes rose up and restored the rule of order. Should have been done by the proper authorities, of course."

Salty said, "There wasn't no law to do it,

so folks had to take care o' things their own selves."

McKendrick sniffed. "Such things would never happen in Canada."

"Do you believe what we've told you, Sergeant?" Frank asked. "We could sure use those horses of ours you've got. I don't think we could walk much farther."

"You have bills of sale or any other sort of proof the animals belong to you?"

"As a matter of fact," Frank said, "we do. We bought them in a place called Powderkeg Bay, on the other side of the mountains."

"I've heard of it. Never been there."

"I'll see if I can find those papers," Frank said.

Frank had the bills of sale from Parkhurst's Livery in his saddlebags, which he had slung over his shoulder along with the pack of supplies. Actually, a couple of these horses hadn't come from there, but the descriptions on the papers were vague enough that McKendrick didn't notice the discrepancy. Anyway, Frank thought, three horses were three horses, under sore-footed circumstances like these.

"Very well," the sergeant said as he handed the bills of sale back to Frank. "Everything you've told me seems reasonable enough to accept, Mr. Morgan, although it does take a bit of imagination. Do you have any idea what the Métis plan to do with those Gatling guns?"

Frank shook his head. "No, but they've been responsible for two armed rebellions against the Canadian government. I have a hunch that whatever their plan is, it won't be anything good."

"Indeed," McKendrick said. "My men and I will proceed with all due haste to Calgary, so I can wire my superiors with this news. You and your companions will accompany us."

"That was what I figured on doing," Frank said.

A hint of an icy smile appeared on McKendrick's lips. "You don't understand. You have no choice in the matter. For the time being you may consider yourselves under arrest."

"Arrest!" Salty yelped in surprise. "What in tarnation are you arrestin' us for, you . . . you danged redcoat!"

"You're being held for questioning as suspicious characters," McKendrick said.

"That don't sound like no real charge to me!"

Frank said, "Take it easy, Salty." To McKendrick, he went on, "We're coming with

330

you anyway, Sergeant. What's the point in placing us under arrest?"

"It gives me the authority to demand that you surrender your weapons." McKendrick carried a revolver in a holster with a flap over the butt of the gun. He rested his hand on that flap now.

Frank could have drawn his own Colt half a dozen times or more in the time it would take McKendrick to unfasten that flap and haul out the holstered revolver. Outnumbered four to one, though, he didn't want to get in a shooting scrape with the Mounties.

It wasn't just a matter of the odds, either. Sergeant McKendrick might be a stiffnecked, overly suspicious son of a gun, but he was just doing his job the best way he knew how. Wrong or not, he didn't deserve a bullet for that.

"All right, Sergeant," Frank said. "We want to go to Calgary anyway, so we'll cooperate . . . for now. Don't get spooked. I'm going to hand you my gun."

"Carefully," McKendrick advised.

Frank reached over with his left hand to slide the Colt from leather and surrender it to the Mountie. Salty grumbled about giving up his gun, but he did it.

That just left Reb. McKendrick turned

toward him and said, "You, too, Mr. Russell. Hand over your weapon."

Reb looked torn. Suddenly, he stepped back, and his hand flashed to his holster with blinding speed. He drew the ivory-handled gun before any of the Mounties could hope to stop him and trained the weapon on McKendrick.

"Hold it right there, Sergeant," Reb said. "I don't want to shoot you, but I will if I have to. You're not gettin' my gun."

Chapter 30

"Reb, what in blazes are you doing?" Frank demanded. He glanced at the Mounties. Several of them had raised their rifles and pointed them at the young man. They might have opened fire if Sergeant McKendrick hadn't lifted a hand to stop them.

"Hold on there, lads," McKendrick said. "No shooting unless we absolutely have to." He glared at Reb. "What's the meaning of this, Mr. Russell?"

"The meanin' is that I ain't handin' over my gun to you," Reb drawled. "I haven't done anything wrong. You can't arrest me, either."

Again that frosty smile touched McKendrick's lips. "I beg to differ with you, sir. I can arrest anyone I please."

The gun in Reb's hand didn't waver as he said, "Well, I reckon you can *try* to arrest me . . . but you're liable to be in mighty hot water with your bosses if you do."

"Oh? Why, pray tell?"

"Because *they'll* be in hot water with the U.S. government. The Canadian government knows I'm here."

Quietly, Frank said, "Reb, I think you've got some explaining to do."

"Yeah," Salty added indignantly.

Reb smiled but didn't lower his gun. "I'm gonna reach in my pocket," he said. "Sergeant, tell your boys not to get itchy trigger fingers."

"You heard the man," McKendrick told the other Mounties. "I'd like to see what this . . . gentleman . . . thinks is going to change my mind."

Reb slid his free hand inside his buckskin shirt. He brought out a small leather folder. "I'll toss it to you, Frank," he said. "You can show it to the sergeant."

Frank nodded. "All right."

Carefully, Reb lofted the folder through the air to Frank, who caught it and flipped it open before handing it to McKendrick. A badge and an identification card were pinned inside the folder.

"So you're really Captain Russell," Frank said.

Reb nodded. "That's right. Attached to the U.S. Secret Service right now. I was sent up here to try to get on the trail of those

Gatlin' guns. Once I did, I was supposed to contact your folks, Sergeant, and let you know where they were so the Mounties could recover 'em. If we were somewhere you could send a wire to Ottawa, you could confirm that pretty quick-like."

"But we're not, are we?" McKendrick snapped. "So I'm left with the decision of whether or not to accept this preposterous story."

"It's not preposterous," Reb said. "You've got my badge and bona fides right there."

McKendrick shook his head. "Anyone can have a badge and an identification card made."

"You don't give up easy, do you?"

McKendrick gave him a flinty look. "I'm a sergeant in the North West Mounted Police. Of course I don't give up easily."

Frank said, "For what it's worth, Sergeant, I believe him. Ever since I met him, my gut's been telling me there was something I didn't know about Reb, and I reckon this is it."

Salty squinted at the young man. "Was you really at the ro-day-o down in Pecos?"

"Yeah," Reb replied with a grin. "I've been travelin' around competin' in rodeos for a while. Gives me a good excuse for bein' where I need to be when the Army and the

Secret Service send me on a job." He looked at McKendrick again. "How about it, Sergeant? Are we gonna work together, the way your government and my government intended, or does there have to be a ruckus?"

"You're heavily outnumbered, you know," McKendrick reminded him. "You can't hope to prevail."

"I'll take my chances. And *you're* the one I've got my sights lined on, remember."

Frank finally lost his temper. "Blast it, while we're standing around here jawing, the varmints we're after are getting farther away. All the signs indicate that they're headed for Calgary, Sergeant, so that's the way we all want to go. There's no need for a bunch of argument."

McKendrick drew in a deep breath, held it for a second, and then said, "I suppose you're right, Mr. Morgan. There's no need to press the issue. Would you like your weapons returned to you?"

"I sure as hell would," Salty said.

McKendrick handed the revolvers back to Frank and the old-timer. "Consider yourselves no longer under arrest."

"I never really did," Salty said as he pouched his iron.

"We'll call this a truce," McKendrick went on.

Frank said, "That works for me. We don't have our saddles anymore, but we can rig blankets on our horses and use rope for hackamores."

Getting ready to ride didn't take long. Frank helped Salty onto one of the horses. The old-timer was still pretty stiff and sore from his wound.

Reb had holstered his gun, but he kept a wary eye on McKendrick and the other Mounties as the party moved out, heading east. The three Americans rode at the head of the group with McKendrick.

"How long do you think it'll take us to get to Calgary?" Frank asked.

"If we're not delayed, we should reach there late this afternoon or early this evening."

Frank nodded slowly. "The Métis have enough of a lead that we can't catch them. They're going to get to the settlement before we do. That's going to make it harder to find them."

"There are several thousand people in Calgary," McKendrick said. "It's going to be a difficult task."

Reb said, "It's worse than that. They're havin' their annual livestock exhibition, with that rodeo comin' up any day now. Folks from all over this part of the country will be in town for that, so the population'll be two or three times what it usually is."

McKendrick looked over at him. Even the sergeant's usual self-control was shaken. "My God," he muttered. "And you say these so-called revolutionaries have Gatling guns?"

"Four of them," Frank said, "and from the sound of it, a perfect opportunity to raise plenty of hell with them."

Calgary was both frontier cowtown and bustling industrial city these days. The downtown area had numerous brick buildings rising several stories high, but around Victoria Park, on the Elbow River where the stream curved up from the south to join with the Bow River, Calgary still looked like the cow country settlement it had been more than fifteen years earlier when it first grew up around the North West Mounted Police post established there.

There was even a hotel called the Drover's Rest. That was where Joseph and Charlotte Marat found themselves this evening, along with Anton Mirabeau.

Joseph had tried all day to talk Mirabeau out of his plan, but the man would not be budged. Attacking the Mountie post was one thing. The Mounties had killed Métis in the past.

But the thought of opening fire with the Gatling guns on the crowd at the rodeo planned for the next day horrified Joseph.

Charlotte didn't like the idea of slaughtering innocent people, either, and she had tried to talk to Mirabeau about it. Mirabeau refused to listen. He just fell back on his stubborn claim that the attack on the rodeo would force the government in Ottawa to take the rebellion seriously.

The three of them sat in the hotel's dining room. Mirabeau had changed from his buckskins before coming into town. Like Joseph and Charlotte, his ancestry was mostly French, so their status as mixed-bloods was not obvious. Anyone who looked like a Cree Indian wouldn't have been allowed to stay here.

The other men in the group were camped outside of the settlement, keeping watch over the all-important crates that contained the rapid-firers.

Mirabeau sipped his wine and said, "First thing in the morning, we'll pick up the wagons and drive out to the camp." He had already made arrangements to purchase two large prairie schooners with canvas covers over the back. The plan called for the Gatling guns to be mounted, two in each wagon, one at the front of the vehicle and one at the rear. The guns would be covered with canvas as well so that no one would be able to see them when the wagons were parked at both ends of the rodeo grandstands that had been erected in Victoria Park.

From there, the Métis manning the guns would be able to spray the crowd with thousands of steel-jacket slugs in a matter of minutes. By the time anyone figured out what was happening, hundreds of people would be dead.

Then it would be up to the men in the wagons to make their getaway as best they could. There would be so much chaos because of the slaughter that the men might actually be able to escape.

Mirabeau went on, "Charlotte, you and Dumond will need to have our horses nearby and ready to ride." He smiled. "We'll be in a hurry."

"I would think so," she said, "considering that you'll be fleeing from the site of mass murder."

Mirabeau's smile disappeared. "Not murder," he said. "Revolution."

"At least let Joseph help me with the horses," Charlotte said.

Mirabeau shook his head. "No offense,

ma cher, but after today, I no longer trust your brother. I would prefer to have him where I can keep an eye on him."

Joseph said tightly, "I'm sitting right here, you know."

"I know," Mirabeau said with a nod. "Joseph, you have been a dear friend to me. You are almost like *my* brother, and someday soon, once Charlotte and I are married, you will be. But our cause is more important than anything else, even that."

"More important than me?" Charlotte asked.

Mirabeau looked coolly at her. "I beg of you not to make me choose."

She grimaced and looked away.

"After tomorrow, you'll see that I'm right," Mirabeau continued. He drank the last of his wine and pushed away the empty plates from their meal. "We should go upstairs and get some rest. Momentous events await us."

Joseph had reached a decision. He nodded and said, "You're right, Anton. We should go upstairs."

Mirabeau looked a little surprised that Joseph would agree with him on anything, even this. But he smiled and said, "Fine."

The three of them left the dining room and walked through the lobby to the stairs.

The Drover's Rest, as its name implied, wasn't a fancy place. It catered to cattlemen, and it was furnished comfortably but simply. A number of men sat in the lobby, talking about cattle prices. These were some of the ranchers who were in town for the livestock exposition and rodeo.

They paid no attention to the two men and the woman who went up the stairs to the second floor of the squarish frame building. Joseph and Charlotte had adjoining rooms on the left side of the corridor. Mirabeau's room was across the hall on the right.

As they approached their doors, Mirabeau put a hand on Charlotte's arm. He might have wished to kiss her good night, but if so he was going to be disappointed, because she pulled away from him. Joseph, walking along the corridor behind them, was glad to see that. The falling-out that his sister had had with Mirabeau meant she was less likely to be upset by what happened next.

Joseph looked swiftly up and down the hallway. It was deserted at the moment. That was perfect for what he needed to do.

He took the pistol from under his coat, pointed it at the back of Mirabeau's head, and pulled the trigger.

CHAPTER 31

But even as Joseph fired, Mirabeau was already moving, twisting around and throwing himself to the side so that the bullet from Joseph's pistol whipped harmlessly past his head.

The big man's arm came up in a vicious backhanded blow that crashed into Joseph's jaw and flung him against the wall. Charlotte screamed as Mirabeau lunged after Joseph and grabbed the wrist of his gun hand.

Bone cracked as Mirabeau gave the wrist a savage twist. Joseph cried out in pain. The gun slipped from suddenly nerveless fingers and thudded to the carpet runner in the center of the hallway.

Mirabeau kept hold of Joseph's broken wrist and used his other hand to pound a couple of swift punches into the smaller man's face. Joseph's head rocked back. His surroundings whirled crazily around him for a second, then a black curtain seemed to drop over his eyes. He was still conscious, but just barely.

He heard a door open, and a second later he felt himself shoved into a room. His legs turned rubbery and collapsed, dumping him on the floor. A kick dug into his belly and drove the air from his lungs. He lay there helplessly, for the moment blinded by pain and gasping for breath.

Another sound came to his ears, but in his stunned state, it took him several seconds to figure out that it was Charlotte crying. The sharp crack of a slap silenced the sobs.

"Quiet," Mirabeau ordered in a harsh whisper. "People will come to see what that shot was about. As far as they know, no one is in this room."

Sure enough, a few moments later footsteps came from the hall, and a man's loud voice asked, "Did anybody see what the hell happened up here? Who fired that shot?"

The red-shot darkness that had descended over Joseph's vision was fading now. He could see a little again. Mirabeau loomed over him. Mirabeau had one arm wrapped around Charlotte's waist, and his other hand was clamped over her mouth to keep her from crying out.

Joseph tried to move, but his muscles

didn't want to cooperate. He shifted just enough to draw Mirabeau's attention. The man kicked him again. Charlotte struggled in Mirabeau's grip, but she was no match for his brutal strength.

The hubbub in the corridor grew louder. Someone knocked on the door. Mirabeau didn't answer, and his iron grip on Charlotte kept her from responding. Eventually the commotion died down, and the people in the corridor went away.

When Mirabeau let go of Charlotte, she tried to slap him. He caught her wrist in mid-swing.

"Settle down and behave, Charlotte, or I'll have to hurt you like I hurt Joseph," he threatened her.

Joseph watched through slitted eyes. His broken wrist throbbed in agony, but he found himself unable to make a sound.

Charlotte stopped struggling with Mirabeau. "How . . . how could you do that to Joseph?" she asked in a wretched voice.

"How could I . . ." Mirabeau shook his head. "That precious brother of yours tried to kill me! Didn't you see?"

"Because he doesn't want to be a party to hundreds of cold-blooded murders!"

"It's not murder," Mirabeau said. "It's politics."

She just stared at him, aghast at his casual pronouncement.

Joseph got his good hand underneath him and pushed himself into a sitting position. By the time he was upright, Mirabeau had drawn a gun and pointed it at him.

"Don't make me kill you, Joseph," Mirabeau warned. "I'm not sure your sister would ever forgive me for that."

"You're already beyond forgiveness," Charlotte said in an icy voice.

Mirabeau's broad shoulders rose and fell in a shrug. "The cause comes before personal considerations. I understand that, even if the two of you don't." He looked at Joseph. "Did you really think I wasn't waiting for you to try something, my friend?"

Joseph had caught his breath enough to say, "You are not . . . my friend. Never again . . . Anton."

Mirabeau shrugged again. "I can live without friendship —" He glanced at Charlotte. "And without love, if it means my people will be free."

"How can you contemplate doing such evil in the name of good?"

"There is no good or evil, only freedom or slavery."

"You're wrong, Anton."

"We shall see." Mirabeau kept the gun

346

trained on Joseph. "But not if the two of you continue to interfere. I don't like to do this, but I have to make sure you won't ruin everything."

"How are you going to do that?" Joseph managed to sneer. "Kill us both?"

Mirabeau shook his head as he stepped closer. "No. But you won't be interfering with me anymore."

Even if he hadn't been in such pain he could barely move, Joseph wouldn't have been fast enough to avoid what happened next. Mirabeau bent down, and the gun in his hand rose and fell. Joseph felt the smashing impact on his head. This time when the black curtain dropped, it enveloped him completely.

He was there, and then abruptly, he wasn't.

"What's to stop me from yelling for help?" Meg wanted to know as she and Palmer stood in the darkened doorway of a business across the street from the Drover's Rest that was closed for the night.

"Go ahead and yell," Palmer said. He pressed the barrel of the pistol he held harder into Meg's side. "I'll just shoot you and be out of here before anybody knows what happened. As many people as there are in Calgary right now, nobody's gonna find me."

It was a bluff — mostly — but he had a point. The exposition and rodeo had swelled Calgary's population to several times its normal size, and it was already the biggest town in this part of the country. If a man wanted to hide from the law, Calgary was a good place to do it right now.

"Anyway," Palmer went on, "you're a smart girl, Meg. You've figured out by now that I don't want to hurt you. Hell, if you play along with me, I might just give you a share of the gold."

"I don't want any of the gold," Meg said coldly. "You killed Frank and Salty and Reb."

Palmer sighed. "You're just not gonna get over that, are you?"

"What do you think?"

"I think you're gonna come with me. I've got to find some place to stash you while I go on about my business."

They had trailed Joseph and Charlotte Marat into Calgary from the place outside of town where the rest of the group had camped. Palmer didn't know the big, bearded man with the Marats, but he seemed to be in charge. Palmer intended to grab the three of them and use them to force the others to turn over the gold.

He couldn't do that if he had to watch Meg like a hawk all the time, though. He prodded her into motion now, herding her at gunpoint through the alleys of this busy neighborhood near Victoria Park.

He'd heard about a place where he might be able to leave Meg and have her guarded. He knew approximately where the house was located, and when they got there he recognized it from the description he'd heard back in Skagway. It was a big house near the railroad tracks, surrounded by aspens.

The woman who answered the door had the pinched, suspicious face of madams all over the frontier. She regarded the two people standing on her porch and said, "Men don't usually bring girls with them, mister."

"Your name Alice Beale?" Palmer demanded.

"What if it is?"

"Owen Lundy sent me."

"Owen . . ." The madam's face softened instantly. "Where is he?"

"He'll be along in a day or two," Palmer lied. "For now, he told me that if I ever needed any help in Calgary, you were the woman to see."

Alice Beale lowered her voice. "What do you want, mister?"

He let her see the gun he had pressed to Meg's side. "You think you could keep up with this little hellcat for me for a day or two?"

A greedy smile curved the woman's mouth as she took in Meg's blond, wholesome good looks. "Want me to put her to work, do you?"

"No," Palmer said quickly. "Just lock her in a room and keep her there. Make sure she stays quiet and doesn't cause any trouble."

The madam didn't ask any questions. She just said, "I reckon I could do that." Then her eyes narrowed again. "But it'll cost you."

"I expect to pay. That won't be a problem."

"Better not be." Alice Beale nodded. "Although if you were to skip out on me, I could get what you owe out of this one. Pretty quick, too."

"It won't come to that," Palmer said. He gave Meg a shove toward the door. "Get in there."

Suddenly she tried to break away and run. Palmer grabbed her and threw her down on the porch. The madam turned her head to call over her shoulder, "Titus!"

A massive man with a bald, bullet-shaped head loomed up behind her. "Yeah, Miss Alice?" he rumbled.

"Take this girl upstairs," she ordered. "Lock her in Desdemona's old room."

"You want me to quiet her down first?"

"No, not unless you have to." As the huge man picked up Meg, Alice Beale leaned closer to her and went on, "You don't want Titus to have to quiet you down, missie. I promise you, you don't."

Meg sagged in Titus's grip. Palmer smiled. He knew despair when he saw it. Meg wouldn't give any more trouble, and she would be here waiting for him when he got back. He'd be a lot richer than he was now, too.

"I appreciate this," he told the madam as Titus and Meg disappeared inside the house. "I'll make it worth your while."

She snorted. "Damn right you will."

Palmer left the house and headed back toward the Drover's Rest. When he got there, he brushed his clothes off before he went in. As he crossed the lobby, he looked around, but he didn't see any familiar faces.

"Howdy," he said to the clerk at the desk. "Couple of friends of mine are supposed to be staying here. Joseph Marat and his sister Charlotte. Have they checked in yet?"

The clerk obviously didn't find anything unusual about the question. He nodded and said, "Yes, sir. They're in Rooms Fourteen and Fifteen upstairs. Their friend Mr. Mirabeau is in Room Five."

Palmer grinned. "Ah, so Mirabeau's here, too. Splendid."

So that was the big man's name. It didn't mean anything to Palmer.

He nodded his thanks to the clerk and headed for the stairs. No one tried to stop him as he climbed to the second floor, but as he passed several men on their way down, he heard them talking about a shot that had gone off upstairs a while earlier. No one seemed to know what it was about.

That was odd, Palmer thought, but probably none of his business.

Since he'd been lucky enough to find out what he needed to know, he went to the door of Room Five. He would brace Mirabeau first, since the man was the most likely to either have the gold or know where it was. He would deal with the Marats later, if he needed to.

The hallway was deserted at the moment. Palmer slipped his gun out of the holster under his coat and used his other hand to knock on the door.

"Mr. Mirabeau?" he called. "Telegram for

you, sir?"

At first he thought there was no response. Then he frowned and leaned closer to the panel. Sure enough, he heard some muffled sounds coming from the other side of it, followed by a bumping noise.

Palmer's instincts told him something was wrong in there, and finding out what it was might prove valuable to him. He tried the knob. Locked.

Well, there were other ways in.

He drew back a little, raised his foot, and drove his heel against the door beside the knob. With a splintering crash, it burst open.

Palmer went in fast, in a low crouch with his gun swinging from side to side. No lamps burned in the room, but enough light spilled in from the hall for him to see a couple of figures lying on the bed. They were tied hand and foot, as well as gagged. Despite the gags, Palmer could see enough of their faces to recognize them.

"Why, Joseph and Charlotte Marat," he said. "Fancy meeting you folks again."

CHAPTER 32

The crowds started streaming into the rodeo grandstands before noon the next day, even though the competition itself wasn't scheduled to start until two o'clock that afternoon.

By that time, Frank, Salty, and Reb were on hand, circulating through the crowd. So were Sergeant McKendrick and some of his men. It wasn't uncommon to see North West Mounted Police constables around Calgary, since the town had grown up around and taken its name from Fort Calgary, the Mountie post that had been the first permanent structure in the area.

Frank and the others had arrived in town the previous evening, and as Reb had predicted, all it had taken to confirm his identity were a couple of wires from the Mountie post to Ottawa. Canadian government officials had ordered McKendrick's superiors to give Reb any help he requested, and they had passed that order on to Mc-Kendrick. The ruddy-faced sergeant didn't particularly like it, Frank knew, but Mc-Kendrick was nothing if not a man who did his duty.

The rodeo seemed the most likely spot for the Métis to strike, and Frank was convinced that Palmer had followed them here to Calgary in an attempt to recover the gold.

"We'll be there when folks start coming in tomorrow," he had suggested to Reb and McKendrick when they made their plans. "If we can spot Palmer, maybe he'll lead us to the Métis."

"What about Meg?" Reb had asked.

"Either she'll be with Palmer, or he'll know where she is. That's why we need to take him alive. I'd appreciate it if you could pass that along to your men, Sergeant."

McKendrick had nodded. "Of course, Mr. Morgan. But I make no guarantees. The most important thing is stopping whatever atrocity those people have planned."

Frank couldn't argue with that. Hundreds of lives might be at stake. But Meg meant a lot to him, so he planned to do everything in his power to keep Palmer alive until the varmint led them to her.

So far Frank hadn't seen anybody he recognized. Neither had Salty or Reb.

"There's too dang many people here," Salty said. "It's like tryin' to pick one ant outta a dang anthill."

"Just keep watching," Frank said.

He wasn't the sort of hombre to get discouraged, but he had to admit that the odds of spotting Palmer and trailing him to the Métis and those Gatling guns were small. Frank had bucked plenty of long odds in the past, though, and was still here to tell about it.

Folks had come from all over to attend this rodeo and exposition. Horses were tied everywhere there was a place to loop their reins, and scores of buggies, buckboards, and even some covered wagons were parked near the arena. The sound of happy, excited voices filled the air on this beautiful summer day.

Frank just hoped that screams of pain and terror wouldn't replace those happy voices before the day was over.

"We should tell the Mounties," Joseph said, although the idea of turning to the constables for help was repulsive to him. This wasn't the first time he had made the suggestion.

"No," Charlotte said. "We have to give Anton a chance to see that he's wrong."

"He's not going to —"

Joseph stopped. Arguing with his sister was a waste of time. Even after everything Mirabeau had done, she couldn't bring herself to betray him.

From behind them, Palmer said, "You two stop wrangling and take me to him. I don't care what he does, I just want the gold."

Joseph glanced over his shoulder. Palmer's hand was under his coat, and Joseph knew that hand gripped the butt of a gun. He and Charlotte had gone from being in the clutches of one madman to another. But where Mirabeau was obsessed with avenging the Métis who had lost their lives in the past rebellions, Palmer's only thought was of the gold.

"He won't have all of it," Joseph said. "I told you that. Some of it went to purchase the wagons."

"Then I'll take what he has," Palmer said. "Keep moving."

The three of them made their way through the thickening crowds. Palmer had held them prisoner since finding them in the hotel room the night before. He had freed Charlotte long enough to bind up Joseph's broken wrist, but that was all the medical attention he had received. The wrist still hurt like blazes, and his hand had gone numb.

After that, Palmer had bound and gagged Charlotte again so that he could get some sleep. They had stayed like that until a short time earlier, when he had finally untied Charlotte and had her untie Joseph in turn. Then he had marched them at gunpoint down here to the rodeo arena in Victoria Park.

Joseph hadn't told Palmer exactly where to find Mirabeau. If he had done that, then Palmer wouldn't have needed to keep them alive anymore. Joseph was confident Palmer would have slit their throats and left them at the hotel.

Palmer was a fool. Mirabeau wasn't going to turn over the gold to Palmer. He wouldn't care that Palmer was holding the two of them hostage. But maybe Palmer's intrusion would disrupt Mirabeau's bloodthirsty plans. That was the only hope Joseph clung to.

Joseph saw the canvas-covered prairie schooner up ahead. He turned to Palmer and nodded toward the wagon.

"There," he said.

A greedy smile creased Palmer's face. "All right," he said. "Go ahead. And if Mirabeau wants the two of you alive, he'd damn well better do what I say."

That was where Palmer had made his fatal mistake, Joseph thought.

Anton Mirabeau didn't care about life. His only concern was death.

Frank climbed to the top of the grandstand, leaving Salty and Reb to keep searching lower down. The broad brim of his Stetson shaded his eyes as he looked from one end of the arena to the other. He still didn't see Palmer anywhere, but another thought had cropped up in his mind.

The Métis couldn't just attach those Gatling guns to their carriages, roll the rapid-firers into place, and start shooting. People would see the guns and panic long before the first shot went off. They would have to hide the Gatlings somehow in order to get them close enough for the massacre they had planned.

He and his friends still didn't know for sure that the revolutionaries were going to strike at the rodeo, Frank reminded himself. But it seemed like such a perfect opportunity that he didn't see how they could pass it up.

The Gatling guns were pretty big. Frank recalled that the guards at Yuma Prison had had one mounted on a wagon. There were a lot of wagons parked near the arena. He turned to look toward one end of the grandstand. . . .

And there was Joe Palmer, following a man and a woman toward a big prairie schooner with an arching canvas cover over its bed.

Frank's eyes narrowed as he peered into the shadows under that cover. Something was in the back of the wagon, something bulky under another sheet of canvas.

"Blast it," Frank breathed. He knew he was looking at one of the Gatling guns. There was something else in the back of the wagon, he realized, probably a second rapid-firer.

He jerked his head toward the other end of the grandstand, saw an identical wagon parked there, angled so that if the other two Gatling guns were in there, they could fire through the canvas cover, tearing it to shreds in seconds, and rake their deadly claws right across the crowded stands.

Frank cupped his hands around his mouth and shouted, "Salty!"

The old-timer didn't hear him at first over all the noise coming from the crowd. Frank yelled again, and this time Salty looked up.

"The Conestoga!" Frank shouted as he waved a hand toward the big wagon. "The

Conestoga!"

Salty jerked his head in a nod and took off at a run, weaving his way awkwardly through the crowd. He couldn't move too fast because of the wound in his side and the press of people all around him, but he hurried as much as he could.

Frank didn't see Reb, but he knew the young Army officer was around somewhere. He made his way down the grandstand as quickly as possible, taking more than one step at a time and dodging around people arriving for the rodeo.

When Frank reached the ground, he spotted McKendrick. "Sergeant!" he called. "I've found what we're looking for."

He didn't want to yell out anything about Gatling guns. That might start a stampede in which innocent people would be hurt or killed.

McKendrick joined him. "Where?" the Mountie asked sharply.

"In that wagon over there. There's another one at the other end of the grandstand. I sent Salty down there."

"That old man?"

"He's a lot tougher than you think he is."

McKendrick reached for the whistle attached to his red coat. "I must summon reinforcements."

Frank grabbed his arm and jerked him into motion. "We can handle this ourselves!"

"You're insane," McKendrick muttered, but he came along.

Frank had lost sight of Palmer, but the man had to still be around somewhere. As he and McKendrick approached the wagon, some sort of scuffle suddenly broke out at the rear of it. Frank threw himself forward in a run.

A shot roared.

Mirabeau stared at Joseph and Charlotte in shock as they came up to the back of the wagon. He looked as if he was about to reach under the canvas to grasp the Gatling gun's crank.

"Take it easy, Mirabeau," Palmer said. "I don't want any trouble. You can see I've got your friends. Give me the rest of that gold, whatever you've got left, and I'll let them go."

"You're one of Lundy's men!" Mirabeau exclaimed. "I thought you were all dead."

"I'm my own man," Palmer snapped, "and I want that loot."

Mirabeau laughed. "You're insane. The gold means nothing now. Anyway, it's long gone. I brought what I needed to buy these wagons, then sent one of my men back into the mountains with the rest of it. It will support our cause for a long time."

"You mean you don't even have it anymore?" Palmer asked as his lips drew up into a snarl.

"That is exactly what I mean."

"You lie! I'll kill these two —"

"Go ahead." Mirabeau turned back to the gun. "Now I have work to do."

Joseph knew this was his last chance to stop the massacre. He turned suddenly and threw himself at Palmer. His right hand was useless for firing a gun, but he could still swing that arm like a club. He smashed a blow across Palmer's face and grabbed for the man's gun with his left hand.

The attack by a supposedly crippled man took Palmer by surprise. As he staggered back a step, Joseph wrenched the gun out of his hand and whirled around, lifting the weapon toward Mirabeau as he tried to get his finger through the trigger guard.

He was too late. Mirabeau had seen what was happening and jerked the canvas off the Gatling gun so he could swivel it around. Joseph found the trigger and fired, the sound of the shot not really all that loud with all the noise of the crowd around them.

Then the Gatling gun began to chatter and spit fire, and Joseph felt himself being driven backward as his flesh shredded under the leaden onslaught.

At the other end of the grandstand, Salty saw Reb and waved a hand at him. "The wagon!" the old-timer yelled. "They're in that wagon!"

Reb fell in alongside him. "Where's Frank?"

"Goin' after the guns at the other end."

"Split up," Reb ordered. "You take the front, I'll take the back end. We'll get 'em in a cross fire."

"Better hurry. Ain't no tellin' when they'll start the ball!"

And just as if Fate were listening, chaos erupted at the other end of the grandstand. Shots churned out, dozens of rounds in a few seconds. The men in this wagon must have been waiting for that, because the canvas on the side facing Salty and Reb suddenly erupted in flame and lead, ripping apart to reveal the death-spewing weapons inside.

"Hit the dirt!" Salty yelled. He hauled out his old revolver as he threw himself to the ground. Pain shot through him from the bullet crease in his side, but he ignored it.

A few feet away, Reb's ivory-handled Colt was already out and roaring. One of the

Gatlings dipped toward him. Reb flung himself to the side and rolled as several dozen slugs kicked up dirt where he had been a second earlier. As he came up on a knee, he fired over the revolving barrels, squeezing off two swift shots. Both bullets hit the gunner in the face, erasing his features in a bloody smear as he was thrown backward. That rapid-firer fell silent.

The other one still poured death toward the now shrieking and stampeding crowd. Salty gripped the wrist of his gun hand with his hand to steady it and fired. The man turning the devil gun's crank doubled over as the old-timer's bullets punched into his midsection. That gun stopped firing as well as the man collapsed.

Hell was still roaring down at the other end of the arena, though.

Frank's Colt was in his hand even before the first shot rang out. When the Gatling began to fire and one of the men at the back of the wagon stumbled back as he was shot to pieces, Frank raised the revolver and triggered three shots, blasting the slugs right through the wagon's canvas cover.

At the same time, Sergeant McKendrick drew the revolver from the holster at his waist and leaped to the front seat of the vehicle. He fired through the opening there as the second Gatling gun began to roar. The gun was abruptly silenced.

Not the one in the rear, though. The canvas ripped apart as whoever was manning the weapon swung it toward Frank. He dived flat as the slugs hammered through the air above him. The shredded canvas fluttered, giving Frank a glimpse of the man turning the crank. He was big and bearded, and his face was covered with blood. He looked positively satanic as he kept the Gatling pounding away.

Another shot came from the rear of the wagon, almost unnoticed in the chaos. Frank glanced in that direction and saw that the woman had picked up the little pistol. Smoke curled from the muzzle, so he knew she had fired the shot.

The man at the Gatling gun let go of the crank and lurched to his feet. One hand clutched at his neck where a bullet had torn through it. Blood flooded over his fingers. With his other hand, he reached for the rapid-firer's crank, evidently determined to fire it even as he was dying.

Frank stood up and shot him in the head.

The man reeled back against the other side of the wagon's canvas cover and then slid down it, leaving a crimson stain behind him.

Frank turned his head to look for Palmer. The battle, eventful though it had been, had lasted only a minute or so.

Palmer was gone. Frank's heart sank when he realized that. Then a second later he spotted what looked like Palmer's back as the man fled from the bloody chaos.

"Morgan, what —" McKendrick called after him as Frank broke into a run.

"Tell Salty and Reb I've gone after Palmer!" Frank shouted over his shoulder as he bulled his way through the crowd, trying desperately not to lose sight of his quarry.

CHAPTER 33

Everybody was trying to get away from the scene of the shooting, but the crowd thinned a little as Frank left the immediate area of the grandstand. He could see the man he was chasing better now, and he was sure it was Joe Palmer. The man glanced back, and Frank would have sworn that Palmer's eyes widened with recognition.

The hombre probably thought he was being chased by a ghost.

Suddenly, Reb Russell flashed past Frank, so quickly it appeared almost as if the older man were standing still. Reb quickly closed the gap with Palmer and left his feet in a flying tackle that sent both of them spilling to the ground.

By the time Frank caught up, Reb was on top of Palmer, slamming punches into the man's face. "Where is she, damn you?" Reb demanded between clenched teeth. "Where is she?"

Frank holstered his gun. He could get it out again quickly enough if he needed to . . . and it didn't look like he would need to.

Reb had just about pounded Palmer's face into raw meat by now. Frank put a hand on the young man's shoulder and said, "You'd better stop hitting him, Reb, or he won't be able to talk at all. He might even be dead."

Reb stopped throwing punches and drew his gun instead. He jammed the muzzle up under Palmer's jaw and said, "He'll be dead, all right, if he doesn't tell me where Meg is *right now.*"

"A . . . a house," Palmer began babbling. "Close by! I'll . . . I'll show you!"

Salty, Sergeant McKendrick, and several more Mounties came hurrying up. "Get that man on his feet," McKendrick ordered. "He's under arrest."

Reb looked like he might argue the point, but he moved aside and let the Mounties take charge of Palmer.

"He's going to tell us where to find our friend Meg," Frank said. "You can wait that long to take him to jail, can't you, Sergeant?"

"Very well," McKendrick said. To Palmer, he said, "You, there. Lead us to your hostage, immediately."

"Jus' . . . jus' don't let that madman near me again," Palmer choked out through smashed lips.

A few minutes later, at a house surrounded by aspens not far from Victoria Park, Meg rushed out onto the porch and into Reb's arms while the woman who ran the place babbled to McKendrick about how she hadn't known anything about Palmer kidnapping anybody, she'd just been doing a favor for a friend of a friend. . . .

The sergeant held up a hand to stop her. "Silence, madam," he ordered. "Just be thankful that the young woman is all right. She *is* all right, isn't she?"

"She's fine," the woman insisted. "Nobody laid a hand on her, Sergeant, I swear. You can ask her yourself."

"I will, have no doubt about that."

Frank and Salty stood at the other end of the porch, thumbs hooked in their gunbelts, grinning as Reb kissed Meg. Salty dug an elbow into Frank's side and chuckled.

"Looks like these young folks don't need us old pelicans around no more," he said.

"I don't reckon they ever really did," Frank said with a smile.

That evening, Frank and Salty sat in the lobby of the Drover's Rest. Salty was smoking a big cigar he had gotten somewhere. Reb and Meg were in the dining room, having supper. Frank had figured it was a good idea to give them some privacy.

"You see the way they was sparkin' each other this afternoon?" Salty said between puffs on the "see-gar," as he called it.

"I saw," Frank said solemnly.

"I reckon Meg ain't gonna be moonin' over you no more."

"You knew about that?"

Salty snorted. "Of course I knowed it. I ain't blind, you know."

"She'll be a lot better off with Captain Russell."

"No doubt about it. You're too old to have much to offer to a gal like that. And I got to admit, I never was all that sold on the idea of her comin' down to Mexico with us. Havin' a gal along might sort'a cramp my style when it comes to the señoritas."

"Speaking of being too old to have much to offer," Frank said drily.

"Oh, there's life in these old bones yet," Salty insisted. He puffed on the cigar again, then sighed and went on, "I just wish I'd got my money back from Palmer."

After being saved from being beaten to death by Reb, Palmer had been eager to talk. He had freely confessed that he no longer had any of the loot he and Yeah Mow Hopkins had taken with them when they escaped from Skagway.

"Hell, I lost most of it in a poker game while Yeah Mow was sleepin' off a drunk in some whore's bed, before we ever got to Powderkeg Bay," Palmer had told them. "I never told Hopkins about it, because I knew as long as he thought I had the loot, I could get him to go along with anything I wanted while he was waiting for his share."

"You mean we chased you halfway across Canada for *nothin'?*" Salty had demanded in astonishment.

"It wasn't for nothing," Frank had pointed out. "We helped save a lot of people from being massacred today."

"Well, yeah, I reckon. But I'm still broke."

"Don't worry about the money," Frank assured the old-timer now as they sat in the hotel lobby. "I've got enough for both of us."

"You're gonna have to tell me sometime how come a driftin' gunfighter's got plenty of dinero," Salty said.

Frank smiled. "Maybe I'll do that."

He looked up and grew more solemn as Sergeant McKendrick came through the hotel's front door. The sergeant looked around, spotted them, and came across the lobby to join them.

"What was the final tally, Sergeant?" Frank asked as McKendrick sat down.

McKendrick sighed. "Six dead — not counting the Métis — and upwards of thirty wounded. Terrible, just terrible. But it would have been much, much worse if not for you and your friends, Mr. Morgan."

"I'm glad we were around to lend a hand."

"What are your plans now, if you don't mind my asking?"

"Is that an official question?" Frank asked with a grin.

"Well . . . it might be. I've spoken to some of my superiors about you. They tell me that you have quite a reputation down in the States. It's said that trouble follows you wherever you go."

"So you'd probably just as soon I went somewhere else besides Canada."

"Indeed. The North West Mounted Police are charged with keeping the peace, you know. I have a feeling that would be much easier without the, ah, Drifter in our midst."

Frank didn't take offense. He had heard it all before. He said, "Don't worry, I'll be moseying on pretty soon. Salty and I have been talking about going down to Mexico." He turned to the old-timer. "In fact, I was thinking about seeing if I can send a wire to

Seattle and see if the fella who's been looking after Stormy, Goldy, and Dog could put
them on a train and ship them over to White
Sulphur Springs in Montana. I've got a
friend named Bob Coburn who owns a
ranch near there. It's really not all that far
from here, as the crow flies. If we could pick
them up there, we wouldn't even have to go
back to Seattle."

Salty nodded. "Sounds like a mighty fine
plan to me. I wouldn't mind takin' a *pasear*
down through that Montana cattle country."

"If I can assist you in any way in making
your plans, Mr. Morgan, please let me
know," McKendrick said.

"I'll do that," Frank promised. "We'll be
outfitted and on our way in a day or two,
more than likely."

McKendrick said his farewells and left.
Frank and Salty resumed their sitting and
musing.

"Reckon they'll ever have another ro-
day-o here, after all the hell that broke loose
at this one?" Salty asked.

"I expect they will. Reb says they're the
coming thing, that they'll be holding rodeos
all over the country before you know it."

"Hmmph. Why in tarnation would they
do that?"

"Because it won't be long until the frontier

that we knew is gone, Salty. Hombres like the two of us are the next thing to relics already. People will want to remember the way things were, though, and rodeos and Wild West shows and things like that will be the only way."

"It won't be the same," Salty warned.

"Nothing ever is," Frank said.

ABOUT THE AUTHOR

William W. Johnstone is the *USA Today* and *New York Times* bestselling author of over 220 books, including the popular Ashes, Mountain Man, and Last Gunfighter series. Visit his website at www.william johnstone.net or by email at dogcia@aol .com.

Being the all around assistant, typist, researcher, and fact checker to one of the most popular western authors of all time. **J. A. Johnstone** learned from the master, Uncle William W. Johnstone. Bill, as he preferred to be called, began tutoring J. A. at an early age. After-school hours were often spent retyping manuscripts or researching his massive American Western History library as well as the more modern wars and conflicts. J.A. worked hard — and learned. "Every day with Bill was an adventure story in itself. Bill taught me all he could about the art of story-telling and creating believable characters. *'Keep the historical facts accurate,'* he would say. *'Remember the readers, and as your grandfather once told me, I am telling you now, be the best J.A. Johnstone you can be.'* "

The employees of Thorndike Press hope you have enjoyed this Large Print book. All our Thorndike, Wheeler, and Kennebec Large Print titles are designed for easy reading, and all our books are made to last. Other Thorndike Press Large Print books are available at your library, through selected bookstores, or directly from us.

For information about titles, please call:
  (800) 223-1244

or visit our Web site at:
  http://gale.cengage.com/thorndike

To share your comments, please write:
  Publisher
  Thorndike Press
  10 Water St., Suite 310
  Waterville, ME 04901